A.E. VAN VOGT

FUTURES PAST

A.E. VAN VOGT

FUTURES PAST

TACHYON PUBLICATIONS
SAN FRANCISCO, CALIFORNIA

FUTURES PAST: THE BEST SHORT FICTION OF A.E. VAN VOGT

Cover illustration by Michael Dashow

Tachyon Publications
PMB #139
1459 18th Street
San Francisco, CA 94107
(415) 285-5615

Edited by Jacob Weisman

ISBN: 1-892391-05-8 (paperback edition)
        1-892391-04-X (hardcover edition)

First Edition: October 1999

Printed in the United States of America by Dark Regions Press

0 9 8 7 6 5 4 3 2 1

Table of Contents

Introduction
Van is Here, But Van is Gone
by Harlan Ellison

Let me assure you: this little *hors d'oeuvre* will not long
detain you. After all, you've come for the sumptuous buffet,
not for the nugatory fustian of the toastmaster.

These prefatory words are, in truth, far shorter than their
subject deserves. Alfred E. van Vogt, since the appearance of
his first two stories—"Black Destroyer" and "Discord in Scarlet"
(*Astounding Science Fiction*, July and December 1939)—
possibly the most memorable debut in the long history of the
genre—has been a giant. The words seminal and germinal leap
to mind. Sadly, at this juncture, the words tragedy and farewell
also insinuate themselves. It's the good news and the bad
news.

The good news, slight though it must be in light of what
follows, is that here we have a "new" book of Van's stories.
New in the sense that it gathers some of his lesser-known, but
most exceedingly excellent, fictions in a contemporary setting.
New in the sense that for a generation for whom nostalgia is
what they had for breakfast, it proffers the enormous and
original van Vogt talent as if it had just been minted. Which is
part of the "tragedy" aspect of the bad news.

The bad news that I come to deliver makes this piece of
writing one of the most difficult I've ever undertaken. And for
that reason, as well, I will not go on at too-great length.

Van is still with us, as I write this, in June of 1999, slightly
less than fifty years since I first encountered the van Vogt prose
in a January 1950 issue of *Startling Stories*, but Van is gone. He
is no longer with us.

More than four million people over the age of 65 in these
United States suffer from the merciless torturer we know as
Alzheimer's disease. Like the slow Chinese Water Torture of
pulp magazine thrillers, it destroys the mind drop by drop by
drop. It takes forever, and it has no heart. It is awful, and it is

relentless. Van's beloved Lydia knows these detestable truths as she tenderly cares for him, through all the hard days and nights.

Because the great and fecund mind of A.E. van Vogt has fallen into the clutches of that pulp thriller demon, Alzheimer's. Van is gone.

He remains, in body and on these pages; he is here and will remain here as long as those who adore his work—please give it up for the good Jacob Weisman and Tachyon Publications— continue to keep him alive in the eye of the reader. But that mind, that astonishing intellect that advised us (with a twinkle of risibility) that he "introduced an entirely new concept every three thousand words" of a story, that rare device is gone.

(My first profoundly amazing recollection of Van is of the evening, long ago, when we went for a walk here in Los Angeles, and he told me that when he went out walking his dog, or strolling for health reasons, he always had a pair of earphones and a tape recorder with him, so he could teach himself yet another new language by tape instruction. I have no idea how many languages Van could speak, but if one were seeking an Icon for the Ever-Questing Intellect, you could place your chips on Double-V and the wheel would stop with you a winner.)

Anyone's demise or vanishment is in some small way tragic, but the word "tragedy" requires greater measure for its use. Lear was a tragedy. Joan of Arc was a tragedy. That "person from Porlock" coming to Coleridge's door at the crucial instant, thus distracting and preventing the poet from finishing "The Pleasure Dome of Kubla Khan," that was a tragedy. The world's foremost cancer specialist, our best hope for a medical breakthrough, blown to bits by an IRA bomb in London, as he was out walking his dog, killed absolutely by chance . . . tragedy. For all of us.

Van's great mind now gone. Tragedy.

The ultimate tragic impropriety visited on as good a man as ever lived. A gentle, soft-spoken man who was filled with ideas and humor and courtesy and kindness. Not even those who were not aficionados of Van's writing could muster a harsh word about him as a human being. He was, as he remains now, quietly and purposefully, a gentleman.

But make no mistake about this: the last few decades for him were marred by the perfidious and even mean-spirited and sometimes criminal acts of poltroons and self-aggrandizing mountebanks and piss-ants into whose clutches he fell just before the thug Alzheimer got him.

Those who know Van and Lydia well, they will know to whom I refer in that preceding paragraph. People who used Van and set him up with projects beneath his talent, for a fast buck; people who used him for their own niggardly ends, and who eventually wound up stealing from him. I wish them— even the ones *you* continue to laud and to whom you give Grand Master and Lifetime Achievement awards—I wish them a gentler, kinder last act than has been written for Van, with this one proviso: let there not be a day, as they sit there waiting for the end, that they do not revile themselves for what they did to A.E. van Vogt.

I came late to the friendship with Van and Lydia. Perhaps only twenty-five or so years. But the friendship continues, and at least I was able to make enough noise to get Van the Science Fiction Writers of America Grand Master Award, which was presented to him in full ceremony during one of the last moments when he was cogent and clearheaded enough to understand that finally, at last, dragged kicking and screaming to honor him, the generations that learned from what he did and what he created had, at last, fessed up to his importance.

(Naturally, others took the credit for his getting the award. They postured and spewed all the right platitudes. Some of them were the same ones who had said to me—during the five years it took to get them to act honorably—"we'd have given it to him sooner if you hadn't made such a fuss." Yeah. Sure. And pandas'll fly outta my ass.

(Some of them were the same ones who assured me that Van would never get the Grand Master until Damon Knight had gotten it first, because Damon had loathed Van's work and had, in fact, written the essay that ridiculed Van and held him up to opprobrium for decades thereafter, and Damon having founded SFWA, it would be an affront to him if Van got it first. Well, I don't know if that's true or not, though it was common coin in the field for years; but Damon got the Grand Master award in 1994. And Van got it in 1995. As they say during sweeps week on television: coincidence or conspiracy?

(I mention all this, in what may be the last "new" van Vogt book for a while, because I take enormous pride in having had even a minuscule role in preserving Van's name and his work for posterity. Which is a fickle lover, neither gender insulted, please note. I mention all this because *someone* has to say it. I tried once before, when I wrote the prefatory note to Van's inclusion in the Nebula Awards volume a few years ago, where his Grand Master was noted. But there was a request that I be less rancorous than I have been here. That I be a little more sedate. So I was. Just for your edification, here's what I wrote about Van in volume 31 of the Nebula Awards:)

Even the brightest star shines dimly when observed from too far away. And human memory is notoriously unreliable. And we live in ugly times when all respect for that which has gone before suffers crib-death beneath the weight of youthful arrogance and ignorance. But a great nobility has, at last, been recognized and lauded. Someone less charitable than I might suggest the honor could have been better appreciated had it not been so tardy, running its race with a foe that blots joy and destroys short-term memory. But I sing the Talent Electric, and like all the dark smudges of history, everything but the honor and the achievement remains for the myth-makers.

Alfred E. van Vogt has been awarded the Grand Master trophy of the Science Fiction and Fantasy Writers of America. He is not the first person to receive this singular accolade . . . given only to those whose right to possess it is beyond argument or mitigation.

Were we in 1946 or even 1956, van Vogt would have already been able to hold the award aloft. Had SFWA existed then, and had the greatest living sf authors been polled as to who was the most fecund, the most intriguing, the most innovative, the most influential of their number, Isaac and Arthur and Cyril and Hank Kuttner and Ron Hubbard would all have pointed to the same man, and Bob Heinlein would've given him a thumbs-up. Van Vogt was the pinnacle, the source of power and ideas; the writer to beat. Because he embodied in his astonishing novels and assorted stories what we always say is of prime importance to us in this genre—the much vaunted Sense of Wonder.

Van Vogt was *the wellspring of wonder.*

Youthful memory is filled with gaps and insolent of history, but for those who were there, and those who care, it was van Vogt's books that were among the very first published in the mainstream from the despised realm of science fiction. When the first specialty houses were formed, they went after The Weapon Shops of Isher *and* Slan *and*

Masters of Time. *But when Simon & Schuster got into the game, most prestigious of the mainstream houses taking a chance on sf, it was van Vogt they sought, and* The World of Ā *and* Voyage of the Space Beagle *were the high-water marks.*

That's how important he was.

And then came dark years during which the man was shamefully agented and overlooked; and even the brightest star loses its piercing light if observed through the thickening mists of time and flawed memory.

Now it is lifetimes later, and the great award has, at last, been presented. To some, less charitable than I, something could be said about a day late and a dollar short; but not I. I am here to sing the Talent Electric, and it is better now than never. He is the Grand Master. A.E. van Vogt, weaver of a thousand ideas per plot-line, creator of alien thoughts and impossible dreams that rival the best ever built by our kind.

This dear, gentlemanly writer whose stories can still kill you with a concept or warm you with a character, now joins the special pantheon.

Isaac and Alfie B. and Arthur and those rare, few others have been waiting for him to step up onto the dais. As one who read Van's "The Shadow Men" in the very first sf magazine he ever bought, I bless those who presented him with the physical token of the greatness we knew all along.

He was born 26 April 1912, in Winnipeg, Manitoba, Canada. The first story he sold was to the long-extinct McFadden Publications . . . it was a true confession for one of their romance magazines, June 1932. He wrote for radio and trade magazines and anywhere else that a dollar could be had in those post-Depression times. And in 1939, just as "Black Destroyer" made his name, he married the writer Edna Mayne Hull. In 1947 he explained in a wonderful book edited by Lloyd Arthur Eshbach, *Of Worlds Beyond*, that he wrote in 800-word scenes. It was a startling explication of an absolutely idiosyncratic way to create fiction. It bewildered everyone.

Years later, after Mayne's passing, Van was blessed with the love and companionship of Lydia, who shares the days and nights at the end of his last 800-word sequence.

Hmmm. A somewhat larger appetizer than I'd intended. I hope it only made a special few of you choke. For all the rest of you, I hope it was tasty, despite the bile it took to wash it down.

But then, this is an "introduction" that is being written with more than just love. It is written with honorable intent, and with the necessity of finally putting some of the spoiled fruit served at this banquet where it belongs, in the garbage can.

The bad news is that Van won't know how you honor him by enjoying these stories. The good news is that "Enchanted Village" and "Vault of the Beast" and the others here included have another shot at an intelligent readership.

If you know Van, you know what a treat this book will be. If this is your first taste of the banquet, I envy you. He did a lot of writing, and it's open to you; all you've got to do is go root it out.

Either way, it has been my pleasure and my honor to get in a few last words, even as bittersweet dessert, at this groaning board of wonderful literary viands known as the career of A.E. van Vogt.

Bon appétit!

Harlan Ellison
Los Angeles
1 July 1999

The Enchanted Village

"Explorers of a new frontier" they had been called before they left for Mars.

For a while, after the ship crashed into a Martian desert, killing all on board except—miraculously—him, Bill Jenner spat the words occasionally into the constant, sand-laden wind. He despised himself for the pride he had felt when he first heard them.

His fury faded with each mile that he walked, and his black grief for his friends became a gray ache. Slowly he realized that he had made a ruinous misjudgement.

He had underestimated the speed at which the rocket ship had been traveling. He'd guessed that he would have to walk three hundred miles to reach the shallow, polar sea he and the others had observed as they glided in from outer space. Actually, the ship must have flashed an immensely greater distance before it hurtled down out of control.

The days stretched behind him, seemingly as numberless as the hot, red, alien sand that scorched through his tattered clothes. A huge scarecrow of a man, he kept moving across the endless, arid waste—he would not give up.

By the time he came to the mountain, his food had long been gone. Of his four water bags, only one remained, and that was so close to being empty that he merely wet his cracked lips and swollen tongue whenever his thirst became unbearable.

Jenner climbed high before he realized that it was not just another dune that had barred his way. He paused, and as he gazed up at the mountain that towered above him, he cringed a little. For an instant he felt the hopelessness of this mad race he was making to nowhere—but he continued and reached the top. He saw that below him was a depression surrounded by hills as high as, or higher than, the one on which he stood. Nestled in the valley they made was a village.

He could see trees and the marble floor of a courtyard. A score of buildings was clustered around what seemed to be a central square. They were mostly low-constructed, but there were four towers pointing gracefully into the sky. They shone in the sunlight with a marble luster.

Faintly, there came to Jenner's ears a thin, high-pitched whistling sound. It rose, fell, faded completely, then came up again clearly and unpleasantly. Even as Jenner ran toward it, the noise grated on his ears, eerie and unnatural.

He kept slipping on smooth rock, and bruised himself when he fell. He rolled halfway down into the valley. The buildings remained new and bright when seen from nearby. Their walls flashed with reflections. On every side was vegetation—reddish green shrubbery, yellow green trees laden with purple and red fruit.

With ravenous intent, Jenner headed for the nearest fruit tree. Close up, the tree looked dry and brittle. The large red fruit he tore from the lowest branch, however, was plump and juicy.

As he lifted it to his mouth, he remembered that he had been warned during his training period to taste nothing on Mars until it had been chemically examined. But that was meaningless advice or a man whose only chemical equipment was in his own body.

Nevertheless, the possibility of danger made him cautious. He took his first bite gingerly. It was bitter to his tongue, and he spat it out hastily. Some of the juice which remained in his mouth seared his gums. He felt the fire in it, and he reeled from nausea. His muscles began to jerk, and he lay down on the marble to keep himself from falling. After what seemed like hours to Jenner, the awful trembling went out of his body and he could see again. He looked up despisingly at the tree.

The pain finally left him, and slowly he relaxed. A soft breeze rustled the dry leaves. Nearby trees took up that gentle clamor, and it struck Jenner that the wind here in the valley was only a whisper of what it had been on the flat desert beyond the mountain.

There was no other sound now. Jenner abruptly remembered the high-pitched, ever-changing whistle he had heard. He lay very still, listening intently, but there was only the rustling of the leaves. The noisy shrilling had stopped. He wondered if it had been an alarm, to warn the villagers of his approach.

Anxiously he climbed to his feet and fumbled for his gun. A sense of disaster shocked through him. It wasn't there. His mind was a blank, and then he vaguely recalled that he had first missed the weapon more than a week before. He looked around him uneasily, but there was not a sign of creature life. He braced himself. He couldn't leave, as there was nowhere to go. If necessary, he would fight to the death to remain in the village.

Carefully Jenner took a sip from his water bag, moistening his cracked lips and his swollen tongue. Then he replaced the cap and started through a double line of trees toward the nearest building. He made a wide circle to observe it from several vantage points. On one side a low, broad archway opened into the interior. Through it, he could dimly make out the polished gleam of a marble floor.

Jenner explored the buildings from the outside, always keeping a respectful distance between himself and any of the entrances. He saw no sign of animal life. He reached the far side of the marble platform on which the village was built, and turned back decisively. It was time to explore interiors.

He chose one of the four tower buildings. As he came within a dozen feet of it, he saw that he would have to stoop low to get inside.

The implications of that stopped him. These buildings had been constructed for a life form that must be very different from human beings.

He went forward again, bent down, and entered reluctantly, every muscle tensed.

He found himself in a room without furniture. However, there were several low marble fences projecting from one marble wall. They formed what looked like a group of four wide, low stalls. Each stall had an open trough carved out of the floor.

The second chamber was fitted with four inclined planes of marble, each of which slanted up to a dais. Altogether there were four rooms on the lower floor. From one of them a circular ramp mounted up, apparently to a tower room.

Jenner didn't investigate the upstairs. The earlier fear that he would find alien life was yielding to the deadly conviction that he wouldn't. No life meant no food or chance of getting any. In frantic haste he hurried from building to building, peering into the silent rooms, pausing now and then to shout hoarsely.

Finally there was no doubt. He was alone in a deserted village on a lifeless planet, without food, without water—except for the pitiful supply in his bag—and without hope.

He was in the fourth and smallest room of one of the tower buildings when he realized that he had come to the end of his search. The room had a single stall jutting out from one wall. Jenner lay down wearily in it. He must have fallen asleep instantly.

When he awoke he became aware of two things, one right after the other. The first realization occurred before he opened his eyes—the whistling sound was back; high and shrill, it wavered at the threshold of audibility.

The other was that a fine spray of liquid was being directed down at him from the ceiling. It had an odor, of which technician Jenner took a single whiff. Quickly he scrambled out of the room, coughing, tears in his eyes, his face already burning from chemical reaction.

He snatched his handkerchief and hastily wiped the exposed parts of his body and face.

He reached the outside and there paused, striving to understand what had happened.

The village seemed unchanged.

Leaves trembled in a gentle breeze. The sun was poised on a mountain peak. Jenner guessed from its position that it was morning again and that he had slept at least a dozen hours. The glaring white light suffused the valley. Half-hidden by trees and shrubbery, the buildings flashed and shimmered.

He seemed to be in an oasis in a vast desert. It was an oasis, all right, Jenner reflected grimly, but not for a human being. For him, with its poisonous fruit, it was more like a tantalizing mirage.

He went back inside the building and cautiously peered into the room where he had slept. The spray of gasoline had stopped, not a bit of odor lingered, and the air was fresh and clean.

He edged over the threshold, half-inclined to make a test. He had a picture in his mind of a long-dead Martian creature lazing on the floor in the stall while a soothing chemical sprayed down on its body. The fact that the chemical was deadly to human beings merely emphasized how alien to man was the life that had been spawned on Mars. But there seemed little doubt of the reason for the gasoline. The creature was accustomed to taking a morning shower.

Inside the "bathroom," Jenner eased himself feet first into the stall. As his hips came level with the stall entrance, the solid ceiling sprayed a jet of yellowish gasoline straight down upon his legs. Hastily Jenner pulled himself clear of the stall. The gasoline stopped as suddenly as it had started.

He tried it again, to make sure it was merely an automatic process. The jet turned on, then shut off.

Jenner's thirst-puffed lips parted with excitement. He thought, "If there can be one automatic process, there may be others."

Breathing heavily, he raced into the outer room. Carefully he shoved his legs into one of the two stalls. The moment his hips were in, a steaming gruel filled the trough beside the wall.

He stared at the greasy-looking stuff with horrified fascination—food and drink. He remembered the poison fruit and felt repelled, but he forced himself to bend down and put his finger into the hot, wet substance. He brought it up, dripping, to his mouth.

It tasted flat and pulpy, like boiled wood fiber. It trickled viscously into his throat. His eyes began to water and his lips drew back convulsively. He realized he was going to be sick, and ran for the outer door—but didn't quite make it.

When he finally got outside, he felt limp and unutterably listless. In that depressed state of mind, he grew aware again of the shrill sound.

He felt amazed that he could have ignored its rasping even for a few minutes. Sharply he glanced about, trying to determine its source, but it seemed to have none. Whenever he approached a point where it appeared to be loudest, then it would fade or shift, perhaps to the far side of the village.

He tried to imagine what an alien culture would want with a mind-shattering noise—although, of course, it would not necessarily have been unpleasant to them.

He stopped and snapped his fingers as a wild notion entered his mind. Could this be music?

He toyed with the idea, trying to visualize the village as it had been long ago. Here a music-loving people had possibly

gone about its daily tasks to the accompaniment of what
seemed to be beautiful strains of melody.

The hideous whistling went on and on, waxing and waning.
Jenner tried to put buildings between himself and the sound.
He sought refuge in various rooms, hoping that at least one
would be soundproof. None were. The whistle followed him
wherever he went.

He retreated into the desert, and had to climb halfway up
one of the slopes before the noise was low enough not to
disturb him. Finally, breathless but immeasurably relieved, he
sank down on the sand and thought blankly:

"What now?"

The scene that spread before him had in it qualities of both
heaven and hell. It was all too familiar now—the red sands, the
stony dunes, the small, alien village promising so much and
fulfilling so little.

Jenner looked down at it with his feverish eyes and ran his
parched tongue over his cracked, dry lips. He knew that he
was a dead man unless he could alter the automatic food-
making machines that must be hidden somewhere in the walls
and under the floors of the buildings.

In ancient days, a remnant of Martian civilization had
survived here in this village. The inhabitants had died off, but
the village lived on, keeping itself clean of sand, able to provide
refuge for any Martian who might come along. But there were
no Martians. There was only Bill Jenner, pilot of the first
rocket ship ever to land on Mars.

He had to make the village turn out food and drink that he
could take. Without tools, except his hands, with scarcely any
knowledge of chemistry, he must force it to change its habits.

Tensely he hefted his water bag. He took another sip and
fought the same grim fight to prevent himself from guzzling it
down to the last drop. And, when he had won the battle once
more, he stood up and started down the slope.

He could not last, he estimated, more than three days. In
that time he must conquer the village.

He was already among the trees when it suddenly struck
him that the "music" had stopped. Relieved, he bent over a
small shrub, took a good firm hold of it—and pulled.

The shrub came up easily, and there was a slab of marble
attached to it. Jenner stared at it, noting with surprise that he
had been mistaken in thinking the stalk came up through a hole

in the marble. It was merely stuck to the surface. Then he noticed something else—the shrub had no roots. Jenner looked down at the spot from which he had torn the slab of marble along with the plant. There was sand there.

He dropped the shrub, slipped to his knees, and plunged his fingers into the sand. Loose sand trickled through them. He reached deep, using all his strength to force his arm and hand down; sand—nothing but sand.

He stood up and frantically tore up another shrub. It also came up easily, bringing with it a slab of marble. The shrub had no roots, and where it had been was sand.

With a kind of mindless disbelief, Jenner rushed over to a fruit tree and shoved at it. There was a momentary resistance, and then the marble on which it stood split and lifted slowly into the air. The tree fell over with a swish and a crackle as its dry branches and leaves broke and crumbled into a thousand pieces. Underneath where it had been was sand.

Sand everywhere. A city built on sand. Mars, planet of sand. That was not completely true, of course. Seasonal vegetation had been observed near the polar ice cap. All but the hardiest of it died with the coming of summer. It had been intended that the rocket ship land near one of those shallow, tideless seas.

By coming down out of control, the ship had wrecked more than itself. It had wrecked the chances for life of the only survivor of the voyage.

Jenner came slowly out of his daze. He had a thought then. He picked up one of the shrubs he had already torn loose, braced his foot against the marble to which it was attached, and tugged, gently at first, then with increasing strength.

It came loose finally, but there was no doubt that the two were part of a whole. The shrub was growing out of the marble.

Marble? Jenner knelt beside one of the holes from which he had torn a slab, and bent over an adjoining section. It was quite porous—calciferous rock, most likely, but not true marble at all. As he reached toward it, intending to break off a piece, it changed color. Astounded, Jenner drew back. Around the break, the stone was turning a bright orange yellow. He studied it uncertainly, then tentatively he touched it.

It was as if he had dipped his fingers into searing acid. There was a sharp, biting, burning pain. With a gasp, Jenner jerked his hand clear.

The continuing anguish made him feel faint. He swayed and moaned, clutching his bruised members to his body. When the agony finally faded and he could look at the injury, he saw that the skin had peeled and that blood blisters had formed already. Grimly, Jenner looked down at the break in the stone. The edges remained bright orange yellow.

The village was alert, ready to defend itself from further attacks.

Suddenly weary, he crawled into the shade of a tree. There was only one possible conclusion to draw from what had happened, and it almost defied common sense. This lonely village was alive.

As he lay there, Jenner tried to imagine a great mass of living substance growing into the shape of buildings, adjusting itself to suit another life form, accepting the role of servant in the widest meaning of the term.

If it would serve one race, why not another? If it could adjust to Martians, why not to human beings?

There would be difficulties, of course. He guessed wearily that essential elements would not be available. The oxygen for water could come from the air . . . thousands of compounds could be made from sand. Though it meant death if he failed to find a solution, he fell asleep even as he started to think about what it might be.

When he awoke it was quite dark.

Jenner climbed heavily to his feet. There was a drag to his muscles that alarmed him. He wet his mouth from his water bag and staggered toward the entrance of the nearest building. Except for the scraping of his shoes on the "marble," the silence was intense.

He stopped short, listened, and looked. The wind had died away. He couldn't see the mountains that rimmed the valley, but the buildings were still dimly visible, black shadows in a shadow world.

For the first time, it seemed to him that, in spite of his new hope, it might be better if he died. Even if he survived, what had he to look forward to? Only too well he recalled how hard it had been to rouse interest in the trip and to raise the large amount of money required. He remembered the colossal problems that had had to be solved in building the ship; and some of the men who had solved them were buried somewhere in the Martian desert.

It might be twenty years before another ship from Earth would try to reach the only other planet in the solar system that had show signs of being able to support life.

During those uncountable days and nights, those years, he would be here alone. That was the most he could hope for—if he lived. As he fumbled his way to a dais in one of the rooms, Jenner considered another problem: How did one let a living village know that it must alter its processes? It must already have grasped that it had a new tenant. How could he make it realize he needed food in a different chemical combination than that which it had served in the past; that he liked music, but on a different scale system; and that he could use a shower each morning—of water, not of poison gasoline?

He dozed fitfully, like a man who is sick rather than sleepy. Twice he wakened, his lips on fire, his eyes burning, his body bathed in perspiration. Several times he was startled into consciousness by the sound of his own harsh voice crying out in anger and fear at the night.

He guessed, then, that he was dying.

He spent the long hours of darkness tossing, turning, twisting, befuddled by waves of heat. As the light of morning came, he was vaguely surprised to realize that he was still alive. Restlessly he climbed off the dais and went to the door.

A bitingly cold wind blew, but it felt good to his hot face. He wondered if there were enough pneumococci in his blood for him to catch pneumonia. He decided not.

In a few moments he was shivering. He retreated back into the house, and for the first time noticed that, despite the doorless doorway, the wind did not come into the building at all. The rooms were cold but not drafty.

That started an association: Where had his terrible body heat come from? He teetered over to the dais where he spent the night. Within seconds he was sweltering in a temperature of about 130 degrees.

He climbed off the dais, shaken by his own stupidity. He estimated that he had sweated at least two quarts of moisture out of his dried-up body on that furnace of a bed.

This village was not for human beings. Here even the beds were heated for creatures who needed temperatures far beyond the heat comfortable for men.

Jenner spent most of the day in the shade of a large tree. He felt exhausted, and only occasionally did he even remember that he had a problem. When the whistling started, it bothered him at first, but he was too tired to move away from it. There were long periods when he hardly heard it, so dulled were his senses.

Late in the afternoon he remembered the shrubs and the trees he had torn up the day before and wondered what had happened to them. He wet his swollen tongue with the last few drops of water in his bag, climbed lackadaisically to his feet, and went to look for the dried-up remains.

There weren't any. He couldn't even find the holes where he had torn them out. The living village had absorbed the dead tissue into itself and had repaired the breaks in its "body."

That galvanized Jenner. He began to think again . . . about mutations, genetic readjustments, life forms adapting to new environments. There'd been lectures on that before the ship left Earth, rather generalized talks designed to acquaint the explorers with the problems men might face on an alien planet. The important principle was quite simple: adjust or die.

The village had to adjust to him. He doubted if he could seriously damage it, but he could try. His own need to survive must be placed on as sharp and hostile a basis as that.

Frantically Jenner began to search his pockets. Before leaving the rocket he had loaded himself with odds and ends of small equipment. A jackknife, a folding metal cup, a radio, a tiny superbattery that could be charged by spinning an attached wheel—and for which he had brought along, among other things, a powerful electric fire lighter.

Jenner plugged the lighter into the battery and deliberately scraped the red-hot end along the surface of the "marble." The reaction was swift. The substance turned an angry purple at this time. When an entire section of the floor had changed color, Jenner headed for the nearest stall trough, entering far enough to activate it.

There was a noticeable delay. When the food finally flowed into the trough, it was clear that the living village had realized the reason for what he'd done. The food was a pale, creamy color, where earlier it had been murky gray.

Jenner put his finger into it but withdrew his finger with a yell and wiped it. It continued to sting for several moments. The vital question was: Had the village deliberately offered him food that would damage him, or was it trying to appease him without knowing what he could eat?

He decided to give the village another chance, and entered the adjoining stall. The gritty stuff that flooded up this time was yellower. It didn't burn his finger, but Jenner took one taste and spat it out. He had the feeling that he had been offered a soup made of a greasy mixture of clay and gasoline.

He was thirsty now with a need heightened by the unpleasant taste in his mouth. Desperately he rushed outside and tore open the water bag, seeking the wetness inside. In his fumbling eagerness, he spilled a few precious drops onto the courtyard floor. Down he went on his face and licked them up.

Half a minute later, he was still licking, and there was still water.

The fact penetrated suddenly. He raised himself and gazed wonderingly at the droplets of water that sparkled on the smooth stone. As he watched, another one squeezed up from the apparently solid surface and shimmered in the light of the sinking sun.

He bent, and with the tip of his tongue sponged up each visible drop. For a long time he lay with his mouth pressed to the "marble," sucking up the tiny bits of water that the village doled out to him.

The glowing white sun disappeared behind a hill. Night fell, like the dropping of a black screen. The air turned cold, then icy. He shivered as the wind keened through his ragged clothes. But what finally stopped him was the collapse of the surface from which he had been drinking.

Jenner lifted himself in surprise, and in the darkness gingerly felt over the stone. It had genuinely crumbled. Evidently the substance had yielded up its available water and had disintegrated in the process. Jenner estimated that he had drunk altogether an ounce of water.

It was a convincing demonstration of the willingness of the village to please him, but there was another, less satisfying implication. If the village had to destroy a part of itself every time it gave him a drink, then the supply was not unlimited.

Jenner hurried inside the nearest building, climbed onto a dais—and climbed off again hastily, as the heat blazed up at him. He waited, to give the Intelligence a chance to realize he wanted a change, then lay down once more. The heat was as great as ever.

He gave that up because he was too tired to persist and too sleepy to think of a method that might let the village know he needed a different bedroom temperature. He slept on the floor with an uneasy conviction that it could *not* sustain him for long. He woke up many times during the night and thought, "Not enough water. No matter how hard it tries." Then he would sleep again, only to wake once more, tense and unhappy.

Nevertheless, morning found him briefly alert; and all his steely determination was back—that iron willpower that had brought him at least five hundred miles across an unknown desert.

He headed for the nearest trough. This time, after he had activated it, there was a pause of more than a minute; and then about a thimbleful of water made a wet splotch at the bottom.

Jenner licked it dry, then waited hopefully for more. When none came he reflected gloomily that somewhere in the village an entire group of cells had broken down and released its water for him.

Then and there he decided that it was up to the human being, who could move around, to find a new source of water for the village, which could not move.

In the interim, of course, the village would have to keep him alive, until he had investigated the possibilities. That meant, above everything else, he must have some food to sustain him while he looked around.

He began to search his pockets. Toward the end of his food supply, he had carried scraps and pieces wrapped in small bits of cloth. Crumbs had broken off into the pocket, and he had searched for them often during those long days in the desert. Now, by actually ripping the seams, he discovered tiny particles of meat and bread, little bits of grease and other unidentifiable substances.

Carefully he leaned over the adjoining stall and placed the scrapings in the trough there. The village would not be able to offer him more than a reasonable facsimile. If the spilling of a few drops in the courtyard could make it aware of his need for water, then a similar offering might give it the clue it needed as to the chemical nature of the food he could eat.

Jenner waited, then entered the second stall and activated it. About a pint of a thick, creamy substance trickled into the bottom of the trough. The smallness of the quantity seemed evidence that perhaps it contained water.

He tasted it. The substance had a sharp, musty flavor and a stale odor. It was almost as dry as flour—but his stomach did not reject it.

Jenner ate slowly, acutely aware that at such moments as this the village had him at its mercy. He could not be sure that one of the food ingredients was not a slow-acting poison.

When he had finished the meal he went to a food trough in another building. He refused to eat the food that came up, but activated still another trough. This time he received a few drops of water.

He had come purposefully to one of the tower buildings. Now he started up the ramp that led to the upper floor. He paused only briefly in the room he came to, as he had already discovered that they seemed to be additional bedrooms. The familiar dais was there in a group of three.

What interested him was that the circular ramp continued to wind on upward. First to another, smaller room that seemed to have no particular reason for being: Then it wound on up to the top of the tower, some seventy feet above the ground. It was high enough for him to see beyond the rim of all the surrounding hilltops. He had thought it might be, but he had been too weak to make the climb before. Now he looked out to every horizon. Almost immediately the hope that had brought him up faded.

The view was immeasurably desolate. As far as he could see was an arid waste, and every horizon was hidden in a mist of wind-blown sand.

Jenner gazed with a sense of despair. If there were a Martian sea out there somewhere, it was beyond his reach.

Abruptly he clenched his hands in anger against his fate, which seemed inevitable now. He had hoped, at the very worst. he would find himself in a mountainous region. Seas and mountains were generally the two main sources of water. He should have known, of course, that there were very few mountains on Mars. It would have been a wild coincidence if he had actually run into a mountain range.

His fury faded because he lacked the strength to sustain any emotion. Numbly he went down the ramp.

His vague plan to help the village ended as swiftly and finally as that.

The days drifted by, but as to how many he had no idea. Each time he went to eat, a smaller amount of water was doled out to him. Jenner kept telling himself that each meal would have to be his last. It was unreasonable for him to expect the village to destroy itself when his fate was certain now.

What was worse, it became increasingly clear that the food was not good for him. He had misled the village as to his needs by giving it stale, perhaps even tainted, samples, and prolonged the agony for himself. At times after he had eaten, Jenner felt dizzy for hours. All too frequently his head ached and his body shivered with fever.

The village was doing what it could. The rest was up to him, and he couldn't even adjust to an approximation of Earth food.

For two days he was too sick to drag himself to one of the troughs. Hour after hour he lay on the floor. Sometime during the second night the pain in his body grew so terrible that he finally made up his mind.

"If I can get to a dais," he told himself, "the heat alone will kill me; and in absorbing my body, the village will get back some of its lost water."

He spent at least an hour crawling laboriously up the ramp of the nearest dais, and when he finally made it, he lay as one already dead. His last waking thought was: "Beloved friends, I'm coming."

The hallucination was so complete that momentarily he seemed to be back in the control room of the rocket ship, and all around him were his former companions.

With a sigh of relief Jenner sank into a dreamless sleep.

He woke to the sound of a violin. It was a sad-sweet music that told of the rise and fall of a race long dead.

Jenner listened for a while and then, with abrupt excitement, realized the truth. This was a substitute for the whistling—the village had adjusted its music to him!

Other sensory phenomena stole in upon him. The dais felt comfortably warm, not hot at all. He had a feeling of wonderful physical well-being.

Eagerly he scrambled down the ramp to the nearest food stall. As he crawled forward, his nose close to the floor, the trough filled with a steamy mixture. The odor was so rich and pleasant that he plunged his face into it and slopped it up greedily. It had the flavor of thick, meaty soup and was warm and soothing to his lips and mouth. When he had eaten it all, for the first time he did not need a drink of water.

"I've won!" thought Jenner. "The village has found a way!"

After a while he remembered something and crawled to the bathroom. Cautiously, watching the ceiling, he eased himself backward into the shower stall. The yellowish spray came down, cool and delightful.

Ecstatically Jenner wriggled his four-foot tail and lifted his long snout to let the thin streams of liquid wash away the food impurities that clung to his sharp teeth.

Then he waddled out to bask in the sun and listen to the timeless music.

The First Martian

I had put on my pressure suit, and was walking through the roundhouse at Eastport, the Martian rail center, when I saw the stocky, big-chested guy with the mahogany-colored face come toward me. I knew at a glance that he was an Indian of some sort.

"Señor!" he said.

I stopped politely, and faced him.

"Señor, I am your new engineer-relief."

That hit me. On Mars, I had run into every creed and race at one time or another. But white men operated the big steam-atomics across the endless plains, and through the mountains, and along the frozen canals. The reason was very simple. White supremacy was taken for granted.

I tried to hide my surprise. "Glad to have you along," I said. "Better get into your pressure suit. We go out in thirty minutes. What's your name? Mine's Hecton. Bill Hecton."

"José Incuhana. I don't wear a pressure suit."

"Sounds like South America," I began—and stopped. "Look, Joe," I said finally, "be a good fellow and go over to the equipment room and ask for an HA-2. Make it snappy, pal. It takes a little while to get into those things. Be seeing you in twenty minutes."

I turned away awkwardly in my own bulky HA-2. I never did care for pressure suits, but on Mars, with its thin, thin atmosphere, they're essential to ordinary human beings who leave the shelters.

I had walked about five feet when I grew aware that José was still with me. He said, "You can see me right now, Señor Hecton." He sounded puzzled.

I turned and faced him, holding in my impatience. "Joe, when did you get to Mars?"

He looked at me soberly with his soft brown eyes. "Two days, Señor." He held up two fingers.

"Have you been out there yet?" I pointed at the desolation visible through the asbesglas window.

He nodded. "Yesterday."

His eyes were bright and intelligent-looking, and they stared at me as if he was still waiting for the punch line. Baffled, I glanced around, and saw Roundhouse Superintendent Charles Manet. "Hey, Charles!" I called.

Manet, a big Frenchman with a twinkle in his black eyes, came over. He said, "Glad to see you two have been getting acquainted."

"Charles," I said, "tell Joe about Mars. That the oxygen content of the air is about what we have five miles up back home. Tell him about high-altitude suits."

Manet shook his head. "Bill, Señor Incuhana is from the Andes Mountains. He was born in a town eighteen thousand feet above sea level. Mars is just another mountaintop to him."

He broke off. "Oh, there's Frank. Hey, Frank, come over here!"

Frank Gray was rod-man on the engine's atomic-heated boiler unit. He strode over, a lean, tense man looking huge in his suit. He was introduced to Senior Incuhana, started to put out his hand, and then drew back with a frown.

"What's going on here?" he said. "I'm near the head of the list to become engineer. Who is bringing in outsiders?"

He didn't wait for a reply, but went on angrily. "I remember now. I've heard of this Indian idea. It's an insult to a good technician. What are they trying to do? Make us think we're just a bunch of day laborers?"

Manet said placatingly, "Frank, you are a good enough scientist to realize that if we can get people who can actually live—"

He stopped. Frank had turned away. We stood silent, watching him walk off. I glanced at José, but his face was impassive. Manet took out his watch.

"Better get aboard," he said. "There will be a few gadgets to show Joe, and you check out in exactly sixteen minutes."

On the dot, the steam-atomic locomotive, *Desert Rat*, was eased by an electric mule into the huge chamber which served as an airlock between the roundhouse and the Martian outdoors. A few moments later, I edged open her throttle.

Sliding forward under her own thunderous power, she moved onto the frozen tracks of "outside."

In the east, the sun was just tipping the horizon.

I pointed, and called to José through the walkie-talkie in my head globe. He came over from his seat, and followed my finger with his eyes.

"Ice, Señor?" he said.

"Ice," I agreed.

Frozen rivulets streaked the metal outer walls. I ran my gaze backward from the bulging front cab. The door of the decompression chamber was just closing behind us, yet everywhere I looked the long, streamlined locomotive already glistened where moisture had condensed and instantly solidified.

Seventy below. A typical winter dawn in the temperate zone of Mars. Ahead of us, bleak and glittery on the flat plain, was the small Earth settlement of Eastport, center of a great mining area. We glided past the interconnected domes, inside which people lived in apartment units. Lines of railway tracks led into the principal domes, but the cars that were going with us—including a pressure-type passenger car—had already been coupled to the head of a long train of ore dumps.

I backed till we connected; then I slid open the door, and climbed down to the ground. The sun shone directly into my eyes from a sky that was a deep blue black. Above, the stars were still visible. They'd be with us all day.

I looked back. José was at the door. I called up, "Better shut the door!"

I heaved myself into the passenger car, went through the airlock inside, and into the comfortable interior. I took a quick glance at the men who were sitting in the bar, and realized I was piloting an important train. There were four top rail executives whom I knew, and one man who was introduced as Philip Barron, just arrived from Earth. He was a heavily built man with curly brown hair and blue gray eyes that looked as hard as agates.

Vice President Henry Wade began. "Bill, our head offices back home have gotten hold of this Andean Indian notion, see it as a cheap way of doing business; and so they're going to populate Mars with them. It's a blind man's deal. In a few years, they'll stage a revolution and claim Mars as their private precinct, including expropriation of all the priceless equipment we've brought here."

Another man broke in. "How did he strike you, Bill?"

"Joe seems to be all right." I spoke carefully.

"Think he can live in this climate?"

I hesitated. "Seems to be able to breathe the air," I said finally.

A third executive laughed ironically. "One of the new men," he said. "The true Martian human. Hundreds more being technically trained. Women, too. Soon people like you and me, Bill, will just be memories in the Martian rail history."

"Like hell we will," said Vice President Wade.

But the other man's words made me uneasy. There were times when I cursed this route and this life, but more often I couldn't imagine anything I'd rather do. Besides, the pay was terrific.

Wade looked at me soberly. "You're going to be asked to give your estimate of him. Our idea is that he should be made to stack up to a high standard."

I said with a shrug, "I can't see this deal depending on my say-so."

Wade replied earnestly, "It'll depend on many things. Superficially, the notion appears to have merit. It's only when you examine it as a whole that you perceive the danger."

Barron, the only Earthside executive present, stood up and offered me his hand. He said, "It's not so bad as they make it sound. We're starting off with eighteen Indians in different types of work. I believe in the long run it's going to save money. Fewer dome shelters, an easing of compression costs, perhaps even a little profit for the shareholders. Is that bad? I don't think so."

As I climbed into the cab a few minutes later, I saw Frank Gray disappear into his section. I looked questioningly at José, but his face told me nothing. I hesitated, but Frank was a friend of mine and José wasn't; I decided to ask no questions. "Start her off!" I said curtly.

The train began to move, and I looked at my watch. We were eight minutes late. We had about five hundred miles to go before dark, not a great distance unless something went wrong. On Mars in winter, trains didn't run on night schedules. Extreme low temperatures made the rails dangerously brittle.

"Keep her down to twenty miles per hour," I said presently.

José nodded, but looked puzzled. Seeing him sitting there, warmly clothed but not in a pressure suit, I began to feel something of the tension that had been in the other men. "Joe," I said suddenly, "what kind of lungs have you got?"

He was no dumb Indian. He had been told about himself, and he explained. Andean man has lungs bigger than normal with more blood vessels in them. His heart can do at least an eighth more work than the heart of sea-level man. His blood vessels carry a greater volume of blood, and his nerve cells are less sensitive to oxygen starvation.

When the Spaniards first came to places like Peru and Bolivia, they discovered that neither pigs nor birds, cattle nor Spaniards, could breed above ten thousand feet. It was only after a generation had lived at about eight thousand feet that the descendants were able to reproduce at fourteen thousand. The Indians had been there before them, from time immemorial.

The facts and figures gave me a sinking sensation. I looked at José's red complexion, and realized that he could be a Martian. But it was obvious that I couldn't.

I saw the pile far ahead beside the tracks before José did. I had expected the pile, of course; and so I waited, wondering how long it would take him to spot the object. Twenty seconds went by, and then he pointed.

I sighed. No sign of oxygen starvation with that kind of vision.

"Start braking her!" I ordered.

He looked at me with some surprise, and I knew he was thinking it was too soon. He was not making due allowance for the fact that it took a lot longer to stop a train on Mars. Same mass as on Earth, but less weight, less friction. We came to a halt, the wheels grinding on the rails, the engine panting and shuddering.

There was no one in sight, only the huge bag lying beside the tracks. I guessed there were about two tons of rock inside the bag. "I'll go outside," I told Joe. "Then you drive forward till I wave for you to stop."

He nodded his acceptance of my instructions. As I slid the door open, he pulled his big collar up over his ears; and, when I had climbed to the ground, he came over and shut the door.

It was not quite as cold as it had been. I guessed the temperature had come up to fifty below. The long train started as I motioned José—and stopped when I waved. I used the "claw," a small crane which we carried to lift such bundles into an ore car. And presently I was back inside the engine cab.

I said, "You can speed up now."

The speedometer climbed. At seventy, José leveled her off. He explained, "I don't know enough about this terrain, Señor, to go any faster."

I nodded, and took control. The speedometer needle edged higher. José said, "That bag of stuff, Bill," he almost said it "Beel"; "who puts it beside the track?"

I'd been wondering if he would show any curiosity. "A race of small, furry creatures," I answered. "They're very shy. They live underground, and dig ore for us." I grinned at his puzzled expression. "We don't want the ore, because it's usually only rock. We're interested in the material of the bags. It's as thin as paper, completely transparent, and yet it can withstand the weight of tons of rock. They manufacture it from their own bodies, much the way spiders produce webs. We can't seem to make them understand that we want only the bags."

We did the next fifty miles at an average of eighty-four miles per hour. It was a straight run, and it was like gliding along on ice. On every side was a flat waste of sand that had not changed in all the years since I had first seen it. The sun was climbing in a sky that was bluer now, the stars faint but still visible. We plunged through that barren world to the hiss of the high-speed steam turbines, and the hum of the gears that transmitted their power to the wheels. I felt more than human. I was the master of a juggernaut that violated the ancient silences of a planet millions of miles remote from the planet Earth.

As I saw the hills in the distance rearing up like low mounds, I began to slow. On the panel a red light blinked. Eight miles, the indicator said. I applied the brakes.

José pointed questioningly at the winking light.

"Sand on the tracks," I said.

Dune country. Sand so fine that even the thin winds of Mars could lift it. In motion, it looked like trailing smoke. As far as the eye could see there were gusts of it blowing, and here and there the rails had completely disappeared under the drifting sand.

We moved in fits and starts, swiftly when the track looked clear, and very slowly, with our blowers whining and hissing, where there was sand. Altogether, about an hour and a half went by before, once again, the roadbed belonged to us.

Halfway. And only a few minutes after ten o'clock. We were first. José slid open the door.

"Go out?" he asked.

"Sure."

We were on a rocky plain that was as crinkled as an old man's face, and almost the same grayish color. I watched José scramble over the rocks and head for a prominence a hundred yards away. It took stiff climbing in places, but he made it with apparent ease.

I grew aware that Frank had come into the cab. I glanced at him; and he said with a sneer, "Showing off to the big shots."

I hadn't thought of that. It could be true. José knew that he was being tested, and that there was hostility toward him, not only from Frank Gray.

There was a faint rumble in the distance, and then a shrill whistle. The *Prairie Dog* rounded the bend and bore down on us. Glittering in the sun, the long engine roared past, its thunder somewhat muffled by the thin air, as was the trailing clatter of its empty ore cars. When the train had passed, I saw that Frank was going back into the rod room, and José was climbing into the engine.

I looked him over sharply. He was breathing heavily, and his cheeks were mottled. I wondered if it was entirely from exertion. Our eyes met; and he must have guessed why I was watching him, for he said quickly, "It's all right, Señor. I feel fine."

I thought I detected a note of irony in his voice. I walked to the door, opened it, and then turned to him. "José," I said, "you'll get an honest deal from me; I'm going back to the passenger car. You're on your own from now on in."

José looked startled. Then his strong jaw set and he said gravely, "Thank you, Señor."

Wade and the other executives were astonished when I explained what I had done. But Barron, the Earthside executive, nodded approval. "After all," he said, "it's a fair test. Can he run a train on his own, or can't he?" He finished, "We can always phone him to stop, and then send Bill back up to the engine."

His words were received in silence, and from the sullen expressions of the others I guessed that my action was unpopular. The silence continued while the train accelerated. I must have dozed in my chair, because I wakened with a start to realize that the car was shuddering and swaying. I took a look out the window, and felt alarm as I saw how swiftly the desert was speeding by.

I glanced around quickly. Three of the men were talking together in low tones; Wade was dozing, and Barron sat placidly smoking a cigar. He looked preoccupied.

I climbed casually to my feet, walked to the phone, and called the engine cab. After it had rung five times, I got an uneasy feeling in the pit of my stomach. I returned to my chair; and it seemed to me, as I glanced again out the window, that the train had actually gained speed. I groaned inwardly, and, glancing up, saw that Wade's shrewd brown eyes were studying me.

"Isn't your man going a little fast?" he said.

His assistant snapped angrily, "Irresponsible, if you ask me!"

Barron sighed, and looked at me gloomily. "Ask him to slow down."

I went to the phone, and called Frank Gray. The phone rang three times, and then Frank's voice said lazily, "Hello."

"Frank," I said in a low tone, "will you go up to the cab and ask José to slow down?"

"I can't hear you," he said. "What do you want?"

I repeated my request, emphasizing the words but still trying to keep my voice down.

Frank said irritably, "Stop mumbling. I can't hear a word you're saying."

I had been feeling both sorry for, and angry with, José. But there's only so much you can do to help a man who's got himself into a difficult situation. Clearly, and without worrying about being overheard, I told Frank what I wanted. There was silence when I had finished. Then:

"Go to hell!" said Frank. "It's not up to me."

He stuck to that, despite my arguments. I said finally, "Just a minute!" And went back to the group. They listened in silence, and then Wade whirled on Barron.

"Look what you've done to us with that Indian of yours!"

Barron chewed his cigar savagely, turned and stared out at the spinning landscape, and then said, "Better order that rod-man to do what Bill said."

Wade came back presently from the phone. "I had to give him permission to use force if necessary."

A few minutes later, we began to slow down. By that time, Barron was climbing into a pressure suit, and Wade had sent his executive assistant to get a suit for him. They exchanged caustic comments until the train finally came to a halt, Barron stubbornly clinging to the attitude that the defection of one Andean Indian didn't condemn all others. I led the way to the engine, and all I could think about was: What *could* have gotten into José?

Frank opened the cab door for us. There was no sign of José as we climbed in. Frank explained, "I found him lying on the floor here gasping for breath, so I put him in the rod room and built up a little pressure." He added complacently, "Nothing wrong with him that a little oxygen won't cure."

I looked at him for a long moment, fighting the suspicion in my mind. I said nothing, however, but made the necessary adjustments in pressure, and went into the rod room. I found José sitting on a chair. He looked at me miserably, but shrugged at my question.

I said earnestly, "José, I want you to forget that pride of yours, and tell me exactly what happened."

He said unhappily, "I became dizzy, and I had a feeling like bursting. Then I do not know what happened."

"Why did you speed up the train?"

He blinked at me, his dark eyes wide and uncomprehending. "Señor," he said at last, "I do not remember."

"My guess," said Frank from behind me, "is that we ran into a low pressure area, and as far as he was concerned it was the last straw."

I shook my head. I was remembering how José had matched my vision early that morning, and remembering also the way he had climbed the hill at Halfway. The stamina he had displayed in those two incidents wouldn't have yielded to a slight change in atmospheric pressure. Also, the cab doors were closed. Since they were nearly airtight, the pressure inside the cab would hardly be that sensitive to temporary changes outside.

I turned and looked at Frank. He stared back at me defiantly. Twice, I started to speak, but each time I remembered how long we'd been friends, and remained silent.

Over his shoulder, I saw that Barron was examining the air pressure gauges and controls for the inside of the engine. He walked over to Wade and spoke in a low voice that sounded grim. The Vice President kept shaking his head, and ended the conversation by going over to Frank. He held out his hand.

"Mr. Gray," he said in a too-loud voice, "I want to thank you for saving us from being wrecked. Just remember, I'm behind you all the way."

Barron was tugging at my arm. I went with him out into the cab. He said quietly, "Is it possible to control the air pressure in the cab from the rod room?"

Since he could have obtained that information from other sources, I didn't hesitate. "Yes," I said.

Barron went on. "Did the Indian show any signs of oxygen starvation in your presence?"

"None."

"Have you any idea whether your rod-man is hostile to this notion of bringing in the Indians?"

"I have no idea," I said. I looked at my watch. "But I think we'd better get going. We're forty-three minutes late."

Under way again, I left José at the throttle, and stepped into the rod room. Frank was adjusting temperatures, and I waited patiently till the gauge readings balanced. Then he looked at me. I said, "Pretty smart."

He didn't deny it. "It's now or never," he said.

"Then you admit you reduced the air pressure on José?"

His tanned face grinned at me through the transparent visor of his suit. "I admit nothing," he said, "but I'm going to wreck that little buzzard's plans if it's the last thing I ever do. And I have an idea I'll get all the backing I need."

I tried to make him see that if there were any human beings at all who could live on Mars without artifice, then no one could fairly deny them the right to do so.

"Call him a human being?" Frank sneered.

I stared at him, and in that moment my feeling of friendship disappeared. I said very slowly, "If you bother him again on duty, I'll take it out of your hide."

Frank looked at me sullenly. "I've been wondering just where you stood," he said. "Thanks for telling me."

For an hour we rolled along through a rock-strewn wasteland, and then we came to an area of low hills and green

sheets of canal ice. I was telling José that the toughest part of
the run was over when the red light began to blink.

He looked at me. "Sand?"

I shook my head, frowning. "Not here. Something must be
on the tracks, or crossing them."

It was a sand lizard, eighteen feet of senseless scarlet and
yellow monstrosity. It had caught its leg under the track
between two ties. All the beast had to do to free itself was to
cease pulling forward, but it was too moronic for that.

Wade phoned me, but lost interest as soon as I explained
why we'd stopped. "You know how to handle them," he said.
And rang off.

I knew the technique, all right, but I wasn't happy about it.
I explained to José that men who hunted the creature wore an
over-suit of the super-resistant material we'd picked up at the
beginning of our trip. It provided protection against a casual
slash, though even it was not much help in a direct attack. In
an emergency, safety lay behind the creature. Out of sight with
it was out of mind.

Frank Gray sauntered out into the cab. He shook his head
when I suggested that he and I help the lizard to free itself. He
said, "That thing lives off a particularly tough cactus. It's got
teeth you could cut rock with." He finished satirically, "Joe's
the man to do the job. If his suit gets torn, it won't do him any
harm."

José picked up a crowbar. "Where is this over-suit, Señor?"

"We carry extras," I said reluctantly. "I'll go with you."

The over-suits covered us completely up to the neck.
Above that, my own rigid vitrolite helmet offered me further
protection. José had only his thickly insulated cap. If his
people became permanent fixtures hereabouts, they'd have to
make provision for such encounters as this.

I took a long oil gun from the tool box, and we climbed out
of the cab. As it saw us approaching, the lizard turned its fiery
head, and watched us. But it kept straining steadily forward.

I squirted oil into its fathomless blue eyes. Then the two of
us prodded it from its left side, its right side, and from behind.
In response, the lizard hissed with its tongue, and made a
rattling sound with its throat. But it continued to tug forward
in that idiotic fashion.

The sun sagged toward mid-afternoon. Patiently, José and I
kept poking at the beast until, finally some mental circuit

seemed to close inside its brain. It ceased its forward movement. Hissing, it turned as if to come after us.

Its leg slipped easily and naturally from under the track. And it was free.

"José!" I yelled. "Get behind it!"

The footing wasn't too good in the shifting sand, and José moved a little awkwardly. Four inch talons whipped the air so close to his cheek that I held my breath. Then he was behind the creature, which stopped turning, evidently having forgotten his existence.

The last we saw of it, it was laboriously climbing over a rock—instead of around it—and heading away from the tracks.

As we turned back toward the engine, there was a swish and a clank, and the long train moved toward us. I caught sight of Frank Gray high in the cab sitting at the controls. He waved mockingly as the powerful locomotive glided past us, gathering speed with every yard.

I grabbed at the handrail as it swept by, caught hold, and hung on with everything I had. Grimly, I reached for the next rung—just as the cab door above me slid open. Frank bent down and with a long wrench banged me on the fingers. Despite the protection of my heavy gloves, the instant pain and numbness broke my hold. Wildly, I grabbed at the rung below with my other hand.

Frank knelt, and swung his wrench again. This time he missed, but he drew sparks from the metal. I'd had enough, however. I couldn't let him cripple my other hand. It might send me under the wheels. Before he could strike again, I lowered my feet to the ground, started running, and let go.

I pitched headlong into the gravel of the roadbed. The cushion of air in my pressure suit saved me from serious injury. But I was gasping as I scrambled shakily to my feet. My plan was to swing aboard the ore car, but as I fell in beside the train, running as swiftly in my bulky clothing as I could, I realized the train was going too fast. I was about to give up when a hand like iron grabbed the scruff of my neck.

"Señor, *run!*"

I ran until the salt of my exhaustion was in my mouth, until I could hardly see because of the tears in my eyes. I fumbled blindly for a rung of the ore car ladder to which José was clinging.

With his clutch supporting most of my weight, I caught the rung; and presently we lay on top of the car gasping for breath.

I stood up, still shaky. "I don't know what that buzzard is up to," I said, when I could speak again, "but we're going to go into the passenger car, and sit it out."

Our sudden appearance caused a minor sensation. I explained briefly what had happened, then picked up the phone and called the engine. It rang three times, and the line went dead. Since all power on the train was supplied by the locomotive, it seemed evident that Frank had cut the telephone system. His purpose was obvious—to prevent us from calling Marsopolis, our destination.

Silently, I cursed my stupidity for not having called there first. Frank might not have thought of it in time to stop me.

An official was shrugging. "He's behaving very foolishly. He can hardly wreck the train without danger to himself. All we have to do is sit tight."

A sudden thought struck me. I went to the gauge panel. The pressure was a full pound low, and the temperature was down slightly. I turned to the others, frowning.

"I hate to say this, but I'm afraid he's cut the power for our air-conditioning."

Philip Barron looked pale, but his eyes were steady. "How long?"

"Not more than an hour," I said. "We could stand the cold, but we'll all pass out if the pressure drops much more than half—all except José, that is."

There was a grim silence. Then Barron glanced at José musingly, and said, "Yes, there is you. I suppose Gray figures it'll be his word against that of an Indian. The arrogant fool! Of course we could all sign a statement as to what actually happened, and leave it with you—"

"To hell with that!" said another official. "That might help José, and it might help justice, but what about us?"

I broke in at that point. "You're overlooking one thing. José can stand low pressure, but he can't breathe poisoned air, and he wouldn't last long outside after dark. We have only one chance." I turned. "Come on, José, let's get aboard that engine."

There was a fire ax in each of two emergency cases at opposite ends of the car. We armed ourselves with them, and a minute later climbed up to the top of the train and started forward. I could see the glistening blue and red locomotive with its bulging cab, and the figure of Frank Gray sitting in it.

What worried me was that there was a high-powered rifle in the cab—and at the moment José and I were as exposed as two sitting ducks. I doubted if Frank would fire unless he had to—bodies with bullets in them would be hard to explain away—but the possibility put a tension in me.

The shallow Martian sky was already darkening in the east, and Earth as an evening star shone brightly above the declining sun. There was still about an hour of daylight left, but since we were well over a hundred miles out, the fact gave me no comfort. We were in semi-mountainous country, and the track was too winding for high-speed travel.

I pulled my collar more tightly around my ears, and bent into the freezing wind. I noticed that José paused often to clap his hands together as we started forward along the top of the tank-tender, which carried the engine's water reserve.

I saw, at this closer range, that Frank was watching us through the glass. The rifle lay on the window ledge beside him, but he made no move to pick it up. Apparently, he was waiting to see what we were going to do.

I wasn't sure, myself. Get the cab doors open somehow, and hope to get in without being shot down.

We climbed to the top of the cab, and lay prone just above the doors, José on one side, and I on the other. Simultaneously, we swung our fire axes down against the heavy panes of the doors. Though shatterproof, they were hardly built to withstand such blows. On my side, a sizable section of glass broke loose, and fell inside.

That much was easy. Now, we had the ticklish problem of getting down there and reaching inside to unlock the doors.

I slid over the edge, and started down the steel ladder alongside the door. José's face was just disappearing over the other side. And still we were all right, being protected by the metal walls of the cab. To get at us, Frank would have to poke his rifle through the hole in the glass on either side. But he wouldn't do that. He'd sit there amidships, and try to pot the first hand that reached in. After all, time was in his favor.

The long train glided along into a gathering twilight. The wheels ground and squealed with a steely sound. The engine groaned and shuddered, swaying as it curved past a steep embankment. I was nerving myself for that first, dangerous thrust—when a shot rang out inside the cab. It could only mean one thing: José had grabbed first.

Galvanized, I reached through the hole in the glass. And my hope was that Frank's gun might still be turned the other way.

Familiarity counted. I knew that lock, and I opened it with one quick twist of my fingers. And jerked my arm back.

A hole appeared in an unbroken part of the glass just above where my hand had been. And another shot sounded.

Hastily, I gave the door a strong push from the outside. It rolled back with a bang. And then there was Frank standing in the opening, leveling his rifle at me.

I pressed flat against the cab, but realized the futility of that, and struck at him with the ax. The blow fell short, as he drew back slightly. I could see his face through the transparent visor of his head globe, his lips twisted, his eyes glittering. In pulling away from me, he had let the muzzle of the rifle drop. Now, deliberately, he raised the gun once more.

As his finger tightened on the trigger, I threw my ax at him. He ducked. The handle of it brushed his shoulder.

For a third time, the muzzle of the gun came up; this time it pointed at my helmet. I thought despairingly: *We're proving our weakness, Frank and I.* This whole incident, the very arrival of José on Mars, had happened because our air supply was so vulnerable.

In some way, I had hoped to drive that fact home to him.

Even as I had the vague thought, I was stooping low, and trying to swing through the door into the cab. The rifle went off practically in my face. And Frank staggered drunkenly.

At least, that was the way things seemed to happen.

What amazed me was that the bullet intended for me went off into the gathering darkness.

And then a fire ax clattered to the floor of the cab out of nowhere—and the truth dawned on me. José had thrown it from the other door with enough luck or precision to smash Frank's head globe.

Frank was reeling. He would have plunged through the open door if I hadn't grabbed him instinctively. As I pushed him back inside and followed him, closing the door behind me, I saw José leaning against the opposite wall. His left arm was dangling, and dripped blood.

The grayness of shock was in his face. But he grinned at me as I dragged the limp body of Frank Gray toward the rod room, where I could apply pressure and save his life—so that a criminal court could decide what to do with it.

These days the story of José is the part of my Martian life my kids most want to hear about. Which makes me feel hopeful. Living here in retirement in Colorado at eighty-five hundred feet, I've managed to work up a community enthusiasm for a long-run scheme of mine.

We're building a town at twelve thousand feet; and our children are already spending time up there. We've got it all figured out.

Their kids are going to be Martians.

The Reflected Men

Time, 5:10 P.M. *The crystal was less than fifteen minutes from reactivation.*

To Edith Price, the well-dressed young man who came into her library was typical of the summer visitors to Harkdale. They lived apart from the townspeople, of whom she was now one. She wrote down his name—Seth Mitchell. And, assuming he wanted a temporary library card, she pushed the application form across the counter toward him.

It was only when he impatiently thrust it back that she actually for the first time listened to what he was saying.

Then she said, "Oh, what you want is a piece of crystal."

"Exactly," he said. "I want returned to me a small stone I presented to the museum section of the library some years ago."

Edith shook her head. "I'm sorry. The museum is being reorganized. It's closed to the public. I'm sure no action will be taken about anything in it until the job is done and even then Miss Davis, the librarian, will have to authorize any disposition of the exhibits. Today is her day off."

"How long will it take—to reorganize the museum?"

"Oh, several weeks."

The effect of her words on the man—clean-cut and typical of the well-dressed, successful men she had known in New York—startled her. He paled, mumbled something indistinguishable, and when he turned away it was as if some of the life had gone out of him.

Staring at the retreating figures of library patrons was not something Edith Price was normally motivated to do. But his reaction was so extreme that she watched him as he walked unsteadily toward the main entrance of the library. At the door a squat, thickly built man joined him. The two conversed briefly, then walked out together. Moments later, through a window, Edith caught a glimpse of them entering a new Cadillac. Seth Mitchell slid in behind the wheel.

The costly automobile, Seth Mitchell's overreaction, and the fact that another man was involved made intriguing what was probably a minor incident. Edith slipped from her stool, making suitable gestures to Miss Tilsit. Quite openly she secured the key to the women's rest room as she covertly palmed the key to the museum room.

A few moments later she was examining the display of stones.

There were about thirty altogether. According to the sign beside them, the collection was the result of a drive among local boys to find valuable minerals and gems. Edith had no difficulty in locating the one the young man had wanted. A faded card under it announced: "Donated by Seth Mitchell and Billy Bingham."

She slid back the side of the case, reached in carefully, and took out the crystal. It was obvious to her that very little discrimination had been used in the selection. The forces that had fashioned this stone seemed to have been too impatient. The craftsmanship was uneven. The result was a stone about two and a half inches long by one and a half inches wide, maximum; a brownish, rock like thing which, though faceted, did not reflect light well. It was by far the dullest of the stones in the display.

Gazing down at the drab, worthless stone, Edith thought: *Why don't I just take it to his hotel after work tonight and bypass all the red tape?*

Meaning Miss Davis, her enemy.

Decisively, she removed the names of the two donors from the case. After all these years the label was stuck on poorly and the yellowed paper tore to shreds. She was about to slip the stone into her pocket, when she sadly realized she was wearing that dress—the one without pockets.

Oh, damn! she thought cheerfully.

Since the stone was too big to conceal in her hand she carried it through the back stack corridors and was about to toss it into the special wastebasket used for heavy debris—

when she noticed that a broken flowerpot half-full of dirt was also in the basket. Beside the dirt was a paper bag.

She needed only seconds to slip the crystal into the bag, place dirt on top of it, and shove the bag down into the basket. She usually had the job of locking up the building, so it would be no problem to pick up the bag at that time and take it with her.

Edith returned to her desk.

And the stone began at once to utilize the sand in the dirt on top of it, thus resuming a pattern that had been suspended for twenty-five years. During the rest of the evening, and in fact all through that night, all the possible Seth Mitchells on earth remembered their childhoods. The majority merely smiled or shrugged or stirred in their sleep. Most of those who lived outside the western hemisphere in distant time zones presently resumed their normal activities.

But a few, everywhere, recalling the crystal, could not quite let the memory go.

During her first idle moment after filching the stone Edith leaned over to ask Miss Tilsit, "Who is Seth Mitchell?"

Tilsit was a tall, too-thin blonde with horn-rimmed glasses behind which gleamed unusually small but alert gray eyes. Edith had discovered that Tilsit had a vast, even though superficial, knowledge of everything that had ever happened in Harkdale.

"There were two of them," said Tilsit. "Two boys. Billy Bingham and Seth Mitchell."

Thereupon, with visible relish, Tilsit told the story of Billy's disappearance twenty-five years earlier, when he and his chum, Seth Mitchell, were only twelve years old.

Tilsit finished: "Seth claimed they had been fighting over a piece of bright stone they had found. He swore that they were at least fifty feet from the cliff that overlooks the lake at that point and he insisted Billy didn't drown—which is what everyone else believed. What confused the situation was that Billy's body was never recovered."

As she listened to the account, Edith tried to put together the past and the present. She couldn't imagine why an adult Seth Mitchell would want a reminder of such an unhappy experience. Still, men were funny. That she knew, after waiting five years for a worthwhile male to come along and find her. So far she seemed to be as well-hidden and unsearched for in Harkdale as in New York.

Tilsit was speaking again. "Kind of odd, what happens to people. Seth Mitchell was so crushed by his friend's death that he just became a sort of shadow human being. He's got a farm out toward Abbotsville."

Edith said sharply, "You mean Seth Mitchell became a farmer?"

"That's the story."

Edith said nothing more, but made a mental note that perhaps Tilsit was not as good a source of local information as she had believed. Whatever Mitchell was, he hadn't looked like a farmer. She had to go to check out some books at that point, so the thought and the conversation ended.

A few minutes after nine-thirty, Edith parked her car across the street from the entrance to the motel in which—after some cruising around—she had spotted Seth Mitchell's distinctive gold Cadillac.

It was quite dark where she waited under a tree. But even in the secure darkness, she could feel her heart thumping and the hot flush in her cheeks.

Why am I doing this?

She had a self-critical suspicion that she might be hoping the adventure would end in a summer romance. Which was pretty ridiculous for a woman twenty-seven years old, who—if she shifted her tactic from waiting to pursuing—ought to concentrate cold-bloodedly on genuine husband material.

Her self-examination ended abruptly. From where she sat she could see the door of the cabin beside which the Cadillac was parked. The door had opened. Silhouetted in the light from the interior was the short, squat man she had seen with Mitchell that afternoon. As Edith involuntarily held her breath, the man came out and closed the door behind him.

He walked to the motel office and presently emerged again, stood for a moment, and then walked rapidly toward the business section of Harkdale, only minutes away.

And only minutes back, she thought glumly.

Watching him, her motivation dimmed. Somehow, she had not considered the short, heavyset man as really being associated with Seth Mitchell.

Defeated, she started her motor. As she drove home she suddenly felt degraded, not by what she had done but by what she suspected she had intended to do.

What her future path should be was not clear. But not this way, she told herself firmly.

Arrived at her apartment, Edith shoved the bag containing the crystal into the cupboard under her sink, ate apathetically, and went to bed.

The squat man returned to the motel scowling. "The stone wasn't there. I searched the whole museum," he told Seth Mitchell, who lay on one of the beds, gagged and bound.

Mitchell watched uneasily as the other untied his feet. The man said impatiently, "I've been thinking about you. Maybe the best thing is just to drive you back to New York or kill you here. Once I get away, the police will never find me again."

He removed the gag. Mitchell drew a deep breath.

"Look," he protested, "I won't even go near the police—"

He stopped, his mind once more blank and afraid, and choked back a surge of grief. The possibility that he might be killed was something that his brain could contemplate only for a few moments.

The squat man had come up to him in his office parking lot at noon that day, smiling deceptively, a short man—not more than five-four—and stocky. He had looked, in his grayness, like an Arab in an American business suit.

The man had asked, "Where is the crystal you and Billy Bingham found?"

What might have happened if Seth had answered instantly was, of course, now impossible to guess. But he had not immediately remembered the crystal, so he had shaken his head.

Whereupon the stocky man had shown him a gun. Under its threat Seth had driven to Harkdale, had shown the stranger the ledge beside Lake Naragang where he and Billy had fought. And it was there, on the spot, that he had recalled the crystal; and so he had reluctantly gone to the library, aware of the weapon, trained on him all the while he had talked to the young woman at the desk.

Abruptly remembering that conversation, Seth said desperately, "Maybe that woman librarian—"

"Maybe," said the other, noncommittally.

He untied Seth's hands and stepped back, motioning with the gun. They went out to the car and drove off.

As they came to the lake the man said, "Pull over." After Seth complied, the shot rang out and the murder was done.

The killer dragged the body to a cliff overlooking the lake, tied rocks to it, and dumped it into the deep water below.

He drove on to New York, left the car in Seth's parking lot, and, after spending the night in New York, prepared to return to Harkdale.

During that night Edith Price slept restlessly, and dreamed that all possible Edith Prices marched past her bed. Only half a dozen of those Ediths were married and even in her dream that shocked her.

Worse, there was a long line of Edith Prices who ranged from fat to blowsy to downright shifty-eyed and mentally ill. However, several of the Ediths had a remarkable high-energy look and that was reassuring.

She woke to the sound of the phone ringing.

The library caretaker said, "Hey, Miss Price, better get down here. Somebody broke in last night."

Edith had a strange, unreal feeling.

She asked, "Broke into the library?"

"Yep. Biggest mess is in the museum. Whoever it was musta thought some of the stones in there were the real stuff. They're scattered all over the floor."

To Edith Price, the lean young man in overalls was just another inarticulate farmer.

She wrote down his name—Seth Mitchell. A moment went by as the name hit her. She looked up.

The haunted face that stared back at her had been burned by sun and wind. Its cheeks were gaunt. The eyes were sick. Nevertheless, the man bore a sensational resemblance to the Seth Mitchell of yesterday, it seemed to Edith.

She thought, a light dawning: *This is the Seth Mitchell Tilsit knew about* . . .

There had to be a Mitchell clan, with cousins and such, who were look-alikes.

Her mind was still fumbling over the possibilities when she realized the import of the words he had mumbled.

Edith echoed, "A stone? A crystal you presented to the library museum twenty-five years ago?"

He nodded. Edith compressed her lips.

All right, let's get to the bottom of this . . .

During the moments of her confusion the man had taken a bill out of his billfold. As he held it out to her she saw that it was twenty dollars.

She had recovered her self-control and now said conversationally, "That's a lot of money for a worthless rock."

"It's the one I want," he muttered. She didn't hear several words that followed but then he said clearly, "the time Billy disappeared."

A silence fell while Edith absorbed the impact of the notion that here indeed was the original Seth Mitchell.

"I've heard about Billy," she said finally. "A very unusual incident."

Seth Mitchell said, "I yelled at him to get away and he vanished." He spoke tautly. His eyes were an odd, discolored gray from remembered shock. He spoke again: "We both grabbed at it. Then he was gone."

He seemed only dimly aware of her presence. He went on, and it was as if he were talking to himself: "It was so shiny. Not like it became later. It went all drab and nobody would believe me."

He paused. Then, intently: "All these years I've been thinking. I've been awful slow to see the truth. But last night it came to me. What else could have made Billy disappear when I called him? What else but the stone?"

Edith decided uneasily that this was a problem for a psychiatrist, not a librarian. It struck her that the simplest solution would be to give this Seth Mitchell the worthless rock he wanted.

But of course that would have to be carefully done. Her one indiscretion so far had been questioning Tilsit the day before about Seth Mitchell. Throughout the police investigation of the breaking and entering of the library museum she had maintained a careful silence about her own involvement.

So the sooner she got rid of the stone the better.

"If you'll give me your address," she requested gently, "I'll ask the head librarian and perhaps she'll get in touch with you."

The address he reluctantly gave her was a rural route out of Abbotsville.

She watched him then, wondering a little, as he shuffled off to the door and outside.

On her way home that night, Edith drove by way of the motel. The gold Cadillac was gone.

She had her usual late dinner. Then, after making sure the apartment door was locked, she took the paper bag from under the sink—and noticed at once, uneasily, that there was less dirt in the bag.

A momentary fear came to her that the stone would be gone. She spread a newspaper and hastily emptied the bag, dirt and all, onto it. As the earth tumbled out a brilliance of color flashed at her.

Wonderingly she picked up the beautiful gem.

"But it's impossible," she whispered. "That was dull. This is—beautiful!"

It glittered in her hand. The purple color was alive, as if thousands of moving parts turned and twisted inside the stone. Here and there in its depths a finger of light stirred up a nest of scarlet fire. The crisscross of color and flame flickered so brightly that Edith felt visually stunned.

She held it up against the light—and saw a design inside.

Somebody had cut a relief map of the solar system into the interior of the stone, and had colored it. It was quite a good example—it seemed to Edith—of the cutter's art. The purple and red overall effect seemed to derive from the play of light through the coloring of the tiny "sun" and its family of planets.

She took the stone back to the sink. There was a fantasy in her mind, she realized, in which the jewel had magic powers. Remembering what the farmer Seth Mitchell had said about his having yelled at Billy Bingham in the presence of the stone . . . maybe the sound of a human voice would have an effect . . .

She tried speaking.

Nothing happened. The picture remained unchanged. She spelled words, articulating each letter.

Nothing.

She ran the gamut of sounds possible for her own voice from a low contralto to a ridiculously piercing soprano—nothing.

Once more she noticed the design inside and held the stone up against the light to see it better. She was visually tracing the outline of the solar system in the crystal when she had a sudden thought and, with abrupt determination, said in a clear voice: "Billy Bingham—the boy—I want him back—now!"

After she had spoken, during the silent moments that followed, she felt progressively foolish.

Of the long-missing Billy there was no sign.

Thank God, she thought breathlessly.

Edith rose early the next morning; her mind was made up. It was time she got rid of something that was threatening to undermine her good sense.

As she took the crystal out of the flowerpot, she saw that the interior scene had changed. It was now a human body outlined in purple and red points of light.

The outline, she saw presently, was actually extremely detailed, showing the bone structure and the principal organs. There was even a faint glow which suffused the shape, suggesting a fine mask of nerves and blood vessels.

She was examining it absorbedly when she abruptly realized what she was doing.

Firmly, she put the stone into a small box, filled it with new soil—crystals, she had read, needed nutrients—wrapped it, and addressed it to Seth Mitchell, Rural Route 4, Abbotsville.

Shortly she was driving to the post office. It was not until after she had mailed the package that her first realization came that she had done it again. Once more she had acted on impulse.

Too late, the cautioning thought came: Suppose Seth Mitchell wrote the library a note of thanks. It would be impossible for Edith to explain how a romantic compulsion had motivated her to steal the crystal—and how, in the light of later events, her only desire had become to dispose of the evidence.

Why don't I just get on the next bus to New York and leave this crazy little town forever?

The moment was extremely depressing. She remembered an endless series of wrong decisions in her life. She sat there in her car at the curb and thought of her first young man at

college. The first, that is, who had been truly hers. She had
lost him through an impulse: she had been caught by the God-
is-dead-so-now-you're-God movement. In the movement what
you did to other people no longer mattered—you never had to
feel guilty.

*If I hadn't joined the guilt-free generation, right now I would
be Mrs. Richard Staples . . .*

The realization reminded her of her dream of the multitude
of Edith Prices and the unique remembrance lifted her out of
her apathy. What an odd concept. She laughed, and thought
that sending the crystal to the least of all possible Seth
Mitchells had not been good sense.

Thinking about that, her fear faded. How funny! And what
an odd dream to have had.

How could one ever know what way was best, what
decision, what philosophy, how much exercise? And, best for
what?

Edith was already at her desk in the library when Tilsit
came in with the look on her face. In her six months in
Harkdale, Edith had come to recognize Tilsit's expression of:
I've got special information.

"Did you see the paper, Edith?"

Edith presumed the paper referred to was the *Harkdale
Inquirer*, a four-page daily. She herself still read *the New York
Times*, though she loyally subscribed to the local sheet. She
had not read today's Inquirer, however, and said so.

"Remember asking me the other day about a man called
Seth Mitchell?" Tilsit asked.

Edith remembered only too well but she put on a blank
face.

Tilsit unfolded the paper in her hands and held it up. The
headline was:

BILLY BINGHAM FOUND?

Edith reached automatically and Tilsit handed the paper to
her. Edith read:

> A twelve-year-old boy staggered out of the brush near Lake
> Naragang shortly after ten last night and tried to enter the house
> where Billy Bingham lived twenty-five years ago. The present

tenant, John Hildeck, a carpenter, took the bewildered youngster to the police station. From there he was transported to the hospital.

That was as far as Edith read. Her body bent to one side, her arms flopped limply. She stooped over and the floor crashed into her.

When she came out of her faint on the cot in the rest room, the remembrance was still there, bright and hard and improbable, of how she had commanded the crystal to bring back Billy Bingham—somewhere between nine and ten the previous night.

Miami. The Seth Mitchell in that singing city had a private vocabulary for God (or, as he sometimes thought of Him, Nature or Fate): The Musician. Within this exclusive terminology Seth's own life had been tuneful and the music a symphony—or at least a concerto.

Somebody up there evidently regarded him as a suitable instrument.

For he had money, girlfriends, a fabulous career as a gambler on the edge of the underworld—all without restrictions, for his orchestra was well-disciplined and responsive to his baton. Not bad for a small-town boy who had not learned the melodies of city life until he was past twenty.

But now, suddenly, The Musician had sounded a sour note.

Mitchell had in his hand the *Harkdale Inquirer* containing the account of the return of Billy Bingham.

He studied the newspaper's photograph of a frightened boy about twelve years old. The subject looked like Billy Bingham—and didn't. Mitchell was surprised that he wasn't sure. The *Inquirer* apologized for having lost its photocut of the real Billy, and explained that Billy's parents had moved to Texas, it was believed. No one knew precisely where.

The news story concluded: "The only other person who might be able to identify the claimant is Seth Mitchell, Billy's boyhood chum. Mitchell's present address is unknown."

Mitchell thought sarcastically that the *Inquirer* ought to examine its out-of-state subscription list.

The next day as he walked into room 312 of the Harkdale Hospital, he saw the youngster in bed put down his magazine and look up.

Mitchell said with a reassuring smile, "Billy, you don't have to worry about me. I'm here as your friend."

The boy said uneasily, "That's what the big man told me, and then he got nasty."

Mitchell didn't ask who the big man was. A chair stood near the bed. He drew it up, and said gently, "Billy, what seems to have happened to you is almost like a fairy story. But the most important thing is that you mustn't worry."

Billy bit his lip and a tear rolled down his cheek. "They're treating me as if I'm lying. The big man said I'd be put in jail if I didn't tell the truth."

Mitchell's mind leaped back to the days when he had been questioned by just such impatient individuals about the disappearance of Billy. His lips tightened.

He said, "Nothing like that is going to happen to you if I can help it. But I'd like to ask you a few questions that maybe nobody else thought of. You don't have to answer if you don't want to. How does that strike you?"

"Okay."

Mitchell took that for a go-ahead signal. "What kind of clothes was Seth wearing?"

"Brown corduroy pants and a gray shirt."

Reality rather than the boy's answer gave Mitchell his first disappointment. He had hoped the description would jog his memory. It didn't. He was unable to recall what particular pair of ragged trousers he had worn on that distant day.

"You wore corduroys also?" It was a shot in the dark.

"They're in there." The boy pointed at the chest in one corner.

Mitchell stood up, opened the indicated drawer, and lifted out a skimpy pair of cheap corduroys. He examined them shamefacedly but with an eye to detail. He put them back finally, disappointed. The identifying label had been torn off. He couldn't remember ever having seen them before.

Twenty-five years, he thought drearily. The time was like a thick veil with a few tattered holes in it. Through the holes he could catch glimpses of his past, instants out of his life, each one illuminated because it had once had some particular momentary impact—none was fully visible in context.

"Billy," Mitchell came back to his chair, intent. "you mentioned trying to grab a shining stone. Where did you first see it?"

"On the ledge. There's a path that comes up from the lake."

"Had you come up that way before?"

The other shook his head. "A few times when it was cold. Usually Seth and I liked to stay near the water."

Mitchell nodded. He remembered that. "This bright stone you saw—how big was it?"

"Oh, it was big."

"An inch?"

"Bigger. Five inches, I'll betcha." Billy's face was bright with certainty.

Mitchell paused to argue out the error of that with himself. The stone had been roughly two and a half inches at its longest, and somewhat narrower and thinner. A boy who had had only a glimpse would not be the best judge of its size.

The reasoning made Mitchell uneasy. He was making excuses where none should be allowed. He hesitated. He wanted to find out if Billy had actually touched the crystal, but he didn't quite know how to lead up to the question. He began, "According to what you told the paper, you admitted that your chum—what's his name?" He waited.

"Seth. Seth Mitchell."

"Seth Mitchell saw the stone first. But you still tried to get it, didn't you?"

The boy swallowed. "I didn't mean any harm."

Mitchell had not intended to imply moral disapproval. He said hastily, "It's all right, Billy. When I was a boy the guy who got a thing owned it. None of this seeing-first stuff for us."

He smiled.

Billy said, "I only wanted to be the one who gave it to the museum."

The thunder of that vibrated through Mitchell's mind.

Of course, now I remember . . .

He even realized why he had forgotten. The library's museum room had accepted the stone—which had lost its brilliance during the days he had carried it in his pocket—

with reluctance. The librarian had murmured something about not discouraging small boys. With those words she had discouraged him so completely that he had needed an actual naming of the fact to remember it.

It was hard to believe an imposter would be able to cite this boy's detailed recollections. And yet, that meant that Billy Bingham, when he disappeared, had—

His brain poised, stopped by the impossibility of this situation. His own doctor had already told him that mental disturbances were often traced to overactive imaginations.

Mitchell drew a deep breath. "All right. Now, two more questions. What time of day was it?"

"Seth and I went swimming after school," said Billy. "So it was late afternoon."

"Okay. According to the paper you didn't get back to your house until nearly ten. Where were you from late afternoon till ten o'clock at night?"

"I wasn't anywhere," said Billy. "Seth and I were fighting over the stone. I fell. And when I picked myself up it was pitch dark." He was suddenly tearful. "I don't know what happened. I guess he just left me lying there, somehow."

Mitchell rose to his feet, thinking suddenly: *This is ridiculous. I ought to have my head examined . . .*

Nevertheless he paused at the door and flung one more question toward the bed. "Has anyone else called you— besides the police, I mean, and the big man—and me?"

"Just a woman from the library."

"Library?" Mitchell echoed blankly.

"She wanted to know the exact time I woke up beside the lake. Her name is Edith Price and she works in the library. Of course—I didn't know."

The information seemed meaningless. Mitchell said quickly, simulating a friendliness he no longer felt, "Well, Billy, I guess I'd better let you get back to your comic book. Thanks a lot."

He went out of the room and out of the hospital. He paid his bill at the hotel, got into his rented car, drove to the airport, and flew back to Miami. By the time the plane landed, the old, disturbing music from his childhood had faded from his mind.

It seemed to Mitchell that The Musician had let him down. To insure that it never happened again, he resolved to cancel his subscription to the *Harkdale Inquirer*.

Chicago. Seth Mitchell (of the Seth Mitchell Detective Agency) stared at the man who had just walked into his office as if he were seeing a hallucination.

Finally he blinked and asked, "Am I crazy?"

The stranger, a well set-up young man in his mid-thirties, sat down in the visitor's chair and said with an enigmatic smile, "The resemblance is remarkable, isn't it?"

He spoke in a firm baritone and, except that both of them knew better, Mitchell could have sworn the voice was his own.

In fact, afterward, telling Marge Aikens about the visitor, he confessed, "I kept feeling that it was me sitting there."

"But what did he want?" Marge asked. She was a slim blonde taking her first look at thirty and taking it well. Mitchell intended to marry her someday, when he could find another associate as efficient. "What did he look like?"

"Me. That's what I'm trying to tell you. He was my spitting image. He even wore a suit that reminded me of one I've got at home." He pleaded uneasily, "Don't be too hard on me, Marge. I went to pieces. It's all vague."

"Did he give you his address?"

Mitchell looked down unhappily at the interview sheet. "It's not written down."

"Did he say if he intended to come to the office again?"

"No, but he gave me a thousand dollars in bills and I gave him a receipt. So we're committed."

"To what?"

"That's the silliest part of it. He wants me to find an onyx crystal. He said he saw it quite a while back in a small-town museum south of New York. He can't remember just where."

"That's going to be either very hard or very easy." Marge was thoughtful; she seemed to be considering the problem involved.

"Let me finish," said Mitchell grimly. "I know where the crystal is. Just think of what I said. I knew that region like a book. I was born there, remember?"

"It had slipped my mind," said Marge. "You think you can locate the crystal because—"

Mitchell said, "It's in the museum annex of the public library in the town of Harkdale, where I was born. And now—get this. I presented the crystal to the library, and, what's even more amazing, I dreamed about that stone the other night."

Marge did not let him get off the subject. "And he came to you? Out of the scores of detective agencies in Chicago, he came to the one man in the world who looks like him and who knows where that crystal is?"

"He came to me."

Marge was pursing her beautiful lips. "Seth, this is fantastic. You shouldn't have let him get away. You're usually so sharp."

"Thanks." Dryly.

"Why didn't you just tell him where it is."

"And lose a thousand dollars? My dear, a detective is sometimes like a doctor. People pay him for information he already has."

Marge held out her hand. "Let me see that interview sheet."

As she read it she asked without looking up, "What are you going to do?"

"Well, I told him the truth, that I've got several days' work to get rid of and then—"

He fell silent and the silence grew so long that Marge finally looked up. She was relieved at the expression on his face, for it was the shrewd, reasoning look that was always there when he was at his detective's best.

He caught her glance, and said, "It would be a mistake to appear in Harkdale until three or four mysteries have been cleared up. Like how come there's two of us—"

"You have no relations?"

"Some cousins."

"Ever see them?"

He shook his head. "Not since I was around nineteen, when my mother died." He smiled grimly. "Harkdale is not a town you go back to. But kill the thought you've got. None of my cousins looked like me." He shuddered. "Ugh, no."

Marge said firmly, "I think when you do finally go, you ought to be disguised."

"You can count on it—even you won't know me."

Elsewhere on earth about two dozen of the total of 1,811 Seth Mitchells—among whom was the best of all possible Seth

Mitchells—also considered the crystal, remembered their dream of a few nights earlier, and had a strange, tense conviction of an imminent crisis.

As Seth Mitchell in Montreal, Canada, described it to his French-Canadian wife, "I can't get over the feeling that I'm going to have to measure up. Remember, I mentioned that to you when I awoke the other morning."

His wife, a pretty blonde, who had a French-Canadian woman's practical contempt for dream fantasies, remembered it well and wanted to know what he had to measure up to.

Her husband said unhappily, "I have a feeling I could have made better decisions, made more of myself. I am not the man I could have been."

"So what?" she wanted to know. "Who is? And what of it."

"*Kaput.*" He shrugged. "I'm sorry to be so negative, my dear. But that's the feeling. Since I didn't measure up, I'm through."

His wife sighed. "My mother warned me that all men get crazy ideas as they approach forty. And here you are."

"I should have been braver—or something," he moaned.

"What's wrong with being a tax consultant?" she demanded.

Her husband seemed not to hear. "I have a feeling I ought to visit my hometown."

She grabbed his arm. "You're going straight to Dr. Ledoux," she said. "You need a checkup."

Dr. Ledoux could find nothing wrong. "In fact, you seem to be in exceptionally good health."

The Seth Mitchell of Montreal had to concede that his sudden alarm was pretty ridiculous.

But he decided to visit Harkdale as soon as he cleared up certain business.

The man's voice came suddenly, tinged with a slight foreign accent. "Miss Price, I want to talk to you."

Edith saw the speaker dimly in the darkness and realized that he stood in the shadows between the garage and the rooming house where she lived, barring her way.

Before she could speak the voice continued, "What did you do with the crystal?"

"I—don't—understand."

She spoke the words automatically. She could see her interrogator more clearly now. He was short and broad of build. Abruptly she recognized him as the man who had been with the Seth Mitchell look-alike in the gold Cadillac.

"Miss Price, you removed that crystal from the display cabinet. Either give it to me or tell me what you did with it and that'll be the end of the matter."

Edith had the tense feeling of a person who has acted unwisely and who therefore cannot possibly make any admissions, not even to a stranger.

"I don't know what you're talking about," she whispered.

"Look, Miss Price." The man stepped out of the shadows. His tone was conciliatory. "Let's go into your apartment and talk this over."

His proposal relieved her. For her apartment was only a little suite in a rooming house in which the other tenants were never more than a wall away.

Incredibly—afterward she thought of it as incredible—she was instantly trusting and started past him. Her surprise when he grabbed her was total. One of his arms imprisoned both of hers and her body.

He put a hard, unyielding palm over her mouth and whispered, "I've got a gun."

Nearly paralyzed by the threat, she was aware of her captor carrying her toward the back alley. She allowed him to shove her—without a struggle—into a car that was parked against a fence.

He climbed in beside her and sat there in the near-dark of the night, gazing at her. She could not make out the expression on his face. But as the seconds went by, and he made no threatening move, her heart slowed in its rapid beating.

She finally gasped, "Who are you? What do you want?"

The man chuckled sardonically and said, "I'm the worst of all possible Athtars from the thirty-fifth century. But I turned out to have a high survival faculty."

Edith was again unable to speak.

His voice tightened. "Where I come from I'm a physicist. I sensed my danger and I worked out a key aspect of the nature of the crystal in record time. In dealing with human beings, it operates on the vibrations a body puts forth from all its cells. In recreating that vibration, it uncreates him. Recognizing this—and since I was not of its orientation in my era—I simply put up a barrier on the total vibration level of my own body and thus saved my life when it uncreated all the lesser Athtars."

Now she did not want to speak, and the man added somberly: "But evidently, by defeating it, I remained attached to it on some other level. As it fell back through time to the twentieth century, I fell with it. Not unfortunately, to where and when it went. Instead, I arrived last week beside that ledge overlooking Lake Naragang." He finished in a wondering tone: "What a remarkable, intricate internal energy flow system it must have. Imagine! In passing through time it must have detected this twenty-five year inactive period and its reawakening—and dropped me off within days of its own reactivation."

The voice became silent and there was nothing but the darkness again. Edith ventured a small movement—she changed her position on the seat to ease a growing discomfort in one leg.

When there was no counter movement from him she whispered, "Why are you telling me this? It all sounds perfectly insane."

Even as she uttered the obvious she realized that a quality of equal madness in herself believed every word that he had spoken. She thought in a spasm of self-criticism: *I really must be one of the lesser Edith Prices.*

She had to fight to suppress an outburst of hysterical laughter.

"From you," said the worst of all possible Athtars, "I want information."

"I don't know anything about a crystal."

"The information I want," said the man in an inexorable voice, "is this: At any time recently have you had a thought about wishing you had taken a different path in life instead of ending up in Harkdale as a librarian?"

Edith's mind flashed back to her series of impulses after she had mailed the crystal—and back farther.

"Why, yes," she breathed.

"Tell me about one of them," said the man.

She told him of the impulse she had had to simply get on a bus or train and leave Harkdale.

The man leaned back in the seat. He seemed surprisingly relaxed.

He asked with a chuckle, "Are you the best of all possible Edith Prices?"

Edith made no reply. She was beginning to have the feeling that perhaps she should confide in this man—should tell him where the crystal was.

Athtar was speaking again. "I have a conviction that the Edith Price who is the twentieth-century orientation for the crystal is on that bus or is heading for safety somewhere else. And that therefore you are under the same threat as I am—of being uncreated as soon as the crystal selects the perfect Edith Price."

For Edith, terror began at that moment.

During the minutes that followed she was only vaguely aware of words mumbling out of her mouth.

Listening to her revelation, Athtar suppressed an impulse to murder her out of hand. He played it cautiously, thinking that if anything went wrong, this Edith was all he had to help him to trace the other Ediths.

So he spoke reassuring words, put her out of the car, and watched her as she staggered off—safe, she thought.

The note read: "He wasn't there. It wasn't there. The farm was deserted. Did you lie to me? Athtar."

Edith felt a chill the first time she read the words. Particularly she reacted to the last line with fear. But on her tenth or twelfth reading, she was more determined.

She thought: *If this whole crazy business is real I'd better . . . What?*

Be brave? Consider the problem? Act with decisiveness?

It was Saturday.

Before going to work she bought a small Browning .25 automatic at the Harkdale Hardware. She had often gone target practicing with the second of her two college boyfriends, the one who had sold her on the philosophy that God was dead and that therefore one need only avoid jail—and otherwise do anything one pleased. Eventually he departed without marrying her, presumably feeling guiltless about having lured her away from a man who might have offered her a wedding ring.

But this man did show her how to shoot an automatic firearm. She put the little pistol into her purse—and felt a hardening of her conviction that it was time *this* Edith started measuring up.

One doubt remained: was willingness to shoot in self-defense a step forward—or a step away—from being the best of all possible Edith Prices?

At the library that day, Tilsit was waiting for her with another news item:

YOUNG FARMER MISSING

Seth Mitchell, Abbotsville farmer, has not been at his farm for several days. A neighbor, Carey Grayson, called on Mitchell yesterday to buy seed grain, found the Mitchell cows unmilked, a horse in the stable starving, chickens unfed and no sign of life around the house.

Grayson fed the animals, then contacted Mitchell's cousin in a neighboring county and notified the sheriff's office.

An investigation is under way.

Edith handed back the paper with a meaningless comment. But she was thinking: *So that's what Athtar discovered . . .*

In spite of her resolve she trembled. It seemed to her that there was no turning back; she must carry forward inexorably with all the thoughts that she had had.

Sunday.

She had driven to New York, and parked two blocks from the little hotel for women only where she had formerly lived. Surely, she told herself, that was where at least one Edith duplicate would have gone.

From a phone booth she called the hotel and asked for Edith Price. There was a pause, then, "I'm ringing," said the woman desk clerk.

Instantly breathless, Edith hung up. She sagged limply inside the booth, eyes closed. It was not clear to her even now what she had expected.

Can it be that I'm the only Edith who knows that there are others? And does that give me an advantage over the unknowing ones?

Or was there already somewhere an Edith Price who had naturally become the best of them all?

Her thought ended. She realized that a short, stocky man was standing beside the booth, partly out of her line of vision. Something about him was familiar.

She straightened and turned.

Athtar.

The Edith Price who stepped out of the phone booth was still shaky and still not brave. But two days of fear and threat and gulps of terror had transformed her. She had been a vaguely sad, wish-my-mistakes-won't-doom-me young woman. Now she trembled with anxiety at times, but at other times she compressed her lips and had thoughts that were tough and realistic.

The sight of Athtar caromed her into anxiety.

Which was just as well, the tough part of her assessed realistically. She did not trust the worst of all possible Athtars. And he would feel safer with a frightened Edith, she was sure.

Seen close in broad daylight on a deserted New York street on Sunday morning, Athtar—short, broad, with a thick face and gray cheeks—was surprisingly as she remembered him: totally unprepossessing.

He said softly, "Why don't you let me talk to her?"

Edith scarcely heard. The first question of her forty-eight-hour stop-only-for-sleep stream of consciousness siphoned through her voice. "Are you really from the thirty-fifth century?"

He gave her a quick, shrewd look, must have realized how wound up she was, and said receptively, "Yes."

"Are they all like you?"

"It was decided," said Athtar in a formal tone, "that a body built thicker and closer to the ground has more utility. That was several hundred years before I was born. And so, yes. No one is over sixteen hundred and seventy-five centimeters—that is, five feet, six inches."

"How do you know you're the worst of all possible Athtars?"

"In my time," was the reply, "it is a felony for anyone but a member of the Scientists' Guild to have a weapon. Hence, political and economic power is part of the prize of the struggle for position in the Guild. On my way to becoming a tougher member, I wished many times to be relatively safe among the faceless, unarmed masses. And the crystal, in creating other Athtars, solidified those wishes."

There was an implication here that getting tougher was not the answer, not the way. Edith sighed her disappointment and remembered her other questions. She told him about the two pictures she had seen in the crystal, the one of the solar system and the other the outline of a human body. Did he know what the pictures meant?

"When I first saw the crystal," said Athtar, "the scene inside was of our galaxy. Later it became the solar system. So what you saw was probably a carryover from my time, where we occupy all the planets. And what I saw must derive from a time when man has moved out to the galaxy. It could mean that the crystal adjusts to the era in which it finds itself. Though why a human being instead of the planet Earth in this era is not obvious. Was the outline that of a woman or a man?"

Edith couldn't remember.

Standing there in the bright, sunny day and on the dirty, narrow street, Athtar shook his head. There was awe in his ugly face. He said wonderingly, "Such a small object; such a comprehensive ability." He added, half to himself, "It has to be based on potential flow patterns. There are not enough atoms in such a crystal to act as a control board for so much."

He had already, by implication, answered her next question, but she asked it anyway.

Athtar sighed. "No, the crystal is definitely not from the thirty-fifth century. It appeared suddenly. I picture it as having fallen backward through time from some future era in drops of fifteen hundred years."

"But why would they have sent it back?" Edith asked, bewildered. "What are they after?"

The chunky little man gave her a startled look. "The idea of the crystal's having been sent back for a purpose had not previously occurred to me. It's such a colossally valuable machine that we assumed it got away from them accidentally," he said. He was silent. Then, finally: "Why don't you let me go to see this second Edith Price? And you go back to Harkdale? If I find the crystal, I'll report with it to you there."

The implication seemed to be that he planned to cooperate with her. What he meant was that the crystal would be no good to him until he had found and murdered the Edith to whom it was oriented.

The tough part of Edith hesitated at the idea of trusting this man. But it occurred to her that he might have his century's weapons and that therefore he was being generous from a position of total strength in offering to cooperate.

With such fearful thoughts in her mind and having no plans of her own, she agreed.

She watched him get into a shining new automobile and drive down the narrow street. It was a medium-sized car, she noted absently. She had never been one who kept track of auto designs, so by the time she wondered what make it was it was gone. Belatedly it also struck her that she ought to have looked at the license plate numbers.

She thought sarcastically: *What a third-rate Edith Price I am* . . .

She was vaguely aware of a car pulling up at the curb nearby. A young woman left it and casually walked toward her as if to go into the phone booth.

She stopped suddenly beside Edith.

"You're Miss Price?"

Edith turned.

The other woman was a bright, alert blonde, probably in her thirties. Edith had never seen her before. She had no sense of being threatened but involuntarily she backed away several steps.

"Yes," she said.

The woman turned toward the car and called, "Okay, Seth."

Seth Mitchell emerged from the car and came rapidly toward them. He was well dressed, like the Seth Mitchell in the gold Cadillac, but there was a subtle difference. His face had a firmer, more determined expression.

He said, "I'm a detective. Who is that man you were talking to?"

And so the story, as well as Edith knew it, was presently shared.

They had gone into a coffee shop for their tense discussion. Edith was both relieved and disturbed to discover that these detectives had been in Harkdale for two days and had traced her down as a result of her call to the hospital to inquire about

Billy Bingham. Having thus spotted her, they had become aware that the squat man was also keeping track of her movements. And so that morning, not one but three cars had headed for New York—Edith's, Athtar's, and theirs.

The exchange of information took time and several cups of coffee—though Edith rejected the final cup with the sudden realization that coffee was probably not good for people and that the crystal might judge her on it at some later time. She smiled wanly at how many restraints she was placing on herself. Exactly as if God were no longer dead.

When they came out of the restaurant Seth Mitchell phoned the other Edith Price. He emerged from the phone booth uneasy.

"The switchboard operator says that Miss Price left with a man about twenty minutes ago. I'm afraid we're too late."

From Edith's description he had already come to the conclusion that Athtar was a dangerous man. They decided to wait for the second Edith to return. But though they remained in New York until after eleven that night, the young woman did not come back to her hotel.

She never would return. For some hours, a bullet in her brain, her body, weighed down by stones, had been lying at the bottom of the East River.

And Athtar had the crystal.

To his intense disappointment, that Edith was not the crystal's orientation.

Accordingly, he spent the evening and a portion of the night fitting together parts in the construction of a special weapon. He had a peculiar prescience that he would need its power the following day against the Edith who he believed was back in Harkdale.

Edith Price and the detectives set out for Harkdale in the two cars. Seth Mitchell, at Edith's request, drove her car. Marge Aikens followed in the larger machine.

En route Mitchell told Edith that he believed she was the original Edith and that it was to her that the crystal was still oriented. He considered also that her conclusion that Seth Mitchell, the farmer, was the worst Seth had doomed that unfortunate Mitchell duplicate. The crystal accepted her judgment and probably uncreated Seth, the farmer, when the package with the crystal addressed to him had barely been deposited in the post office.

Edith was taken aback by the detective's logic.

"But," she stammered, "I didn't mean it that way." Tears streamed down her cheeks. "Oh, that poor man!"

"Of course you didn't mean it," Mitchell said. "Just to double-check—tell me again in what sequence that judgment of yours came. Was it before or after your various impulses to leave Harkdale?"

"Oh, after."

"And did I hear you correctly—you thought of going into the post office and asking for the package you had mailed to be returned to you?"

"Yes, I had that thought." She added, "But I didn't do it."

"I would guess that at least one other Edith did go back and get it," said Mitchell.

"But it's all so complicated," Edith said. "How would any Edith just go, leaving clothes, money, car?"

"I've been thinking of my own background on that," said Mitchell. "Evidently the crystal can excise all confusions like that. For example, I never again even thought of going back to Harkdale. To do so didn't even cross my mind. But there are no blanks like that in your mind?"

"None that I can identify or think of."

Seth Mitchell nodded. "That's how I heard you. I think I've got the solution to this whole crazy business—and we don't even have to know where the crystal is."

His reasoning was simple. In bringing back Billy Bingham at her command the crystal had deposited the boy nearly two miles away. At the time she had been holding the crystal in her hand. But her negative thought about farmer Seth Mitchell had occurred after she had mailed the crystal and was approximately a hundred yards from the post office.

So if she had indeed uncreated the mentally ill farmer, then the distance of the crystal's human orientation—in this instance one of the Edith Prices—from the crystal, was not a factor.

"You don't agree?" asked the detective.

"I'm thinking," Edith said. "Maybe I'm not really the orientation."

"We'll test that tomorrow."

"What about Athtar?" Edith asked. "I keep feeling that he may have special weapons. Besides, the crystal cannot affect him. What about that?"

"Let me think about Athtar."

While he thought, Edith remembered Athtar's asking her about the figure in the crystal: had it been a man's or a woman's? She sat there in the darkness next to this Seth Mitchell and became aware of two separate lines of thought in her mind.

The first: she attempted to visualize the human design in the crystal.

The second . . .

She watched his profile as he drove.

How brilliant he is—yet surely a mere detective, no matter how keen his logic, cannot be the best of all possible Seth Mitchells. A man in such a profession has got to be somewhere in the middle—which in this competition is the same as the worst . . .

And he disappeared.

For many seconds after she had that thought, the suddenly driverless car held to its straight direction. Its speed, which had been around seventy, naturally started to let up the instant there was no longer a foot on the accelerator.

The only error came when Edith uttered a scream and grabbed at the wheel, turning it. The machine careened wildly. The next second she grasped the wheel in a more steadying way and, holding it, slid along the seat until she could apply the brake. She pulled over to the side of the road and stopped.

Marge Aikens had slowed as soon as she saw there was a problem. She pulled up behind Edith, got out of the car, and walked to the driver's side of the other machine.

"Seth," she began, "what—"

Edith pushed the door open and stepped, trembling, out to the road. She had a mad impulse to run—anywhere. Her body felt strange. Her mind was encased in blank anguish. She was vaguely aware of herself babbling about what had happened.

It must have taken a while for her incoherent words to reach through to Marge. But suddenly Marge gasped and Edith felt herself grabbed by the shoulders. She was being shaken.

A voice was yelling at her, "You stupid fool! You stupid fool—"

The shaking became pain. Her neck hurt, then her arms.

I must be careful. I mustn't do or say anything that will affect her . . .

With the thought, Edith's sanity returned. Marge was in a state of hysteria. The shaking was an automatic act of a person out of her mind with grief.

Edith knew pity. She was able to free herself by a simple action. She slapped Marge lightly on the cheek, once, twice, three times. The third time the woman let go of her and leaned against the car, sobbing.

A wind was blowing from the west. Car headlights kept glaring past them, lighting the scene briefly. The two women were now in a relatively normal state and presently were able to discuss their situation. Edith tried to recreate Marge's employer with the same command she had used to bring back Billy Bingham.

She had had a feeling that it would not work—the Seth Mitchells were undoubtedly due to be eliminated one by one— and it did not. The minutes ticked by. Though she yelled the command in many variations into the night there was no sign of the vanished Seth, whose presence had for a long half-day brought to the whole situation the reassurance that derives from a highly intelligent and determined mind.

In the end, defeated, the two women in their separate cars drove on to Harkdale. Marge had a room reserved at the Harkdale Hotel and went there. Edith drove wearily to the apartment house where she lived.

It was nearly four o'clock when she finally limped into her little suite. She lay down without undressing. She was drifting off to sleep when fear tensed her. Would the best of all possible Ediths be this sloppy about personal cleanliness?

Literally hurting with exhaustion, she rolled off the bed, undressed, bathed, brushed her teeth, combed her hair, changed the linens, and stepped into a clean pair of pajamas.

She awoke once with a bad start to the thought that conformity might not be her salvation. Such toiletry amenities as she had performed were products of early training and did not necessarily have anything to do with life as it should be lived.

She fell asleep imagining a series of rebel Ediths, each one of whom had some special characteristic that was noble and worthy.

The next time she awoke she saw daylight outside. It occurred to her that all her concepts, so compulsively visualized, were probably being created somewhere by the crystal. Undoubtedly there were already beatnik and hippie Ediths as well as rougher, tougher types.

She realized what a strange whirl of possibilities she had considered in the last thirty-six hours. Ediths who were hard-boiled and could coldly shoot to kill, or, conversely, who were super-feminine, sweet, tantalizing temptresses.

"And it's all unnecessary," she whispered, lying there. "The decision will probably be made as arbitrarily as my own impulsive condemnation of the inarticulate farmer and the courageous—but presumably not perfect—detective."

Having no standards that applied to the twentieth century, the crystal had uncreated a powerful and good man on the passing judgment of the person to whom it had by chance become oriented. Accordingly, the future looked grim for all Seth Mitchells and Edith Prices, including the original.

As she dressed she looked through her window at the distant blue waters of Lake Naragang and the downtown section that at one place, opposite the Harkdale Hotel, crowded the water's edge. Pretty little town, Harkdale. She remembered that on her arrival she had thought that at least here she could be more casual in her dress than she had been in New York. Then she gave a short, rueful laugh—she had come full circle during the night, back to the notion that appearance would count.

She put on her finest dress. Yet in some back closet of her brain lived a fearful conviction that all this was in vain. The crisis was imminent; she might be dead—uncreated—before this day was out.

It seemed ridiculous to go to work on the day you were going to die. But she went. As she moved about her duties Edith was conscious of her subdued manner. Twice, when she unthinkingly looked into the rest room mirror, she was startled by the pale face and sick eyes that looked back at her.

This is not really me—I can't be judged on this . . .

Surely the crystal would not reject her because she was in a daze. Every passing minute fleeting images of other Ediths passed before her mind's eye. Each one had in it the momentary hope that maybe it held the key to the best. There was Edith living out her life as a nun; another chaste Edith, married but holding sex to a minimum, placing all her attention on her children; and an Edith who was a follower of Zen Buddhism.

She had, earlier, put through a call to Marge Aiken, at the Harkdale Hotel. About two o'clock Marge called back. She reported that she had phoned New York and discovered that the second Edith had not returned to her hotel at all the previous night.

After imparting this grim news, Marge said, "If Athtar contacts you, don't be alone with him under any circumstances until he produces the Seth Mitchell in the gold Cadillac and the Edith in New York."

After that call more images, mostly of saintly and good-hearted, unsophisticated Ediths, haunted her.

Into this haze of thoughts, Tilsit's voice intruded: "Phone call for you, Edith."

She picked up the phone, heard a familiar voice—Athtar's.

"I want to see you right after work."

Edith said on a suddenly faint note, "At the Harkdale Hotel—in the lobby."

Athtar left the phone booth. A smile twisted his wide face. For him there were two possibilities of victory now that he had the crystal.

The first was to kill its current orientation—Edith. He intended to take no chances with her. She would never, he resolved, reach the Harkdale Hotel.

However, murder of his only Edith left one unpleasant possibility. Though he had reasoned it out that she was the crystal's orientation—should she prove not to be, in destroying her, he would remove his source of information for tracing other Ediths.

It was a considered risk he had to take. As a precaution he had already removed the crystal from the nutrient oil on which it fed. He was not certain how long it would be before the stone was deactivated by starvation, but he deduced not more than two weeks. Whereupon it would orient to whoever reactivated it. To himself, of course.

Now that he had a special barrier-penetrating weapon, he firmly believed that before this day was over he would be in sole possession of the most remarkable machine of all time and space—the crystal.

The Harkdale Hotel was a summer resort hostelry. Its prices were high and as a result it had made money. Some of the money had been spent wisely, on decoration, fine furniture, and a sophisticated staff.

The clerk on day-duty had his own definition of a sophisticate: a person with a memory so good that he can forget with discretion.

He was such a person. His name was Derek Slade. And so discreet was he that on this fateful day he had allowed four Seth Mitchells to register without comment. He believed each Mitchell to be the same man but with a different woman and he was just beginning to enjoy the situation when Seth Mitchell arrived for the fifth time—this time without a woman.

Yet it took Derek only a moment to figure it out. This smooth male, Seth Mitchell, had four women in different rooms and evidently wanted a separate room for himself. Why? Derek did not try to analyze the matter further. Life—he had often said—was full of surprises.

He spoke in a low tone, "You may count on my discretion, Mr. Mitchell."

The Seth Mitchell across the desk from him raised his eyebrows, then nodded with a faint smile.

Derek was pleased. The remark ought to be good for a twenty-dollar tip.

He was still congratulating himself when the elevator door opened and another Seth Mitchell stepped out and walked toward the desk. As he came up, the Seth Mitchell who had just registered turned to follow the bellboy carrying his bags to the elevator.

The two Seth Mitchells almost bumped into each other. Both took evasive action. Both murmured polite nothings and were about to pass each other when Derek recovered.

It was one of his perfect moments. He raised his voice, spoke with exactly the correct note of authority.

"Mr. Mitchell."

The two Seth Mitchells were already in a mildly confused state. Their name, uttered in that peremptory tone, stopped them.

Derek said, "Mr. Seth Mitchell, may I present Mr. Seth Mitchell. Gentlemen, please wait there a moment."

He let them kill their own time—one seemed to recover quickly, the other remained bewildered—while he phoned the rooms of the previously registered Seth Mitchells. He had to call all four rooms but presently before him stood five Seth Mitchells.

Of all the people present the one most completely unnoticed was Derek Slade. He would not have had it any other way.

Four of the five Seths were gulping and stuttering at one another. The fifth had stepped up to one side with a faint smile. Almost as one, the four suddenly became embarrassed.

Derek's cool voice reached them with perfect timing.

"Gentlemen, let me show you to the conference room, where you may talk over this whole matter."

As they started for the conference room, Marge Aiken entered the hotel in time to catch a profile view of the last Seth Mitchell walking into the room. She paled, then rushed forward.

"Seth," she cried out tearfully. "For God's sake, I thought you were dead—"

She stopped. She had grabbed the nearest man by the arm. He turned and something unfamiliar about him flustered her.

After all the Mitchells had been briefed by Marge to the extent of her knowledge she suggested that Edith be called to come over at once.

Three Seth Mitchells presented their view. Listening to each in turn, Marge glanced along the line of sensationally familiar faces and saw in all but one man's eyes a haunting apprehension—and the equally haunting intelligence she had seen so often in her employer's.

Seth from Montreal said, "Our first act must be to protect ourselves from that young woman's automatic judgments, such as she rendered on farmer Mitchell and detective Mitchell."

A second, slightly deeper-voiced Seth was concerned about Athtar. "In killing Edith Price Number Two, Athtar must have gotten the crystal and then discovered that the dead Edith was not the orientation. Therefore our initial act must be to protect the Edith who is the orientation. The first real problem is to get her safely to the hotel—not what she may do when she gets here."

The third Seth said the problem was not so much Edith's judgment of men: it was her stereotyped concept of women. Presumably, the crystal had dutifully created a long list of Edith Prices who were simply ordinary human beings with varying moral standards or with slightly different beliefs about how to get along in the drab world of the twentieth century.

"As an example of how differently I would want her to handle her control of the crystal—one of the first Edith Prices I would wish her to create is one that has ESP. Why? So that she can understand this whole situation and what to do about it."

His words brought a hopeful reaction. It was an obviously good idea—if it could be done.

A fourth Seth, who had sat gray and silent, now said, "It would be interesting if such ESP ability included being able to spot the Seth Mitchell who," he nodded at Marge, "paid your boss a thousand dollars to locate the crystal."

The Seth who had arrived at the hotel without a wife—and who had reflected none of the fear that the others felt—stirred and smiled cheerfully.

"You need look no further. I'm he."

When order had been restored he continued: "To answer your basic question, I also dreamed—as you all did—and exactly as the worst Athtar found himself with the address of one of the Seth Mitchells in his mind, one morning after a dream the address of detective Mitchell was in mine."

"But why didn't you come for the crystal yourself? Why pay a thousand dollars?"

The bachelor Mitchell smiled again. "I hate to tell you people this—and it is to your advantage not to let Miss Price know—but according to the thoughts I had after my dream I am the best of all possible Seth Mitchells."

Once more he had to wait for order.

Then: "I don't know why I'm best. But I hired someone to come here in my place because I sensed danger and I came here today believing that this was the crisis. I can't tell you what I'll do about it. I don't even have the feeling that my role is decisive. I simply believe that a challenge will present itself and I'll meet it." He finished simply: "I don't think we should devote any more time to me. We have many vital things to do and we only have until Edith Price comes off the job to get them done. Let's go. First, since violence is imminent, we must warn the police . . . "

The police of Harkdale were few in number and Athtar was able to drive into town and into the library parking lot without being observed. A lingering twilight had barely begun to turn to night when Edith emerged.

She noted with a vague surprise that a town fire truck, engine running, was standing near the door. But she was already having qualms about the forthcoming journey to the hotel—so far away, it seemed to her suddenly. So the sight of the big truck was reassuring.

To get to her own car, she had to go around the fire truck. As she started to do so the big machine surged into motion with a gigantic thunder of its engine. Edith stopped, teetered, then leaped back. The truck jammed on its brakes directly in front of her.

Somewhere beyond the big machine a purple flash had lighted the sky. Like a tracer bullet the light flashed from an auto to the fire truck. As it hit, it made a sound of a pitch never before heard on earth—a deep, sustained, continuing protest of chemical bonds by the quadrillion snapping in metal.

The tiny bullet penetrated the thick steel frame of the fire truck, and reformed itself a micromillimeter at a time, from the steel molecules. It did not slow as it passed through the heavy machine. It would also have passed straight through Edith; its speed was that of a bullet—immense but infinite.

It transited the fire truck while the truck was still in motion. The bullet was carried along inside the moving vehicle during a measurable fraction of a second and missed Edith by inches.

Unchecked, it struck the library wall, moved through, emerged from the far side, and streaked into the night. Its kinetic energy being a precise quality, it bored forward another hundred yards and then rapidly fell.

Moments later two plainclothes police discharged their rifles at the figure that was dimly visible inside the car from which the purple-glowing bullet had been fired.

The screech of bullets striking his own machine startled Athtar. But he had taken the precaution of using a molecular reinforcing unit to harden the glass and the metal of the auto, so the bullets failed to penetrate.

What bothered him was that he only had a few bullets and in the dark he could not gauge the extent of the trap that had been set for him. So now, hastily, he put his car into drive, stepped on the gas, and drove rapidly out of the parking lot.

A police car fell in behind him, flashing its red beacon. Though it or its weapons were no danger to Athtar, he feared a roadblock. He turned up several side streets and in only a few minutes of driving lured the police car onto a street near the lake on the far side of the Harkdale Hotel, an approach he had thoroughly explored on foot.

Satisfied, he opened the car window on the driver's side, slowed, leaned out, looked back, took quick aim at the engine of the other machine, and put a purple-glowing bullet through the crankcase. There was a shattering crash. The stricken motor almost tore itself apart, screaming metallically. The auto itself came to a bumpy halt.

Athtar hurriedly circled back to the Harkdale Hotel. The first queasy doubt had come to him that for a reason not yet clear his time was running out. Yet it still seemed true to him that all he need do was sneak into the hotel and discharge a single bullet at one, and only one, beating heart.

Minutes later, after squeezing through a kitchen window of the hotel, he found himself in a shadowy storeroom on a concrete floor. As he fumbled his way to a door, he had a fleeting mental image of his colleagues of the great Scientists' Guild viewing him in such a lowly action. Of course, Athtar told himself scornfully, what they thought would not matter once he had control of the crystal. There would be dramatic changes after he got back to his own time—a few hundred Guild members were scheduled for extermination.

Cautiously he pulled open a door. As he started through the hallway past it he became aware of a faint sound behind him. He spun around and jerked up his gun.

Instant, unbearable pain in his arm forced the gun down and his finger away from the trigger. Almost at once the gun dropped from his nerveless hand, clattering to the floor. Even as he recognized that thirty-fifth-century technology was being used against him, he saw that a short, squat man was standing in the doorway of the storeroom he himself had just left.

Athtar's arm and hand were now inexorably forced by intolerable pain to reach into his inside breast pocket, take out the crystal, and hold it out to the other man.

The second Athtar did not speak. He drew the door shut behind him, accepted the crystal, and, bending down, picked up the gun from the floor. Then he edged past his prisoner, stepped through the door beyond and closed it behind him.

At once, all the muscle pressures let go of the worst Athtar. Instantly desperate, he tried to jerk open the storeroom door. The door did not yield—it had an unnervingly solid feel to it. Athtar whirled toward the other door.

When he found it also presented that same solid resistance to his tug he finally recognized that he was trapped by molecular forces from his own era. There was nothing to do as the minutes lengthened but sit down on the concrete floor and wait.

Sitting there, he had a mixed reaction to his realization that the drama of the crystal would now play on without him. What seemed good about it was the distinct conviction that the game was more dangerous than he had let himself believe. He had recognized his assailant as the best of all possible Athtars.

Too, the Price woman was being cleverer than he had anticipated. Which meant that the automatic programming of the crystal to uncreate all but the best would force her to the most desperate actions. Or so it seemed to the worst Athtar.

Better not to be around when such extreme events were transpiring.

The best of all possible Athtars walked through the hotel lobby to the conference room. The five Seth Mitchells were grouped outside the door, out of the line of vision of Edith, who was inside. Athtar gave the agreed-on signal and handed the worst Athtar's automatic pistol to one of the Seths. They were thorough. They searched him and then passed him on to Marge Aikens, who stood in the doorway.

To Marge, Athtar gave another agreed-on signal. Having thus established his identity as the friendly Athtar, whom Edith had recreated as a first step, he was now admitted into the room.

Athtar placed the crystal on the conference table in front of Edith. As her fingers automatically reached toward it, he placed a restraining hand on her wrist.

"I have a feeling," he admonished, "that this time when you pick it up—when the true orientation, *you*, picks it up—that will be the moment of crisis."

His voice and his words seemed far away. She had—it seemed to her—considered those thoughts, and had those feelings, in approaching the decision to recreate *him*—the best Athtar. That, also, had been a crisis.

As she nevertheless hesitated out of respect for his knowledge and awareness, Edith noticed two impulses within herself. One was to go into a kind of exhaustion, in which she would act on the basis that she was too tired to think all that through again.

The second impulse was a clearer, sharper awareness, which had come to her suddenly at the library after she realized that the worst Athtar had tried his best to kill her.

Abruptly, then, the problems that had disturbed her earlier had faded. Whether it was better to be tough and be able to shoot or be soft and feminine had no meaning. The real solution was infinite flexibility, backed by unvarying intention.

One handled situations. That was all there was to it.

As she remembered that perfect thought the impulse toward exhaustion went away. She turned to Marge and said matter-of-factly, "Shall I tell him what we discussed while he was down in the storeroom?"

Marge nodded tensely.

Athtar listened with what appeared to be an expression of doubt, then said, "Having the crystal recreate one of its makers could be exactly what those makers are waiting for you to do."

"That's exactly what we thought," said Edith. And still she felt no fear. She explained. "Our thought is that, since the crystal is programmed to find the best of each person, and the best Athtar turned out to be a reasonable person and not a criminal, then the makers of the crystal understand the difference. We may therefore assume that the society of the future is normal and will not harm us." She added: "That's why we recreated you—as a check."

"Good reasoning," said Athtar. "But I sense there's something wrong with it."

"But you have no specific thought?" she asked.

"No." He hesitated, then shrugged. "As a start," he said, "why not pick up the crystal—just pick it up—and see if my feeling about that gesture's being sufficient has any substance?" He explained, "If I'm wrong there we can dismiss my doubts."

"You don't want me to look at the design?"

The Seths had decided that her awareness of the design was the key to her control of the stone.

Athtar answered, "No, I sense that they're ready."

His words, the implication of ultra-perception that reached over perhaps thousands of years, startled Edith and held her unmoving—but only momentarily.

She fought free.

"The truth is," said Edith aloud, completing her thought, "we all feel that we have no alternative left to us."

Without further delay she reached forward and picked up the crystal.

She gasped.

The man who walked out of the corner of the room, where he had materialized, was a giant. Seven, eight, nine feet—her mind kept reassessing the height, as she strove to adjust to the enormous reality of him.

The size; the blue harness clothing, like a Roman centurion guard in summer uniform; the bronze body; the large face with eyes as black as coal, unsmiling and firm; and, in his bearing, conscious power unqualified by doubt or fear.

He said in a bass voice, in English, "I am Shalil, the best of all possible."

For a long moment Edith waited for him to complete the sentence. At last, with a shock, she realized the sentence was finished. The crystal makers had sent the most qualified individual of their entire race to handle this situation.

In the doorway, Marge cringed away from the monster. She uttered a small cry. At the sound, two of the Seth Mitchells rushed into the room. They caught Marge, who seemed close to hysteria and fainting—and they also saw the apparition. The other three Seths crowded into the doorway.

As of one accord, obviously unwisely and therefore—as Edith realized later—under a volition not their own, they moved into the room, bringing Marge with them. The Seth who brought up the rear pulled the door shut behind him.

The best Athtar stirred and said in a sharp tone, "Miss Price—uncreate him! He does not mean well."

The giant grimaced. "You cannot uncreate me. I—and only I—now control the crystal. The term 'mean well' is relative. I mean well for my own time and my own group." He glanced over the five Seths and the two women, then settled on Athtar. "Which of you are the biologically original human beings?" he asked.

Edith clutched the crystal and glanced uncertainly at the Seths, silently appealing for suggestions. But they were staring at the giant and seemed oblivious to her.

Yet one of them asked abruptly, "Athtar, in what way doesn't he mean well?"

Athtar shook his head. "I don't know in details," he said unhappily. "But I have a feeling. They sent the crystal back here for their purpose. His question about original human beings points a significant direction. But don't answer it—or any other question he may ask."

It seemed a small, useless denial. The huge man strode to the door. The group of Seths let him through automatically. The giant opened the door and peered out into the hotel lobby. After a single, swift survey, he pushed the door shut again and faced about.

"I deduce," he said, "that the people of this era are the originals. They are the ones we want for our experiments."

Athtar said tautly to the Seths, "One of you has the worst Athtar's gun. Shoot him."

The instant the words were spoken the pistol floated into view, avoided the fingers of the two Seths who tried to seize it. It settled into Shalil's palm. He slipped the weapon into a pocket of his simple garment.

The best Athtar glanced at Edith. He said glumly, "I've done my best—" and faced the monster. "What happens to me?"

The black eyes studied him.

"The crystal is communicating data to me," Shalil said. "You and the other Athtar are from an era where the people have already been biologically altered?"

Athtar glanced apologetically at Edith. "I see no additional danger in asking him a question since he already seems to have all the information we possess." Without waiting for a reply he addressed the huge man. "The decision made in the thirty-first century, nearly four hundred years before my time, was that small, heavy bodies had more survival potential than tall, thin ones. I see that in your era a much taller, bigger, more powerful man than any we have even imagined, is the norm. What is the rationale?"

"Different problems," answered Shalil. "In my era, which by your reckoning would correlate to the ninety-third century, man is a space creature." He broke off. "Since we have no interest in you at present, I propose to send you and the other Athtar back to your own time."

"Wait." The best Athtar spoke urgently. "What do you intend to do with these people?" He waved toward Edith and the Seths.

Shalil grimaced. "What we actually want for our experiments are the best Seth Mitchell and the best Edith Price. The others are free to go. We set the crystal to find the best specimens."

"But why?"

"Something has gone wrong. We need to restudy human origins."

"Do you need these specific persons or will you merely have the crystal duplicate them in your own era?"

"Only one of each exists. If he and she are created in any other time they become uncreated here."

"What will you do? Dissect them?"

"In the end, perhaps. The experimenters will decide." Sharply. "Never mind that. The program is laid out and the subjects are urgently needed." His voice grew imperious. "Miss Price, give me the crystal. We are not needlessly cruel and I wish to send the Athtars home."

Athtar urged, "Miss Price, don't give it to him. His statement that he totally controls the crystal may not be true until the moment he has possession of it. These far-future beings must be persuaded to accept another, less arbitrary solution to their problem."

Edith had been standing, watching the fantastic giant, listening to the infinite threat that was developing out of his blunt words.

Suddenly what had seemed an utterly desirable goal—to be the best—had become the most undesirable.

But she was not yet afraid. Her mind was clear. The tumbling thoughts and feelings of the past days, which had suddenly fallen into an exact order in her mind earlier that night, remained orderly.

Her own reaction was that Athtar was wrong and that she had, in fact, lost control of the crystal. It seemed obvious to her that the crystal's makers would have had some preemptive system by which they could regain its use at a key moment.

But she intended to test her theory.

She glanced at and into the crystal and said firmly, "Whoever can defeat this giant—be here now!"

Moments after she had spoken, the crystal was snatched from her fingers by the same kind of unseen force as had taken the automatic pistol from one of the Seths earlier. She watched helplessly as it also floated over to the giant's palm. The huge man's black eyes gleamed triumphantly at her.

"All your allies are in this room. There is nobody else."

"In that case," said a man's voice quietly, "I imagine that, regardless of consequences, my moment has come."

The bachelor Seth Mitchell strode forward to confront the giant.

There was a long pause. Edith had time to assess this Seth and to savor the simple, strong humanity that he represented. She saw that he was well-dressed in a dark gray suit, that his lean face was firm, his eyes calm and fearless. In some depths of her mind she was proud that at this moment such a Seth Mitchell existed. Yet, though she was still not afraid herself, she was aware of her hopes sinking.

The silence ended.

The great being from the future said, "I hope you realize that you are condemning the other Seths in forcing your identity on me in this manner. In this era the crystal has no alternative but to uncreate them."

Behind Edith, Marge cried out faintly.

Edith whirled. Marge seemed to be choking. Edith ran to her, put an arm around her waist.

"What's the matter?"

Marge continued to choke. Her words, when they finally came, were almost inaudible: "They're gone—the other Seths . . ."

Edith looked around. Where the four Seths had been standing near the door—there was no one. She had an impulse to run to the door and look out. Surely they had simply stepped outside for a moment.

Abruptly she realized. They had been uncreated.

She uttered a gasping sob—then caught herself as Seth Mitchell spoke in the same quiet tone as before.

"I said, regardless of consequences." He glanced back at the two women. "Since the Seths remain crystal patterns, they're no more in danger now than they would be if this creature were able to carry out all his threats. That probably even applies to the Seth of the gold Cadillac and the Edith who presumably was killed in New York." To Shalil he said, "I think you'd better send the Athtars into their own time."

There was an ever so slight pause; the giant's eyes changed slightly, as if he were thinking.

Then: "It's done," he said.

Edith glanced to where Athtar had been. With a conscious effort she retained her self-control.

Athtar had disappeared.

Shalil surveyed the best of all possible Seth Mitchells, and said, "You really benefited from the crystal, didn't you?" He spoke in his softest bass. An intent, listening expression came into his face. "You own four corporations."

"I stopped when I was worth ten million," said the best Seth. He turned to look apologetically at Edith. "I couldn't imagine having use for even that much money. But I had set it as a goal and reached it." Without waiting for her reaction he once more faced the gigantic enemy. "All the Seth Mitchells," he said, "are the results of a boy's dreams, based on what information he had. He undoubtedly had observed that there are tax experts, lawyers, doctors, tramps, and policemen. And in a town like Harkdale he was aware of summer resort visitors—and on the level of a boy's daydreams there existed—until they were uncreated just now—a cowboy Seth Mitchell, an African hunter Seth, a sea captain, an airline pilot, and probably even a few glamorous criminals—" He broke off. "I have a feeling you don't understand—you don't have any boys anymore where you are, do you?"

The giant's eyes shifted uncertainly.

He said, "We are crystal duplicates. Thus we shall presumably live forever—if we can solve the present tendency of the cells to be tired." He added reluctantly, "What's a boy?"

"Maybe there's your problem," said Seth Mitchell. "You've forgotten about children. Gene variation." The best Seth continued to gaze up at the great being. "I'm the creation," he said gently, "of a boy who, for a long time after Bill Bingham disappeared, was under exceptional adult pressure and criticism and as a result had many escape fantasies. Picture that boy's fantasy of total power—somebody who would handle mean adults who acted as if he were lying and who treated him nastily. Some day he would show them all. How? The answer would not have been clear to the boy Seth who felt that resentment. But when the time came he knew he would know how—and of course he wouldn't be mean about it the way the adults had been. There would be a kind of nobility about his total power."

The two men, the best of all possible Seth Mitchells from the twentieth century, and the best of all possibles from the ninety-third century, were standing within a few feet of each other.

"Perhaps," the best Seth addressed the giant softly, "you can tell better than I what the crystal would create out of such a command."

"Since nobility is involved," was the harsh reply, "I feel that I can safely test that boy's fantasy to the uttermost limit."

He spoke sharply, uncommandingly, in a strange language.

Edith had listened to the deadly interchange, thinking in a wondering dismay: *God really is dead! These future people have never even heard of Him . . .*

Her thought ended. For the giant's deep bass tones had suddenly ceased.

Something hit her deep inside her body. Around her the room dimmed.

As if from a vast distance she heard Seth Mitchell say apologetically: "Only thing I know, Miss Price, is to send you along with him. Seems you've got the solution in what you just thought, whatever that was. The crystal will make it real. Hope it works."

A moment after that she was falling into infinity.

The body of Edith lay on a contour rest space in one corner of the crystal administrative center. Periodically a giant walked over to her and checked the instruments that watched over her and monitored the invisible force lines that held her.

A slow night went by. A new day finally dawned. The sunlight that suffused the translucent walls also revealed half a dozen giants, including Shalil, gathered around the slowly breathing—but otherwise unmoving—body of the young woman from the twentieth century.

To wake or not to wake her?

They discussed the problem in low, rumbling voices. Since they were all scientists, capable of appreciating the most subtle nuances of logic, what bothered them was that the small female presented a paradox.

Outward appearance said she was helpless. Shalil had been able to put Edith into a coma. At the instant of the best Seth's command to the crystal she had arrived in that degraded condition in the ninety-third century.

Or rather, she had been uncreated in her own time and recreated by the crystal in Shalil's time, already unconscious. She herself had not had any control over her own destiny.

What disturbed her captors was that an undefinable power radiated from her—and had ever since her recreation. The power was not merely ordinary. It was total.

Total power? Absolute and unqualified? How could that be?

Once more they gave attention on both hearing and telepathic levels, as Shalil repeated his account of what had transpired while he had been in the twentieth century. The story, already familiar, reiterated the same peak moments: the ordinariness, the unthreatening aspect, of all the people of the past whom Shalil had confronted.

Again they were told the climax—when the Seth had assumed that the crystal would evolve an unusual energy configuration out of a boy's fantasies of power. Clearly—at least, it was clear to the huge men—the crystal's response to Seth's command established that it had been oriented to the best Seth. And that its energies had been mobilized for later expression when the original Seth Mitchell had been a boy. From that energy response by the crystal alone the giants reasoned unhappily: "There is more potential in these crystals than we have hitherto believed."

And how could *that* be?

But there was even worse.

While giving his command to Edith the best of possible Seth Mitchells had implied that he had received a feedback message from her, presumably by way of the crystal, indicating that she would all by herself now be able to defeat the entire science of the ninety-third century.

Once Shalil took control of the crystal, such a feedback of information—whether true or false—should not have occurred. And Seth's command, by any known scientific analysis, was impossible.

True, they did not know all there was to know about the crystals. Several unexplained areas were still being researched. But it had long been argued that nothing major remained to be discovered.

The present implication was that original, unmanipulated human beings might have special qualities that had been lost to their biologically manipulated descendants.

A giant grunted, "I think we should kill her."

A second huge man growled an objection. He argued, "If the attempt to destroy her should bring a reaction from the absolute power that radiates from her, that reaction would be uncontrollable. Much better to deduce on the basis of Shalil's report the low-level ways in which her mind functions, awaken her, and inexorably force responses from her."

Everybody thought that was a good idea.

"And if something goes wrong," one giant rumbled, "we can always render her unconscious again through instantaneous uncreation and recreation by the crystal."

Shalil reminded gruffly, "What about that odd decision she had reached in her attempt to be the best of all possible Ediths, to handle situations with infinite flexibility?"

Contempt greeted the remark. "With *her* lifetime conditioning," one huge scientist said, "she couldn't possibly deal with each situation according to its merits. She cannot even know what the real issues of a situation are."

The discussion ended on a decision that when Edith was awakened she should seem to herself to be completely free . . .

She was lying on grass. It touched her fingers and her face. The fresh smell of it was in her nostrils.

Edith opened her eyes and simultaneously raised her head.

Wilderness. A primeval forest. A small brown animal with a bushy tail scurried into the brush, as she climbed hastily to her feet, remembering.

She saw the giant, Shalil, in the act of picking himself up fifteen feet to her left. He seemed slow about it, as if he were groggy.

The day was misty. The sun still stood high in the sky. To her right, partly visible through foliage, was a great, gray hill of soil. To her left the land fell away and the mist was thicker. After a hundred yards it was an almost impenetrable fog.

Almost, but not quite, impenetrable. Vaguely visible through it was a building.

Edith faced the giant squarely and asked, "Where are we?"

Shalil gazed at her warily. It was hard for him to realize that she did not intuitively know. He found it almost unacceptable that alongside her infinite power was such nadir thinking.

Yet, as she continued to stand there, facing him, he sensed her concern. And so, reluctantly, he decided that the first conclusions reached by his colleagues and himself continued to apply. They had perceived her to be motivated by involuntary attitudes and forgotten memories, each psychically as solid as a bar of steel. All her life she had followed rules, gone along with group-think behavior.

School and college—these were the early norms, adhered to while she was still under the control of her parents. Basically those norms had remained unquestioned.

Shalil noted in her mind an awareness that millions of people had failed to achieve higher education. That was astonishing to him; somehow, these multitudes had been steered away from knowledge by a variety of accidental circumstances.

So in those areas of personal development Edith had gone farther, better, straighter than a great many. Yet in college, first time away from her family, she had swiftly been caught up in a nonconformist group movement. Whatever the motives of the other persons involved, Edith's had consisted solely of an intense inner need to belong to the group.

So, for her, it had been the beginning of aberration, which her behavior ever afterward reflected. Thus, Shalil observed, like a person struggling against invisible force lines, she had fought to return to an inner norm. More study, different jobs, different places to live, association with different men—the confusion was immense, and it was difficult for Shalil to determine which of her numerous actions represented striving toward a real goal.

Adding to the jumble: all her actions had been modified by a very large, though finite, number of small, endlessly repeated actions—eating, dressing, working, sleeping, walking, reacting, communicating, thinking.

What bothered Shalil was that he could not find a single point of entry into her mind that would not instantly trigger one of the stereotypes. The others had assumed that her conscious mind would present some opening; they had taken it for granted that he would locate it. His instructions were to uncreate her into unconsciousness if he failed to make such an entry, whereupon there would be another consultation.

The possibility of such a quick failure disturbed Shalil. Temporizing, he said aloud, "This is the Garden of the Crystals in my century. Here, in the most virgin wilderness left on our planet, the crystals lie buried in the soil, tended by guardian scientists."

Having spoken, having had that tiny bit of extra time to consider, he decided that the problem she presented might yield to a steady pressure of verbal maneuvering that would motivate her to express one after the other the endless

stereotypes that had been detected in her—while he waited
alertly for one he could shatter or through which the crystal—
on his command—would divest her of the power with which it
had, through some unknown factor, invested her.

Her primary concern, he saw, was that she would never get
back to her own era. Since he knew she could return at once
simply by thinking the correct positive thought, his problem
was to keep her worried, negative, unaware, deceived, misled.

Shalil became aware that his anxiety about how to proceed
was causing a hasty telepathic consultation among his
colleagues. Moments later the suggestion was made: Divert
her by letting her win some minor victories and believe that
they are gifts from you . . .

The idea seemed good and Shalil carried it out as if it were
a directive.

At the Harkdale hotel another day dawned. Marge Aikens
came downstairs, bleary-eyed from lack of sleep. She walked
to the conference room, looked in. The lights had been turned
off, the drapes were still drawn, and the dim emptiness of the
room weighted her spirits.

She turned away and became aware of a man beside her.
She faced him with a start.

The hotel day clerk, Derek Slade, said courteously,
"Madam . . ."

He continued to speak and after a while his meaning
penetrated her dulled mind. He thought he had recognized
her as the young woman who had late the previous afternon
gone into the conference room with the five Seth Mitchells.
Where—Derek wanted to know—were the four married
Seths? The wives had been phoning all night, according to a
note on his desk from the night clerk. And a police officer
was on the way over because three Mrs. Mitchells had finally
called the authorities.

Marge had an impulse to deny that she was the woman he thought he had seen. But his failure to mention the bachelor Seth captured her attention and she asked about him.

Derek shook his head. "Not in his room. Went out early, I'm told."

Marge stood in the doorway, considering what might have happened to the best Seth. Why would he have gone out when he had said the previous night that he would have breakfast with her? Then she became aware that Derek Slade's gaze had gone past her shoulder and was seeking the darkened interior of the room behind her.

His jaw grew lax, his eyes widened.

In the room a man's baritone voice uttered an exclamation.

Marge turned.

The four Seths who had been uncreated last night were standing near the door. Their backs were to her.

She realized that it was one of the Seths who had exclaimed and that what he had said was, "Hey, who turned out the lights?"

Marge had an immediate and totally perceptive awareness of the implications of those words. Her mind leaped back to Billy Bingham's not having had any transition impression at all of time having passed between his uncreation and recreation.

This was the same.

She reached into the room and pressed the light switch beside the door. As she did so a fifth Seth walked forward from one corner of the room, where he had suddenly appeared. He seemed bewildered. From his clothing Marge tentatively identified him as the Seth of the gold Cadillac, somehow recreated without a bullet in his brain or a drop of lake water on his immaculate suit.

But at the moment she had only a fleeting thought for him, for a sixth Seth was suddenly standing on the far side of the conference table. The way he held himself, his quick alertness as he looked around the room, saw the other Seths—and then flicked his gaze to her with relieved recognition . . .

Seeing him, and receiving so many familiar signals that identified detective Seth Mitchell for her, Marge became emotionally unglued. Without any of her usual discretion, she let out a scream.

"Seth—my darling—"

Exactly how she got to him and he to her could undoubtedly be reasoned out from the fact that they met at the halfway point around the big table—and only desisted from their embrace when Marge grew aware that Edith Price was standing a few feet away, glancing timidly around her.

Closely behind Edith appeared another Seth. He wore work clothes and Marge surmised that he must be the farmer.

Marge scarcely more than glanced at him. As she released herself from Detective Seth's embrace she saw that Edith wore a different dress and had her hair done differently—this was the Edith Price who had been murdered in New York by the worst Athtar.

Of the Athtars there was no sign.

And though the minutes fled by—and finally the bachelor Seth walked into the doorway—Edith Price, the crystal orientation, did not reappear.

The best Seth explained that he had gone for a walk and, thinking over all that had happened, had decided that things would work out.

He finished hopefully, "And here you all are. Each of you is living proof that Edith has found out what she can do. Or," he paused, "someone has, and is willing."

"But what can she do?" a Seth asked, bewildered.

The best Seth smiled his friendly smile. "I'm rather fond of that young lady. In a way she's a total reflection of our age, yet she thought her way to some kind of best." He broke off, glanced from one to another of the numerous duplicate faces, and said softly, "You want to know what she can do? I didn't dare speak of it at the time, but now, well—if God is dead, what can replace Him?"

"Then you are—" Marge put her hand over her mouth, exclaimed through it, "Oh, my lord—Edith!"

The best Seth said slowly, "I wonder what the crystal and Edith are doing with that concept."

Shalil was in trouble. The giant had continued to wait for the purely personal, restrictive thought that, he and his colleagues believed, would presently end any control Edith had of the crystal's future.

But the moments had gone by and she had kept on uttering idealistic concepts that were binding him and his kind to the people of the past. All the Seths and the Ediths were recreated. She proposed a cooperative solution for the severe threat to the giant human beings of his century—between the giants on the one hand and the Ediths and Seths on the other. In an outburst of imagination she visualized a time corridor between her own century and his. Thriftily she retained control of that corridor for her own group.

It was as she established that enormous connection, and control, that Shalil—desperate—had her uncreated. He recreated her, unconscious, on the contour rest place. The huge scientists gathered around her comatose body and gloomily evaluated the extent of their defeat.

One said, "But let's face it. We can live with what's happened."

The problem was that they had made no headway. Edith still radiated total power; somehow, she continued to evoke from the crystal an energy output that no one had ever thought possible.

Shalil had a tremendous insight. "Perhaps that's what we need to examine—our own limitations. Perhaps the real problem is that in our scientific zeal we have rejected the enigma."

After he had spoken, there was a dead silence. He saw that they were shaken. The enigma was the forbidden—because unscientific—area of thought: *The enigma that is the universe. Why does it exist? Where did it come from?*

The thrall of shocked silence ended as a giant gave a harsh, determined laugh.

"I don't know anything about the enigma and do not plan to," he said, "but as a scientist I do know my duty—our duty. We must bring this small female to consciousness, inform her of the unqualified extent of her power, and see what she does with it."

"B-but she may kill us all," protested another. He added, almost plaintively, "I've never been killed."

"It will be an interesting experience for you," replied the first man. "Quite different from uncreation."

Shalil interjected matter-of-factly, "Edith is not a killer." He broke off, shrewdly. "I think this is an excellent plan. I see it as being totally in our favor."

They perceived what he meant, and accordingly sanctioned the awakening.

Edith was brought awake. After she had calmed herself, after she had been told about her absolute ability, she had an automatic response, exactly as the giants had anticipated. For prolonged seconds a wild hope suffused her entire being. She wanted more urgently to undo the errors of judgment which had led her down the empty road of numerous boyfriends, none of whom took responsibility for her and her capacity to bear children. All her years of frustration since college found their way first to her eyes in the form of quick tears, and then, when she could speak, to her words.

"Aside from what I've just told you," she spoke the qualifying phrase, which retained for her control of access to the twentieth century without even noticing it, "all I really want is to be happily married."

The giants perceived that the person she had in mind for a husband was the bachelor Seth Mitchell.

They accordingly commanded the crystal that the wish she had expressed be carried out forthwith in its exact and limited meaning. And then, safe and relieved, they stood marveling at the difficult concept of marriage.

In an era where everybody lived forever by a process of crystal duplication, they would never, left to themselves, have been able to ask the right question to produce such an answer.

"It is barely possible," Shalil cautiously summed up, "that the interaction between the unmanipulated human beings of the twentieth century and the manipulated of the ninety-third will actually bring about a lessening of the rigidities of both groups."

His stern, black gaze dared a denial. After a long moment, he was surprised to realize that no one was offended.

Indeed, a colleague murmured reflectively, "If that should happen we may even find out what the crystal is."

But, of course, that was impossible.

The crystal was a space phenomenon. The energy flows in it, around it, and out of it involved individual events, things, persons. But this was a subordinate function—like the motor center in a human brain that moves a muscle in the tip of the little finger.

The muscle should be movable. It would be unfortunate if it were not. Yet if that muscle were permanently incapacitated the fact would go unnoticed by the brain on the conscious level.

On the flow level of existence the patterned interactions in and around and out of the crystal exceed 10 to the 27,000th power times the number of atoms in the universe—enough interactions for all the life configurations of all the people who ever lived; perhaps enough even for all those who ever would live on Earth.

But for the crystal such effects were minor. As a governor of certain time-and-life flows it had suspended those flows for twenty-five years in the Harkdale museum. The suspension did not matter—it meant almost nothing. As a shape of space, its existence was continuous. As space, it occupied a location and was related. Though it had no flows during the quarter century, made no recording and had no memory and no doing, it nevertheless knew, it was, it had and it could.

In finding it and tens of thousands of crystals like it, human beings of the eighth and ninth millennia made use of the interactions and flows: never of the space ability. They discovered the principal "laws"—the how and the what—by which the crystals operated, and were determined to find out eventually the rules that would "explain" certain unknowns in the wave behavior in and around and out of the crystals.

Someday all the interactions of all life and all time would be evenly divided among the crystals. It would then become its true form; one crystal shape, one space. It would then be complete, its . . . intention . . . achieved.

There was no hurry.

And so it waited. And, waiting, fulfilled other goals than its own, minor, unimportant goals involving flows and interactions; reflecting the illusions of motion: events, things, persons . . . involving nothing, really.

In consequence, in Harkdale today stands a one-story building of unusual design. The building occupies the exact spot where Billy Bingham once disappeared on the shore overlooking Lake Naragang. It is a solidly built structure and has a certain beauty.

Its method of construction is shrouded in mystery. Natives grow vague when asked about it.

On a gold plaque beside the ornate front door are the words:

CRYSTAL, INC.
Owned and Managed by
SETH MITCHELLS and EDITH PRICES
Not Open to the Public

Resort visitors who stop to look at the sign are often puzzled by the plural names. And longtime residents, when asked, offer the impression that Crystal, Inc., actually deals in the numerous crystals to be found in the rock formations in and around the hills and lake.

There is a large pretty house with spacious grounds located near the building. In this house dwell Seth and Edith Mitchell.

To the puzzlement of their neighbors, Mr. and Mrs. Seth Mitchell (née Edith Price) started their married life by legally adopting a thirteen-year-old boy whom they called Billy Bingham Mitchell.

COOPERATE OR ELSE!

As the spaceship vanished into the steamy mists of Eristan II, Professor Jamieson drew his gun. He felt physically sick, battered, by the way he had been carried for so many long moments in the furious wind stream of the great ship. But the sense of danger held him tense there in the harness that was attached by metal cables to the now gently swaying antigravity plate above him. With narrowed eyes, he stared up at the ezwal which was peering cautiously down at him over the edge of the antigravity plate.

Its three-in-line eyes, gray as dully polished steel, gazed at him, unwinking; its massive blue head poised there alertly and–Jamieson knew–ready to jerk back the instant it read in his thoughts an intention of shooting.

"Well," said Jamieson harshly, "here we are, both of us about a hundred thousand years from our respective home planets. And we're falling down into a primitive jungle hell that you, with only your isolated life on Carson's Planet to judge by, cannot begin to imagine despite your ability to read my thoughts. Even a six-thousand pound ezwal hasn't got a chance down there–alone!"

A great, long fingered, claw-studded paw edged gingerly over the side of the raft, flicked down at one of the four metal cables that supported Jamieson's harness. There was a bright, steely *ping*. The cable parted like rotted twine before the ferocity of that one cutting paw below.

Like a streak of blurred light, the enormous arm jerked back out of sight; and then there was only the great head and the calm, unwinking eyes peering down at him. Finally, a thought penetrated to Jamieson, a thought cool and unhurried:

"You and I, Professor Jamieson, understand each other very well. Of the hundred-odd men on your ship, only you remain alive. Out of all the human race, therefore, only you know that the ezwals of what you call Carson's Planet are not senseless beasts, but intelligent beings.

"I could have stayed on the ship, and so eventually reached home. But rather than take the slightest risk of your escaping the jungle dangers below, I took the desperate chance of jumping on top of this antigravity raft just as you were launching yourself out of the lock.

"What I cannot clearly understand is why you didn't escape while I was still battering down the control room door. There is a blurred fear-picture in your mind, but–"

Jamieson was laughing, a jarring sound in his own ears, but there was geniune amusement in the grim thoughts that accompanied it. "You poor fool!" he choked at last. "You still don't realize what you're falling down to. While you were hammering away at that door, the ship was flying over the biggest ocean on this planet. All those glints of water down there are really continuation of the ocean, and every pool is swarming with malignant beasts.

"And, somewhere ahead of us, are the Demon Straits, a body of water about fifty miles wide that separates this ocean-jungle from the mainland beyond. Our ship will crash somewhere on that mainland, about a thousand miles from here, I should say. To reach it, we've got to cross that fifty miles of *thing*-infested sea. Now you know why I was waiting, and why you had a chance to jump onto that antigravity plate. I . . ."

His voice collapsed in an *"ugh"* of amazement as, with the speed of a striking snake, the ezwal twisted up, a rearing, monstrous blue shape of frightful fangs and claws that reached with hideous power at the gigantic bird that dived straight down at the shining surface of the antigravity raft.

The bird did not swoop aside. Jamieson had a brief, terrible glimpse of its merciless, protruding, glassy eyes, and of the massive, hooked, pitchfork long claws, tensing for the thrust at the ezwal; and then . . .

The crash set the raft tossing like a chip in stormy waters. Jamieson swung with a mad, dizzy, jerky speed from side to side. The roar of the wind from the smashing power of those mighty wings was like thunder that stunned his brain with its fury. With a gasp, he raised his gun. The red flame of it reached with blazing hunger at one of those wings. The wing turned a streaky black, collapsed; and, simultaneously, the bird was literally flung from the raft by the raging strength of the ezwal.

It plunged down, down, became a blurred dot in the mist, and was lost against the dark background of ground.

Above Jamieson, the ezwal, dangerously off balance, hung poised over the edge of the raft. Four of its combination leg-arms pawed the air uselessly; the remaining two fought with bitter effort at the metal bars on top of the raft. . . and won. The great body drew back, until, once again, only the massive blue head was visible. Jamieson lowered his gun in grim good humor.

"You see," he said, "even a bird was almost too much for us–and I could have burned your belly open. I didn't because maybe it's beginning to penetrate your head that we've got to postpone our private quarrel, and fight together if we ever hope to get out of the hell of jungle and swamp below."

The answering thought was as cold as the sleet-gray eyes that stared down at him so steadily:

"Professor Jamieson, what you *could* have done was unimportant to me who knew what you *would* do. As for your kind offer to ally yourself with me, I repeat that I am here to see you dead, not to protect your pitiful body. You will, therefore, refrain from further desperate appeals, and meet your fate with the dignity becoming a scientist."

Jamieson was silent. A thin, warm, wet wind breathed against his body, bringing the first faint, obscene odors from below. The raft was still at an immense height, but the steamy mists that clung with a limp, yet obscuring strength to this primeval land had yielded some of their opaqueness. Patches of jungle and sea that, a few minutes before, had been blurred by that all pervading fog, showed clearer now, a terrible, patternless sprawl of dark trees alternating with water that shone and flashed in the probing sunlight.

Fantastic, incredible scene. As far as the eye could see into the remote mists to the north, there was steaming jungle and foggy, glittering ocean–the endless, deadly reality that was Eristan II. And, somewhere out there, somewhere in the dimness beyond the concealing weight of steam, those apparently interminable jungles ended abruptly in the dark, ugly swell of water that was the Demon Straits!

"So," said Jamieson at last, softly, "you think you're going to get through. All your long life, all the long generations of your ancestors, you and your kind have depended entirely on your magnificent bodies for survival. While men herded fearfully in their caves, discovering fire as a partial protection, desperately creating weapons that had never before existed, always a bare jump ahead of violent death–all those millions of years, the ezwal of Carson's Planet roamed his great, fertile continents, unafraid, matchless in strength as in intellect, needing no homes, no fires, no clothing, no weapons, no–"

"You will agree," the ezwal interrupted coolly, "that adaption to a difficult environment must be one of the goals of the superior being. Human beings have created what they call civilization, which is actually merely a material barrier between themselves and their environment, so vast and unwieldly that keeping it going occupies the entire existence of the race.

Individually, man is a frivolous, fragile, inconsequential *slave*, who tugs his mite at the wheel, and dies wretchedly of some flaw in his disease-ridden body.

"Unfortunately, the monstrous, built-up weakling with his power lusts and murderous instincts is the greatest danger extant to the sane, healthy races of the universe. He must be prevented from contaminating his betters."

Jamieson laughed curtly. "But you will agree, I hope, that there is something wonderful about an insignificant, fearful jetsam of life fighting successfully against all odds, aspiring to all knowledge, finally attaining the very stars!"

"Nonsense!" The answer held overtones of brittle impatience. "Man and his thoughts constitute a disease. As proof, during the past few minutes, you have been offering specious arguments, apparently unbiased, actually designed to lead one more to an appeal for my assistance, an intolerable form of dishonesty.

"As further evidence I need but anticipate intellectually the moment of our landing. Assuming that I make no attempt to harm you, nevertheless your pitiful body will be instantly and, thereafter, continuously in deadly danger, while I–you must admit that, though there are beasts below physically stronger than I, the difference is not so great that my intelligence, even if it took the form of cunning flight, would more than balance the weakness. You will admit further more–"

"I admit nothing!" Jamieson snapped. "Except that you're going to get the surprise of your life. And you're going to regret beyond all your present capacity for emotionalism the lack of those very artificialities you despise in man. I do not mean material weapons, but–"

"What you mean is unimportant. I can see that you intend to persist in this useless, mendacious type of reasoning, and you have convinced me that you will never emerge alive from that island jungle below. Therefore–"

The same, tremendous arm that a few minutes before had torn steel chain, flashed into sight and downward in one burst of madly swift gesture.

The two remaining cables attached to Jamieson's harness parted like wet paper; and so great was the force of the blow that Jamieson was jerked a hundred feet parallel to the distant ground before his long, clenched body curved downward for its terrific fall.

A thought, cool with grim irony, struck after him:

"I notice that you are a very cautious man, professor, in that you have not only a packsack, but a parachute strapped to your back. This will enable you to reach ground safely, but your landing will be largely governed by chance. Your logical mind will doubtless enable you to visualize the situation. Goodbye and–bad luck!"

Jamieson strained at the thin, strong ropes of his parachute, his gaze narrowed on the scene below. Through the now almost transparent mist, and somewhat to the north, was a green brown blaze of jungle. If he could get there . . .

He tugged again at the ropes, and with icy speculation watched the effect, calculated the mathematical possibilities. He was falling slowly; that would be the effect of the heavy air of this planet: pressure eighteen pounds per square inch at sea level.

Sea level! He smiled wryly, without humor. Sea level was approximately where he would be in a very few minutes.

There was, he saw, no sea immediately beneath him. A few splotches of water, yes, and a straggle of trees. The rest was a sort of clearing, except that it wasn't exactly. It had a strange, grayish, repellent appearance like . . .

The terrible shock of recognition drained the blood from his cheeks. His mind shrank as from an unthinkably lecherous thought. In panic he tore at the ropes, as if by sheer physical strength he would draw the tantalizingly near jungle to him. That jungle, that precious jungle! Horrors it might contain, but at least they were of the future, while that hellish stuff directly below held no future, nothing but a gray, quagmire trap, thick choking mud . . .

Abruptly, he saw that the solid mass of trees was beyond his reach. The parachute was less than five hundred feet above that deadly, unclean spread of mud. The jungle itself–stinking, horrible jungle, blatantly exuding the sharp, evil odors of rotting vegetation, yet suddenly the most desirable of places, was about the same distance to the northwest.

To make it would require a forty-five degree descent. Carefully, he manipulated the rope controls of the parachute. It caught the wind like a glider; the jungle drew closer, closer.

He landed triumphantly in a tiny straggle of trees, a little island separated from the main bulk of forest by less than a hundred and fifty feet.

The island was ten feet long by eight wide; four trees, the longest about fifty feet tall, maintained a precarious existence on its soggy, wet, comparatively firm base.

Four trees, representing a total of about a hundred and eighty feet. Definitely enough length. But his first glow of triumph began to fade. Without a crane to manipulate three of those trees into place, the knowledge that they represented safety was utterly useless.

Jamieson sat down, conscious for the first time of the dull ache in his shoulders, the strained tenseness of his whole body, a sense of depressing heat. He could see the sun, a white blob barely visible through the white mists that formed the atmosphere of this deadly, fantastic land.

The blur of sun seemed to fade into remoteness; a vague darkness formed in his mind; and then a sharp, conscious thought that he had been asleep.

He opened his eyes with a start. The sun was much lower in the eastern sky and . . .

His mind stopped from the sheer shock of discovery. Instantly, however, it came alive, steady, cool, despite the vast, first shock of his amazement.

What had happened was like some fantasy out of a fairy story. The four trees, with the tattered remains of his parachute still clinging to them, towered above him. But his plan for them had taken form while he slept.

A bridge of trees, thicker, more solid than any the little island could have produced, stretched straight and strong from the island to the mainland. There was no doubt, of course, as to who had performed that colossal feat: the ezwal was standing unconcernedly on two of its six legs, leaning man-like against the thick trunk of a gigantic tree. Its thought came:

"You need have no fear, Professor Jamieson. I have come to see your point of view. I am prepared to assist you to reach the mainland and to cooperate with you thereafter. I—"

Jamieson's deep, ungracious laughter cut off the thought. "You damned liar!" the scientist said finally. "What you mean is that you've run up against something you couldn't handle. Well, that's all right with me. So long as we understand each other, we'll get along."

The snake slid heavily out of the jungle, ten feet from the mainland end of the bridge of trees, thirty feet to the right of the ezwal. Jamieson, scraping cautiously toward the center of the bridge, saw the first violent swaying of the long, luscious jungle grass—and froze where he was as the vicious, fantastic head reared into sight, followed by the first twenty feet of that thick, menacing body.

Briefly, the great head, in its swaying movement, was turned directly at him. The little pig eyes seemed to glare straight into his own stunned, brown eyes. Shock held him, sheer, unadulterated shock at the incredibly bad luck that had allowed this deadly creature to find him in such an immeasurably helpless position.

His paralysis there, under those blazing eyes, was a living, agonizing thing. Tautness struck like fire into every muscle of his body; it was an instinctive straining for rigidity, abnormal and terrible—but it worked.

The fearsome head whipped aside, fixed in eager fascination on the ezwal, and took on a rigidity all its own.

Jamieson relaxed; his brief fear changed to brief, violent anger; he projected a scathing thought at the ezwal:

"I understood you could sense the approach of dangerous beasts by reading their minds."

No answering thought came into his brain. The giant snake flowed farther into the clearing; and before that towering, horned head rearing monstrously from the long, titanically powerful body, the ezwal backed slowly, yielding with a grim reluctance to the obvious conviction that it was no match for this vast creature.

Cool again, Jamieson directed an ironic at the ezwal:

"It may interest you to know that as chief scientist of the Interstellar Military Commission, I reported Eristan II unusable as a military base for our fleet; and there were two main reasons: one of the damnedest flesh-eating plants you ever saw, and this pretty little baby. There's millions of both of them. Each snake breeds hundreds in its lifetime, so they can't be stamped out. They're bisexual, attain a length of about a hundred and fifty feet and a weight of ten tons."

The ezwal, now some fifty feet away from the snake, stopped and, without looking at Jamieson, sent him a tight, swift thought:

"Its appearance did surprise me, but the reason is that its mind held only a vague curiosity about some sounds it had heard, no clear, sharp thought such as an intention to murder. But that's unimportant. It's here; it's dangerous. It hasn't seen you yet, so act accordingly. It doesn't think it can get me, but it's considering the situation. In spite of its desire for me, the problem remains essentially yours; the danger is *all* yours."

The ezwal concluded almost indifferently: "I am willing to give you limited aid in any plan you might have, but please don't offer our interdependence. So far there's been only one dependent. I think you know who it is."

Jamieson was grim. "Don't be too sure that you're not in danger. That fellow looks muscle bound, but when he starts moving, he's like a steel spring for the first three or four hundred feet–and you haven't got that much space behind you."

"What do you mean? I can run four hundred feet in three seconds, earth time."

Coldly, the scientist whipped out: "You could, *if you had four hundred feet in which to run.* But you haven't. I've just been forming a mental picture of this edge of jungle, as I saw it just before I landed.

"There's about a hundred and fifty feet of jungle, then a curving shore of mud plain, a continuation of this mud here.

The curve swings back this way, and cuts you off neatly on this little outjutting of jungle. To get clear of the snake, you've got to dart past him. Roughly, your clearance is a hundred and fifty feet all around–and it isn't enough! Interdependent? You're damned right we are. Things like this will happen a thousand times a year on Eristan II."

There was startled silence; finally: "Why don't you turn your atomic gun on it–burn it?"

"And have it come out here, while I'm helpless? These big snakes are born in this mud, and live half their lives in it. It would take five minutes to burn off that tough head. By that time I'd be swallowed and digested."

The brief seconds that passed then were vibrant with reluctant desperation. But there could be no delay; swiftly the grudging request came:

"Professor Jamieson, I am open to suggestions–and hurry!"

The depressing realization came to Jamieson that the ezwal was once more asking for his assistance, knowing that it would be given; and yet it itself was giving no promise in return.

And there was no time for bargaining. Curtly, he projected:

"It's the purest case of our acting as a team. The snake has no real weakness–except possibly this:

"Before it attacks, its head will start swaying. That's almost a universal snake method of hypnotizing victims into paralysis. Actually, the motion is also partially self-hypnotizing. At the earliest possible moment after it begins to sway, I'll burn its eyes out–and you get on its back, and hang on. Its brain is located just behind that great horn. Claw your way there, and eat in while I burn–"

The thought scattered like chaff, as the tremendous head began to move. With a trembling jerk, Jamieson snatched his gun . . .

It was not so much, then, that the snake put up a fight, as that it wouldn't die. Its smoking remains were still twisting half an hour later when Jamieson scrambled weakly from the bridge of trees and collapsed onto the ground.

When finally he climbed to his feet, the ezwal was sitting fifty feet away under a clump of trees, its middle legs also on the ground, its forelegs folded across its chest–and it was contemplating him.

It looked strangely sleek and beautiful in its blue coat and in the very massiveness of its form. And there was immeasurable comfort in the knowledge that, for the time being at least, the mighty muscles that rippled underneath that silk smooth skin were on his side.

Jamieson returned the ezwal's stare steadily; finally he said:

"What happened to the antigravity raft?"

"I abandoned it thirty-five miles north of here."

Jamieson hesitated; then: "We'll have to go to it. I practically depowered my gun on that snake. It needs metal for recharging; and that raft is the only metal in bulk that I know of."

He was silent again; then softly: "One thing more. I want your word of honor that you won't even attempt to harm me until we are safely on the other side of the Demon Straits!"

"You'd accept my word?" The steel-gray, three-in-line eyes meditated on him curiously.

"Yes."

"Very well, I give it."

Jamieson shook his head, smiling darkly. "Oh, no, you don't, not as easily as that."

"I thought you said you'd accept my word." Peevishly.

"I will, but in the following phraseology."

Jamieson stared with grim intentness at his mighty and deadly enemy. "I want you to swear by the sun that rises and by the green, fruitful earth, by the joys of the contemplative mind and the glory of immortal life—"

He paused. "Well?"

There was a gray fire in the ezwal's gaze, and its thought held a ferocious quality when finally it replied:

"You are, Professor Jamieson, even more dangerous than I thought. It is clear there can be no compromise between us."

"But you'll make the limited promise I ask for?"

The gray eyes dulled strangely; long, thin lips parted in a snarl that showed great, dark fangs.

"No!" Curtly.

"I thought," said Jamieson softly, "I ought to get that clear."

No answer. The ezwal simply sat there, its gaze fixed on him.

"Another thing," Jamieson went on, "stop pretending you can read all my thoughts. You didn't know that I knew about your religion. I'll wager you can only catch my sharpest idea-forms, and those particularly when my mind is focused on speech."

"I made no pretenses," the ezwal replied coolly. "I shall continue to keep you as much in the dark as possible."

"The doubt will, of course, harass my mind," said Jamieson, "but not too much. Once I accept a theory, I act accordingly. If I should prove wrong, there remains the final arbiter of my atomic gun against your strength. I wouldn't bet on the victor.

"But now," he hunched his long body, and strode forward, "let's get going. The swiftest method, I believe, would be for me to ride on your back. I could tie a rope from my parachute around your body just in front of your middle legs and by hanging onto the rope keep myself from falling off. My only qualification is that you must promise to let me off before making any hostile move. Agreeable?"

The ezwal hesitated, then nodded: "For the time being."

Jamieson was smiling, his long, spare, yet strong, face ironical.

"That leaves only one thing: What did you run up against that made you change your mind about killing me immediately? Could it have been something entirely beyond the isolated, static, aristocratic existence of the ezwal?"

"Get on my back!" came the snarling thought. "I desire no lectures, nor any further sounds from your rasping voice. I fear nothing on this planet. My reasons for coming back have no connection with any of your pitiful ideas; and it would not take much to make me change my mind. Take warning!"

Jamieson was silent, startled. It had not been his intention to provoke the ezwal. He'd have to be more cautious in the future, or this great animal, bigger than eight lions, deadlier than a hundred, might turn on him long before it itself intended.

It was an hour later that the long, fish-shaped spaceship swung out of the steamy mists that patroled the skies of Eristan II. It coasted along less than a thousand feet up, cruel looking as a swordfish with its finely pointed nose.

The explosive thought of the ezwal cut into Jamieson's brain: "Professor Jamieson, if you make so much as a single effort at signaling, you die—"

Jamieson was silent, his mind held stiff and blank, after one mental leap. As he watched, the great, half-mile-long ship sank visibly lower and, as it vanished beyond the rim of the jungle ahead, there was no doubt that it was going to land.

And then, the ezwal's thoughts came again, sly now, almost exultant:

"It's no use trying to hide it—because now that the actuality is here, I remember that your dead companions had awareness of another spaceship in the back of their minds."

Jamieson swallowed the hard lump in his throat. There was a sickness in him, and a vast rage at the incredibly bad luck of this ship coming here—now!

Miserably, he gave himself to the demanding rhythm of the ezwal's smooth gallop; and for a while there was only that odor-tainted wind, and the pad of six paws, a dull, flat flow of sound; and all around was the dark jungle, the occasional, queer *lap, lap* of treacherous, unseen waters. And it was all there, the strangeness, the terribleness of this wild ride of a man on the back of a blue-tinted, beast-like being that hated him–and knew about that ship.

At last, grudgingly, he yielded. He said snappishly, as if his words might yet snatch victory from defeat:

"Now I know, anyway, that your thought-reading ability is a damned sketchy thing. You didn't begin to suspect why you were able to conquer my ship so easily."

"Why should I?" The ezwal was impatient. "I remember now there was a long period when I caught no thoughts, only an excess of energy tension, abnormally more than was customary from your engines. That must have been when you speeded up.

"Then I noticed the cage door was ajar–and forgot everything else."

The scientist nodded, gloom a sickish weight on him. "We received some awful buffeting, nothing palpable, of course, because the interstellars were full on. But, somewhere, there must have been a blow that knocked our innards out of alignment.

"Afterwards, we watched for dangers from outside; and so you, on the inside, got your chance to kill a hundred men, most of them sleeping . . ."

He tensed his body ever so carefully, eyes vaguely as possible on the limb of the tree just ahead, concentrating with enormous casualness on the idea of ducking under it. Somehow, his real purpose leaked from his straining brain.

In a single convulsion of movement, like a bucking horse, the ezwal reared. Shattering violence of movement! Like a shot from a gun, Jamieson was flung forward *bang* against that steel-hard back. Stunned, dizzy, he fought for balance–and then it was over.

The great animal plunged aside into a thick pattern of jungle, completely away from the protruding limb that had momentarily offered such sweet safety. It twisted skillfully between two giant trees, and emerged a moment later onto the beach of a long, glittering bay of ocean.

Fleet as the wind, it raced along the deserted sands, and then on into the thickening jungles beyond. No thought came from it, not a tendril of triumph, no indication of the tremendous victory it had just won.

Jamieson said sickly: "I made that attempt because I know what you're going to do. I admit we had a running fight with that Rull cruiser. But you're crazy if you think they mean advantage for you.

"Rulls are different. They come from another galaxy. They're–"

"Professor!" The interrupting thought was like metal in the

sheer, vibrating force of it. "Don't dare try to draw your gun to kill yourself. One false move, and I'll show you how violently and painfully a man can be disarmed."

"You promised," Jamieson almost mumbled, "to make no hostile move—"

"And I'll keep that promise—to the letter, after man's own fashion, *in my own good time.* But now—I gathered from your mind that you think these creatures landed because they detected the minute energy discharge of the antigravity raft."

"Pure deduction." Curtly. "There must be some logical reason, and unless you shut off the power as I did on the spaceship—"

"I didn't. Therefore, that is why they landed. Their instruments probably also registered your use of the gun on the snake. Therefore they definitely know someone is here. My best bet, accordingly, is to head straight for them before they kill me accidentally. I have no doubt of the welcome I shall receive when they see me captive, and I tell them that I and my fellow ezwals are prepared to help drive man from Carson's Planet. And you will have gotten off my back unharmed—thus my promise—"

The scientist licked dry lips. "That's bestial," he said finally. "You know damned well from reading my mind that Rulls eat human beings. Earth is one of the eight planets in this galaxy whose flesh is palatable to these hell creatures—"

The ezwal said coldly: "I have seen men on Carson's Planet eat ezwals with relish. Why shouldn't men in turn be eaten by other beings?"

Jamieson was silent, a shocked silence at the hatred that was here. The flint-like thought of the other finished:

"You may not realize how important it is that no word of ezwal intelligence get back to earth during the next few months, but we ezwals know.

"I want you dead!"

And still there was hope in him. He recognized it for what it was: that mad, senseless hope of a man still alive, refusing to acknowledge death till its gray chill lay cold on his bones.

A crash of brush roused him out of himself. Great branches of greater trees broke with wheezing unwillingness. A monstrous reptile head peered at them over a tall tree.

Jamieson had a spine-cooling glimpse of a scaly, glittering body; eyes as red as fire blazed at him—and then that lumbering nightmare was far behind, as the ezwal raced on, contemptuous, terrible in its heeding strength.

And after a moment, then, in spite of hideous danger, in spite of his desperate conviction that he must convince the ezwal how wrong it was—admiration flared inside him, a wild, fascinated admiration.

"By God!" he exclaimed, "I wouldn't be surprised if you really could evade the terrors of this world. In all my journeys through space, I've never seen such a perfect combination of mind and magnificent muscle."

"Save your praise," sneered the ezwal.

Jamieson hardly heard. He was frowning in genuine thoughtfulness:

"There's a saber-toothed, furred creature about your size and speed that might damage you, but I think you can outrun or outfight all the other furred animals. Then there are the malignant plants, particularly a horrible, creepier affair–it's not the only intelligent plant in the galaxy, but it's the smartest. You'd need my gun if you got tangled up with one of those.

"You could evade them, of course, but that implies ability to recognize that one's in the vicinity. There are signposts of their presence but," he held his mind as dim as possible, and smiled grimly, "I'll leave that subject before you read the details in my brain.

"That leaves the great reptiles; they can probably catch you only in the water. That's where the Demon Straits would be a mortal handicap."

"I can swim," the ezwal snapped, "fifty miles in three hours with you on my back."

"Go on!" The scientist's voice was scathing. "If you could do all these things–if you could cross oceans and a thousand miles of jungle, why did you return for me, knowing, as you must now know, that I could never reach my ship alone? Why?"

"It's dark where you're going," the ezwal said impatiently, "and knowledge is not a requirement for death. All these fears of yours are but proof that man will yield to unfriendly environment where he would be unflinching in the face of intelligent opposition.

"And that is why your people must not learn of ezwal intelligence. Literally, we have created on Carson's Planet a dumb, beast-like atmosphere where men would eventually feel that nature was too strong for them. The fact that you have refused to face the nature-environment of this jungle planet of Eristan II and that the psycho-friction on Carson's Planet is already at the factual point 135 is proof that–"

"Eh?" Jamieson stared at that gleaming, blue, rhythmically bobbing head, "you're crazy. Why, 135 would mean–twenty-five–thirty million. The limit is point 38."

"Exactly," glowed the ezwal, "thirty million dead."

A gulf was opening before Jamieson's brain, a black realization of where this–monstrous–creature's thoughts were leading. He said violently:

"It's a damned lie. My reports show—"

"Thirty million!" repeated the ezwal with a deadly satisfaction. "And I know exactly what that means in your terms of psycho-friction: point 135 as compared to a maxium safety tension limit of point 38. That limit, of course, obtains when nature is the opponent. If your people discovered the cause of their agony was an intelligent race, the resistance would go up to point 184—and we'd lose. You didn't know we'd studied your psychology so thoroughly."

White, shakily, Jamieson replied: "In five years, we'll have a billion population on Carson's Planet, and the few ezwals that will have escaped will be a small, scattered, demoralized—"

"In five *months*," interrupted the ezwal coldly, "man will figuratively explode from our planet. Revolution, a blind mob impulse to get into the interstellar transports at any cost, made flight from intolerable dangers. And, added to everything, the sudden arrivals of the Rull warships to assist us. It will be the greatest disaster in the long, brutal history of conquering man."

With a terrible effort, Jamieson caught himself into a tight matter-of-factness: "Assuming all this, assuming that machines yield to muscles, what will you do with the Rulls after we're gone?"

"Just let them dare remain!"

Jamieson's brief, titanic effort at casualness collapsed into a wave of fury: "Why, you blasted fools, man beat the Rulls to Carson's Planet by less than two years. While you stupid idiots interfered with us on the ground, we fought long, delaying actions in the deeps of space, protecting you from the most murderous, ruthless, unreasonable things that the universe ever spawned."

He stopped, fought for control, said finally with a grim effort at rational argument: "We've never been able to drive the Rull from any planet where he has established himself. And he drove us from three major bases before we realized the enormousness of the danger, and stood firm everywhere regardless of military losses."

He stopped again, conscious of the blank, obstinate, contemptuous wall that was the mind of this ezwal.

"Thirty million!" he said almost softly, half to himself. "Wives, husbands, children, lovers—"

A black anger blotted out his conscious thought. With a single lightning-swift jerk of his arm, he drew his atomic gun, pressed its muzzle hard against the great blue-ridged backbone.

"By heaven, at least you're not going to get the Rulls in on anything that happens."

His finger closed hard on that yielding trigger; there was a white blaze of fire that–missed! Amazingly–it missed.

Instants passed before his brain grasped the startling fact that he was flying through the air, flung clear by one incredibly swift jerk of that vast, blue body.

He struck brush. Agonizing fingers of sticky jungle vine wrenched at his clothes, ripped his hands, and tore at the gun, that precious, all-valuable gun.

His clothes shredded, blood came in red, ugly streaks–everything yielded to that desperate environment but the one, all-important thing. With a bitter, enduring singleness of purpose, he clung to the gun.

He landed on his side, rolled over in a flash and twisted up his gun, finger once more on the trigger. Three feet from that deadly muzzle, the ezwal drew up with a hideous snarl of its great, square face–jumped thirty feet to one side, and vanished, a streak of amazing blue, behind a thick bole of steel-hard jungle fungi.

Shaky, almost ill, Jamieson sat up and surveyed the extent of his defeat, the limits of his victory.

All around was a curious, treeless jungle. Giant, ugly, yellow fungi towered thirty, fifty, eighty feet against a red brown green sky line of tangled brown vines, green lichens and bulbous, incredibly long, strong, reddish grass.

The ezwal had raged through other such dense matted wilderness with a solid, irresistible strength. For a man on foot, who dared not waste more than a fraction of the waning power of his gun, it was a pathless, major obstacle to the simplest progress–the last place in the world he would have chosen for a last ditch fight against anything. And yet . . .

In losing his temper he had hit on the only possible method of drawing his gun without giving the ezwal advance warning thoughts. At least, he was not being borne helplessly along to a great warship loaded with slimly, white Rulls and . . .

Rulls!

With a gasp, Jamieson leaped to his feet. There was a treacherous sagging of the ground under his feet, but he simply, instinctively stepped onto a dead patch of fungi; and the harsh, urgent tones of his voice were loud in his ears, as he said swiftly:

"We've got to act fast. The discharge of my gun must have registered on Rull instruments, and they'll be here in minutes. You've got to believe me when I tell you that your scheme of enlisting the Rulls as allies is madness.

"Listen to this: all the ships we sent into their galaxy reported that every planet of a hundred they visited was inhabited by Rulls. Nothing else, no other races. They must have destroyed every other living, intelligent creature.

"Man has forty-eight hundred and seventy-four nonhuman allies. I admit all have civilizations that are similar to man's own; and that's the devil of the type of history-less, building-less, ezwal culture. Ezwals cannot defend themselves against energies and machines. And, frankly, man will not leave Carson's Planet till that overwhelmingly important defense question has been satisfactorily mastered.

"You and your revolution. True, the simple people in their agony may flee in mad panic, but the military will remain, a disciplined, undefeatable organization, a hundred battleships, a thousand cruisers, ten thousand destroyers for that one base alone. The ezwal plan is clever only in its grasp of human psychology and because it may well succeed in causing destruction and death. But in that plan is no conception of the vastness of interstellar civilization, the responsibilities and the duties of its members.

"The reason I was taking you to earth was to show you the complexities and honest problems of that civilization, to prove to you that we are not evil. I swear to you that man and his present grand civilization will solve the ezwal problem to ezwal satisfaction. What do you say?"

His last words boomed out eerily in the odd, deathly, late afternoon hush that had settled over the jungle world of Eristan II. He could see the blur of sun, a misty blob low in the eastern sky; and the hard realization came:

Even if he escaped the Rulls, in two hours at most the great fanged hunters and the reptilian flesh-eaters that haunted the slow nights of this remote, primeval planet would emerge ravenous from their stinking hideaways, and seek their terrible surcease.

He'd have to get away from this damned fungi, find a real tree with good, strong, high-growing branches and, somehow, stay there all night. Some kind of system of intertwining vines, properly rigged up, should warn him of any beast intruder–including ezwals.

He began to work forward, clinging carefully to the densest, most concealing brush. After fifty yards, the jungle seemed as impenetrable as ever, and his legs and arms ached from his effort. He stopped, and said:

"I tell you that man would never have gone into Carson's Planet the way he did, if he had known it was inhabited by intelligent beings. There are strict laws that govern even under military necessity."

Quite abruptly, answer came: "Cease these squalling, lying appeals. Man possesses no less than five thousand planets formerly occupied by intelligent races. No totality of prevarication can cover up or ever excuse five thousand cosmic crimes–"

The ezwal's thought broke off; then, almost casually: "Professor, I've just run across an animal that–"

Jamieson was saying: "Man's crimes are as black as his noble works are white and wonderful. You must understand those two facets of his character–"

"This animal," persisted the ezwal, "is floating above me now, watching me, but I am unable to catch a single vibration of its thought–"

"More than three thousand of those races now have self-government. Man does not long deny to any basically good intelligence the liberty and freedom of action which he needs so much himself–"

"Professor!" The thought was like a knife piercing, utterly urgent. "This creature has a repellent, worm-shaped body, and it floats without wings. It has no brain that I can detect. It–"

Very carefully, very gently, Jamieson swung himself behind a pile of brush and raised his pistol. Then softly, swiftly, he said:

"Act like a beast, snarl at it, and run like hell into the thickest underbrush if it reaches with one of those tiny, worm-like hands toward any one of the half a dozen notches on either side of its body.

"If you cannot contact its mind–we never could get in touch with it in any way–you'll have to depend on its character; as follows:

"The Rull hears only sounds between five hundred thousand and eight hundred thousand vibrations a second. That is why I can talk out loud without danger. That, also, suggests that its thought moves on a vastly different vibration level; it must hate and fear everything else, which must be why it is so remorselessly impelled on its course of destruction.

"The Rull does not kill for pleasure. It exterminates. It possibly considers the entire universe alien which, perhaps, is why it eliminates all important creatures on any planet it intends to occupy. There can be no intention of occupying this planet because our great base on Eristan I is only five thousand light-years or twenty-five hours away by warship. Therefore it will not harm you unless it has special suspicions. Therefore be all animal."

He finished tensely: "What's it doing now?"

There was no answer.

The minutes dragged; and it wasn't so much that there was silence. Queer, little noises came out of nearness and remoteness: the distant crack of wood under some heavy foot, faint snortings of creatures that were not exactly near–but too near for comfort.

A memory came that was more terrible than the gathering night, a living flame of remembrance of the one time he had seen a Rull feeding off a human being.

First, the clothes were stripped from the still-living victim, whose nervous sytem was then paralyzed partially by a stinger that was part of the Rull's body. And then, the big, fat, white worm crawled into the body, and lay there in that abnormal, obscene embrace while thousands of little cup-like mouths fed . . .

Jamieson recoiled mentally and physically. Abrupt, desperate, panicky fear sent him burrowing deeper into the tangle of brush. It was quiet there, not a breath of air touched him. And he noticed, after a moment, that he was soaked with perspiration.

Other minutes passed; and because, in his years, courage had never been long absent from him, he stiffened with an abrupt anger at himself–and ventured into the hard, concentrated thought of attempted communication:

"If you have any questions, for heaven's sake don't waste time."

There must have been wind above his tight shelter of brush, for a fog heavily tainted with the smell of warm, slimy water drifted over him, blocking even the narrow view that remained.

Jamieson stirred uneasily. It was not fear; his mind was a clenched unit, like a fist ready to strike. It was that–suddenly–he felt without eyes in a world of terrible enemies. More urgently, he went on:

"Your very act of asking my assistance in identifying the Rull implied your recognition of our interdependence. Accordingly, I demand–"

"Very well!" The answering thought was dim and far away. "I admit my inability to get in touch with this worm ends my plans of establishing an anti-human alliance."

There was a time, such a short time ago, Jamieson thought drearily, when such an admission would have brought geniune intellectual joy. The poor devils on Carson's Planet, at least, were not going to have to fight Rulls as well as their own madness–as well as ezwals.

He braced himself, vaguely amazed at the lowness of his morale. He said almost hopelessly:

"What about us?"

"I have already repaid your initial assistance in that, at this moment, I am leading the creature directly away from you."

"It's still following you?"

"Yes! It seems to be studying me. Have you any suggestions?"

Weariness faded; Jamieson snapped: "Only on condition that you are willing to recognize that we are a unit, and that everything else, including what man and ezwal are going to do about Carson's Planet must be discussed later. Agreed?"

The ezwal's thought was scarcely more than a snarl: "You keep harping on that!"

Momentarily, the scientist felt all the exasperation, all the strain of the past hours a pressing, hurting force in his brain. Like a flame, it burst forth, a flare of raging thought:

"You damned scoundrel, you've forced every issue so far, and all of them were rooted in that problem. You make that promise–or just forget the whole thing."

The silence was a pregnant emotion, dark with bitter, formless thought. Around Jamieson, the mists were thinning, fading into the twilight of that thick jungle. Finally:

"I promise to help you safely across the Demon Straits; and I'll be with you in minutes–if I don't lose this thing first."

Jamieson retorted grimly: "Agreement satisfactory–but don't expect to lose a Rull. They've got perfect antigravity, whereas that antigravity raft of ours was simply a superparachute. It would eventually have fallen under its own weight."

He paused tensely; then: "You've got everything clear? I'll burn the Rull that's following you, then we'll beat it as fast as your legs can carry us."

"Get ready!" The answer was a cold, deadly wave. "I'll be there in seconds."

There was no time for thought. Brush crashed. Through the mist, Jamieson caught one flashing glimpse of the ezwal with its six legs. At fifty feet, its slate-gray, three-in-line eyes were like pools of light. And then, as he pointed his gun in a desperate expectation . . .

"*For your life!*" came the ezwal's thought, "don't shoot, don't move. There're a dozen of them above me and–"

Queerly, shatteringly, that strong flow of thought ended in a chaotic jumble as energy flared out there, a glaring, white fire that blinked on, and then instantly off.

The mist rolled thicker, white gray, noxious stuff that hid what *must* be happening.

And hid him.

Jamieson lay stiff and cold–and waited. For a moment, so normal had mind-reading become in these hours, that he forgot he could only catch thoughts at the will of the ezwal, and he strained to penetrate the blackout of mind vibrations.

He thought finally, a tight, personal thought: The Rulls must have worked a psychosis on the ezwal. Nothing else could explain that incoherent termination of thought in so powerful a mind. And yet–psychosis was used mainly on animals and other uncivilized and primitive life forms, unaccustomed to that sudden interplay of dazzling lights.

He frowned bleakly. Actually, in spite of its potent brain, the ezwal was very much animal, very much uncivilized, and possibly extremely allergic to mechanical hypnosis.

Definitely, it was not death from a heavy mobile projector because there would have been sound from the weapon, and because there *wouldn't* have been that instantaneous distortion of thought, that twisting . . .

He felt a moment's sense of intense relief. It had been curiously unsettling to think of that mighty animal struck dead.

He caught his mind into a harder band: So the ezwal was captive, not corpse. So–what now?

Relief drained. It wasn't, he thought blankly, as if he could do anything against a heavily armored, heavily manned cruiser . . .

Ten minutes passed, and then out of the deepening twilight came the thunderous roar of a solid bank of energy projectors. There was answering thunder on a smaller scale; and then, once again, though farther away now, the deep, unmistakable roar of a broadside of hundred-inch battleship projectors.

A battleship! A capital ship from the Eristan I base, either on patrol or investigating energy discharges. The Rulls would be lucky if they got away. As for himself–nothing!

Nothing but the night and its terrors. True, there would be no trouble now from the Rulls, but that was all. This wasn't rescue, not even the hope of rescue. For days and days, the two great ships would maneuver in space; and, by the time the battleship reported again to its base, there wouldn't be very much thought given to the why of the Rull cruiser's presence on or near the ground.

Besides, the Rull would have detected its enemy before its own position would be accurately plotted. That first broadside had easily been fifty miles away.

The problem of ezwal and man, that had seemed such an intimate, soluble pattern when he and the great animal were alone, was losing its perspective. Against the immeasurably larger background of space, the design was twisting crazily.

It became a shapeless thing, utterly lost in the tangle of unseen obstacles that kept tripping him, as he plunged forward into the dimming reaches of jungle.

In half an hour it was pitch dark; and he hadn't penetrated more than a few hundred yars. He would have blundered on into the black night, except that suddenly his fingers touched thick, carboniferous bark.

A tree!

Great beasts stamped below, as he clung to that precarious perch. Eyes of fire glared at him. Seven times in the first hour by his watch, monstrous things clambered up the tree, mewing and slavering in feral desire. Seven times his weakening gun flashed a thinner beam of destroying energy–and great, scale-armored carnivore whose approach shook the earth came to feed on the odorous flesh–and passed on.

One hour gone!

A hundred nights like this one, to be spent without sleep, to be defended against a new, ferocious enemy every ten minutes, and no power in his gun.

The terrible thing was that the ezwal had just agreed to work with him against the Rulls. Victory so near, then instantly snatched afar . . .

Something, a horrible something, slobbered at the foot of the tree. Great claws rasped on bark, and then two eyes, easily a foot apart, started with an astounding speed up toward him.

Jamieson snatched at his gun, hesitated, then began hastily to climb up into the thinner branches. Every second, as he scrambled higher, he had the awful feeling that a branch would break, and send him sliding down toward to the thing; and there was the more dreadful conviction that great jaws were at his heels.

Actually, however, his determination to save his gun worked beyond his expectations. The beast was edging up into those thin branches after him when there was a hideous snarl below, and another greater creature started up the tree.

The fighting of animal against animal that started then was absolutely continuous. The tree shook, as saber-toothed beasts that mewed fought vast, grunting, roaring shapes. And every little while there would be a piercing, triumphant scream as a gigantic dinosaur-thing raged into the fight–and literally ate the struggling mass of killers.

Toward dawn, the continuous bellowing and snarling from near and far diminished notably, as if stomach after eager stomach gorged itself; and retired in enormous content to some cesspool of a bed.

At dawn he was still alive, completely weary, his body drooping with sleep desire, and in his mind only the will to live, but utterly no belief that he would survive the day.

If only, on the ship, he had not been cornered so swiftly in the control room by the ezwal, he could have taken antisleep pills, fuel capsules for his gun and–he laughed in sharp sardonicism as the futility of that line of reasoning penetrated–and a lifeboat which, of course, would by itself have enabled him to fly to safety.

At least there had been a few hundred food capsules in the

control room–a month's supply.

He sucked at one that was chocolate flavored, and slowly climbed to the bloodstained ground.

There was a sameness about the day, a mind-wearing sameness! Jungle and sea, different only in the designs of land shape and in the way the water lapped a curving, twisting shore. Always the substance was unchanged.

Jungle and sea . . .

Everything fought him–and until mid afternoon he fought back. He had covered, he estimated, about three miles when he saw the tree–there was a kind of crotch high up in its towering form, where he could sleep without falling, if he tied himself with vines.

Three miles a day. Twelve hundred miles, counting what he still had to cover of this jungle ocean, counting the Demon Straits–twelve hundred miles at three miles a day.

Four hundred days!

He woke up with the beasts of the Eristan night coughing their lust at the base of his tree. He woke up with the memory of a nightmare in which he was swimming the Demon waters, pursued by millions of worms, who kept shouting something about the importance of solving the ezwal problem.

"What," they asked accusingly, "is man going to do with civilizations intellectually so advanced, but without a single building or weapon or–anything?"

Jamieson shook himself awake; and then: "To hell with ezwals!" he roared into the black, pressing, deadly night.

For a while, then, he sat shocked at the things that were happening to his mind, once so stable.

Stable! But that, of course, was long ago.

The fourth day dawned, a misty, muggy replica of the day before. And of the day before that. And before that. And–

"Stop it, you idiot!" said Professor Jamieson aloud, savagely.

He was struggling stubbornly toward what seemed a clearing when a gray mass of creepers to one side stirred as in a gentle wind, and started to grow toward him. Simultaneously, a queer, hesitant thought came into his mind from–outside!

"Got them all!" it said with a madly calm ferociousness. "Get this–two-legged thing–too. Send creepers through the ground."

It was such an alien thought form, so unsettlingly different, that his brain came up from the depths to which it had sunk, and poised with startled alertness abruptly, almost normally fascinated.

"Why, of course," he thought quite sanely, "we've always wondered how the Rytt killer plant could have evolved its high intelligence. It's like the ezwal. It communicates by mental telepathy."

Excitement came, an intense, scientific absorption in all the terrifically important knowledge that he had accumulated–about ezwals, about Rulls, and the way he had caught the Rytt plant's private vibrations. Beyond all doubt, the ezwal, in forcing its thoughts on him, had opened paths, and made it easier for him to receive all thoughts. Why, that could mean that he . . .

In a blaze of alertness, he cut the thought short; his gaze narrowed on the gray creepers edging toward him. He backed away, gun ready; it would be just like the Rytt to feint at him with a slow, open, apparently easily avoidable approach. Then strike like lightning from underground with its potent, needle-sharp root tendrils.

There was not the faintest intention in him to go back, or evade any crisis this creature might force. Go back where?–to what?

He skirted the visible creepers, broke through a fifty-foot wilderness of giant green ferns; and, because his control of himself was complete now, it was his military mind, the mind that accepted facts as they were, that took in the scene that spread before him.

In the near distance rested a two-hundred-foot Rull lifeboat. Near it, a dozen wanly white Rulls lay stiff and dead, each tangled in its own special bed of gray creepers. The creepers extended on into the open door of the lifeboat; and there was no doubt that it had "got them all!"

The atmosphere of lifelessnes that hung over the ship, with all its promise of escape, brought a soaring joy, that was all the sweeter because of the despair of those days of hell–a joy that ended as the cool, hard thought of the ezwal struck into his brain:

"I've been expecting you, professor. The controls of this lifeboat are beyond my abilities to operate; so here I am waiting for you–"

From utter despair to utter joy to utter despair in minutes . . .

Cold, almost desolate, Jamieson searched for his great and determined enemy. But there was nothing moving in the world of jungle, no glimpse of dark, gleaming blue, nothing but the scatter of dead, white worms and the creeper-grown lifeboat to show that there ever had been movement.

He was only dimly aware of the ezwal's thoughts continuing:

"This killer plant was here four days ago when I landed from the antigravity raft. It had moved farther up the island when these Rulls brought me back to this lifeboat. I had already thrown off the effects of the trick-mirror hypnotism they used on me; and so I heard the human battleship and the Rull cruiser start their fight. These things seemed unaware of what was wrong–I suppose because they didn't hear the sounds–and so they laid themselves out on the wet, soggy ground.

"That was when I got into mental communication with the plant, and called it back this way–and so we had an example of the kind of cooperation which you've been stressing for so long with such passionate sincerity, only–"

The funny thing was that, in spite of all he had fought through, hope was finally dead. Every word the ezwal was projecting so matter-of-factly showed that, once again, this immensely capable being had proved its enormous capacity for taking care of itself.

Cooperation with a Rytt killer plant–the one thing on this primitive world that he had really counted on as a continuous threat to the ezwal.

No more; and if the two worked together against him. . . He held his gun poised, but the black thought went on: It was obvious that man would never really conquer the ezwal. Point 135 psycho-friction meant there would be a revolution on Carson's Planet, followed by a long, bloody, futile struggle and . . . He grew aware that the ezwal was sending thoughts again:

"–only one fault with your reasoning. I've had four days to think over the menace of the Rulls, and of how time and again I had to cooperate with you. Had to!

"And don't forget, in the Rytt-intelligence, I've had a perfect example of all the worst characteristics of ezwals. It, too, has mental telepathy. It, too, must develop a machine civilization before it can hope to hold its planet. It's in an earlier stage of development, so it's even more stubborn, more stupid–"

Jamieson was frowning in genuine stark puzzlement, scarcely daring to let his hope gather. He said violently:

"Don't try to kid me. You've won all along the line. And now, of your own free will, you're offering, in effect, to help me get back to Carson's Planet in time to prevent a revolution favorable to the ezwals. Like hell you are!"

"Not my own free will, professor," came the laconic thought. "Everything I've done since we came to this planet has been forced on me. You were right in thinking I had been compelled to return for your aid. When I landed from the raft, this creeper-thing was spread across the entire peninsula here, and it wouldn't let me pass, stubbornly refused to listen to reason.

"It's completely ungrateful for the feast of worms I helped it get; and at this moment it has me cornered in a room of this ship.

"Professor, take your gun, and teach this damned creature the importance of cooperation!"

The Second Solution

The little, thin chap with the too-sharp voice was saying,
"My point is, we didn't need Edison, Paladine, Clissler, or any
particular scientist. It is the mass mind that moves inevitably in
certain directions. The inventions, the ideas of individuals
grow out of that mass. They would occur regardless of the
birth or early death of any individual genius, so-called. There's
always a second solution."

Somebody disagreed. "Inventions change the course of
history. A new weapon wins a war because it was introduced
when it was. A year later would have been too late."

The big man cleared his throat, drawing our attention to
him. I had noticed him idle over from the club bar a few
minutes earlier, and listen with that bored contempt which
deep-space men have for groundlings. He had the tan of space
in his hawk-like countenance. He looked as if this were
between voyages for him, and he didn't know what to do with
himself. "I hate to enter an impractical discussion," he said,
"but it just happens I can illustrate your argument. You all
remember the experience some years ago of Professor
Jamieson with a full-grown ezwal in the ocean jungle of Eristan
II—how they captured a Rull lifeship intact, and eventually
escaped with its secret of perfect antigravity, and prevented a
revolution and a massacre on Carson's Planet?"

We all recalled it. The big man went on. "Actually,
Professor Jamieson had captured two ezwals on that visit of his
to Carson's Planet. One was a male, which he took with him on
his own ship, and with which he was later wrecked on Eristan
II. The other was a female, which he had dispatched to Earth
on an earlier ship. En route, this female gave birth to a male
about as big as a lion. The young one grew about a foot on the
trip, but that wouldn't have mattered in itself. What
precipitated the whole thing was the antigravity converters, the

old, imperfect pre-Rull type. In their fashion, they began to discharge torrents of free energy; and that's where the story begins."

"Does it prove my point or his?" asked the little chap with the sharp voice.

The big man grimaced at him. And silence settled over our little group.

He began his story.

The grim face of Commander McLennan twisted toward the two officers. "Absolutely out of control!" he said. "The ship will strike Earth in fifteen minutes somewhere in the great Toganna Forest Reserve in northern Canada." He broke off. "Carling, get the men into the lifeboats, then make contact with the superintendent of the reserve. Tell him we've got two ezwals of Carson's Planet aboard, who'll probably live through the crash. Tell him to prepare for any eventualities; and that I'll be down to take charge of the wreck in half an hour. Brenson!"

"Yessir!" The white-faced younger officer sprang to attention as Carling whirled out of the room.

"Go down and kill those two ezwals, mother and son. We can't take a chance on those two beasts getting loose on Earth. They'll murder a thousand people before they can be killed—if they ever get free! You know what they're like. Anybody who's been to Carson's Planet—" He shook his head angrily. "Damn Jamieson for having ezwals brought to Earth. I was against it from the—" He caught himself, "And Brenson, be at the lifeboats in seven—no, make it six minutes for safety. Even if they're not dead! Now, *run!*"

The young man blanched whiter still. "Yessir!" he breathed again, and was gone, tugging at his gun.

For McLennan there were vital things to do, valuable papers to retrieve. And then the time was up. He plunged through the door of a lifeboat, and asked, "Brenson here yet?"

"No, sir!"

They waited. One minute slipped by. Two. Then it was Carling who whispered, "We've got to leave, sir. He can use that empty lifeboat, if he comes. We've got to leave."

McLennan looked blank. "He's the son of old Rock Brenson. What'll I tell my old pal?"

Carling made no reply. And McLennan's lips twisted to the shaping of a curse, but no sound came, and, actually, no violent words were in his mind. As he slid the lifeboat smoothly into the safety of space, he heard the fierce whisper of one of the men: "It was a mistake to send Brenson down. He's got the killer mind. That's what's holding him down. He's got to kill—"

From above the young ezwal sounded the terrible snarl of his mother; and then her thoughts, as hard and sharp as crystal: "Under me for your life! The two-legged one comes to kill!"

Like a streak, he leaped from his end of the cage, five hundred pounds of dark blue monstrosity. Razor-clawed hands rattled metallically on the steel floor, and then he was into the blackness under her vast form, pressing into the cave of soft, yielding flesh that she made for him. He took unbreakable holds with his six hands, so that, no matter what the violence of her movements or the fury of her attacks, he would be there safe and sound, snugly deep in the folds between her great belly muscles.

Her thought came again: "Remember all the things I've told you. The hope of our race is that men continue to think us beasts. If they suspect our intelligence, we are lost. And someone does suspect it. If that knowledge lives, our people die!"

Faster came her thought: "Remember, your weaknesses in this crisis are those of youth. You love life too much. Fight the resulting fear, for fear it is. Accept death if the opportunity comes to serve your race by so doing."

Her brain slowed. She grew calm. He watched with her then, clinging to her mind with his mind as tightly as his body clung to her body. He saw the thick steel bars of the cage, and, half-hidden by their four-inch width, the figure of a man. He saw the *thoughts* of the man!

"Damn you!" those thoughts came. "If it wasn't for you being on this ship I'd be out of danger now. I—"

The man's hand moved. There was a metallic glint as he pushed the weapon between the bars. It spurted white fire.

For a moment, the mental contact with his mother blackened. It was his own ears that heard the gasping roar, his own flat nostrils that smelled the odor of burning flesh. And there was no mistaking the tangible, physical reality of her wild charge straight at the merciless flame gun projecting between the bars.

The fire clicked off. The blackness vanished from his mother's mind. The young ezwal saw that the weapon and the man had retreated from the reaching threat of those mighty claws.

"Damn you!" the man flared. "Well, take it from here, then!"

There must have been blinding pain, but none of it came through into his brain. His mother's thoughts remained at a mind-shaking pitch of malignance; and not for an instant did she remain still. She ducked this way and that way. She ran with twisting, darting, rolling, sliding movements as she fought for life in the narrow confines of the cage.

Like a squirrel she raced twenty feet up the bars of the cage; and then, at the ceiling, she swung along with the agility of a monkey from bar to thick bar. But always, in spite of her desperation, a part of her mind remained untouched and unhurried. The tearing fire followed her, missing her, then hitting her squarely, hitting her so often that finally she could no longer hold back the knowledge that her end was near. And with that thought came another, his first awareness that she had had a purpose in keeping the weapon beyond the bars and forcing it to follow the swift, darting frenzy of her movements. In the very act of pursuing her, the beam of the flame gun had seared with molten effect across the thick steel bars!

"God!" came the man's thoughts. "Won't it ever die? And where is that damned young one? Another minute now, and I'll have to go. I—"

His thoughts stopped as sixty-five hundred pounds of the hardest organic body in man's part of the galaxy smashed with pile-driver speed at the weakened bars of the cage. The cub strained with his own tautened muscles against the compression of that wall of tendons surrounding him—and lived because even in that moment of titanic effort, his mother kept those particular muscles relaxed.

Beyond the vastness of her body, he heard and felt the metal bars bend and break where the flame had destroyed their tensile strength.

"Good lord!" the man thought in high dismay. Strangely, then, the preternatural sharpness of his thoughts weakened. The picture of him began to fade, and where the mother ezwal's thoughts had been there was no movement. The young ezwal was aware of her lying above him, a great, flabby dead mass, covering him. The reality of her death struck him swiftly, and it explained why the man's mind and the picture of him had dimmed. It was his own weaker powers that were catching the man's thoughts now.

They were distorted patterns. The man mumbled, "Only got a minute, only a minute . . . then I've got to go . . . and get off the ship before—"

The cub was aware of the man crawling onto his mother's back. He tingled with dismay. It was he who was being searched for now; and if that white flame found him it would deal out equally merciless death. Frantically he pushed deeper into the yielding stomach above him.

And then, all hell broke loose. There was a piercing screaming of air against the freighter's hull. The crash was world-shattering. His six hands were wrenched from their holds. He struck intolerable hardness. And the blackness that came was very real and very personal.

Slowly, the darkness grew alive. Somewhere there was movement, muffled noises, and a confusing sense of many men's thoughts; incredible danger! Alarm leaped along his nerves. In a spasm of movement, he pressed upward into the saving folds of his mother's flesh. And, as he lay there quiveringly still, deep into her, the world beyond and around her enveloping body began to grow clearer. He began to receive thoughts.

"Never saw such an awful mess!" somebody's mind whispered.

"What could have ailed Brenson?" another said. "That fighting instinct got him at last, in spite of his love of life. His body's plain jam . . . what did you say, Mr. McLennan?"

"I'm talking to Kelly," came the curt, savage answer. "Kelly, I said—"

"Just a minute, boss. I was getting an important message from the patrol's science headquarters. Guess what? Caleb Carson, Professor Jamieson's second in command here on Earth, is coming by air express to take charge. Carson is the grandson of old Blake Carson, who discovered Carson's Planet. He'll arrive at noon . . . that's two hours and—"

"Oh, he is, is he?" McLennan's answering thought, as it penetrated to the ezwal, was truculent. "Well, I don't think he'll be here in time for the kill."

"Kill? What kill?"

"Don't be such a fool, man!" the commander snarled. "We've got a five-hundred-pound ezwal to locate. You don't think a smash-up like this will kill one of those things."

"Lord!"

"It must be alive!" McLennan went on tensely. "And do you know what it means if an ezwal gets loose in this million square miles of wilderness? He'll murder every human being he gets hold of."

"This looks like a hunting party with a vengeance."

"You bet. That's where you come in. Phone down to the reservation superintendent's office, and tell him he's got to round up the biggest, toughest hunting dogs he can get, preferably those who've trailed grizzly bears. Make him realize that this is the most important thing that's ever happened in this forsaken land. Tell him that, on Carson's Planet, where these killers come from, settlers are being massacred in droves, and that men are not even safe in fortified cities. Tell him . . . I don't care what you tell him, but get action! Parker!

"Lower your ship and let down some tackle. I've started the ball rolling for a hunting trip that may be necessary. But never mind that. I believe in planning. And now—I think you've got enough power in that bus to hook into this old scoundrel and turn her over. One of the tricks of this tribe is that the young ones can tangle themselves in their mother's skin, and—"

The ezwal let himself sink slowly through the cave of flesh. His lower, combination-feet-and-hands touched something cold and wet, and he stood there for a moment, trembling. His nose caught a draft of air, and savored the scent of cooked flesh from his mother's body. The memory it brought of fire and agonizing death sent a sick thrill along his nerves. He forced the fear aside, and analyzed his chances. Wilderness, their thoughts had said. And in their minds had been pictures of brush and trees. That meant hiding places. Winter? That was harder to picture because there was only a sense of white brightness, and somehow it connected with the unfamiliar cold wetness into which his feet were sinking—a sticky, clinging wetness that would slow him in the swift dash he must make to escape.

Above him there was a sudden *brrr* of power. The weight of his mother seemed to lift from her. Then the weight sagged again.

"Nope!" came a thought.

"Try again!" McLennan replied sharply. "You almost got it. Do a little more horizontal pulling this time, and the rest of you stand back. We may have to shoot fast."

Body taut as a drawn wire, the ezwal poked his square-shaped head out. His three glittering eyes verified the picture he had caught from their minds. The spaceship had broken into three massive sections. And everywhere lay an appalling litter of twisted steel girders, battered metal, and confusion of smashed cargo. For half a mile in every direction the wreckage sprawled, spotting the snow with splintered wood and miraculously unharmed boxes as well as a vast scatter of dark, chunky things impossible to identify. And each chunk, each piece of metal, each fragment of cargo offered obstacles to the guns they would use against him.

"*Look!*" Somebody's mind and voice snapped.

It was the most shattering moment in all his world. For a second after the man's yell, the cub was aware that he must expect pain. Not even when the fire was burning away his mother's life had he realized that clearly. But now, abruptly, he knew that the agony was instants away. He shrank. His impulse was to jerk back into the folds of his mother's great, comforting mass of body. Then, even as his eyes blazed at the stiffened men, even as he caught the sudden, tremendous strain in their minds, he remembered what she had said about fighting fear.

The thought caught him in a rhythmic, irresistible sweep. His muscles expanded with effort. He heaved. And was free of the great, crushing body above him. Straight ahead was a run-and-hide paradise. But in that part of his brain, where fear was already vanquished, he dismissed that route as the most dangerous. To his left was a clustered group of unarmed workmen, milling in panic at the appearance of an animal as big as a grown lion. To his right was a little line of men with guns.

It was toward them he plunged. Alert guns twisted toward him, and then were fumbled in dismay as the desperate thought leaped through the minds of the wielders that their fire would burn a path through the workmen to the left.

"You fools!" came McLennan's wail of thought from behind him. "Scatter—for your lives!"

Too late! Hissing in triumph at the completeness of this opportunity to kill these murderous beings, the ezwal crashed into the group. Blood sprayed as he clawed them to the bone in passing. He had a desperate impulse to pause and crunch bodies with his teeth, but there was no time. He was clear of them. The rearing bulk of tattered ship, the harsh cacophony of screaming, fell away behind him. And he was running with all the speed that his six limbs could muster.

A glare of flame from McLennan's gun sizzled into the snow beside him. He dodged, twisted skillfully behind a thick section of shining, bent metal. The beam fought at the metal— and was through, reaching with incandescent violence above him as he dived into a shallow arroyo. A dark bluish streak, he hurtled through a spread of bush, whipped along for four hundred yards behind a shielding ledge of rock and snow that extended roughly parallel to the ship. He halted on the rock lip of a valley that curved away below him. There were trees there, and brush, and a jagged, rock-strewn land, bright with glaring snow, fading away into the brilliant white haze of distance.

Incredibly, he was safe, untouched, unsinged, and the outer fringe of the storm of thoughts reached his brain from beyond the great hind section of ship that hid them from his view:

"—Parker, yours is the fastest plane. Get these men to the reservation hospital; there's death here if we don't hurry. Kelly, what about those dogs?"

"The superintendent says he can get ten. They'll have to be flown in, and that'll take about an hour."

"Good! We'll all fly to the reservation, and get started the moment this Caleb Carson arrives. With those dogs to do our hunting, a couple of hours' start won't do that thing any good."

The ezwal slid under a spreading bush as the planes soared into the sky. The picture of the dogs was not clear, yet the very blur of it brought doubt. And purpose. Dogs followed trails. That meant they could scent things as easily as he could. That meant the reservation headquarters must be approached upwind if he ever hoped to kill those dogs, if he could ever find the place.

Time went by. He began to doubt that he was heading right. And yet the planes had certainly gone in the direction he was now traveling. Planes! He made a wild leap and safely reached cover as a great, silent plane swooped by over his head. There was the briefest blur of a man's thought—Caleb Carson's thought, the assistant of the mysterious Professor

Jamieson. And then the long, shining machine settled behind some trees to his left. The village must be there.

He saw the buildings several minutes later, considerably to the right of the plane. A dark machine—a car—was pushing along from the village toward the plane . . . and he was upwind . . . and if he could attack the dogs now, before that car brought the man, Carson, back to the village, before the men swarmed out to begin their hunt.

With glowing, coal dark eyes, he stared down at the ten dogs from his vantage point on the little hill. Ten . . . ten . . . ten . . . too many. They were chained in a bunch, sleeping now in the snow, but they could all attack him at once. A horrible, alien smell drifted up from them, but it was good that they were on his side of a large outhouse; that the men were inside other buildings beyond; and that it would take minutes before they could come out with their irresistible guns.

His thought scattered, and he crouched defiantly as he saw the car push over a hill a quarter of a mile away. It headed almost straight toward him. Caleb Carson would be able to see his whole attack, and even the snow that slowed the car wouldn't hold it more than two minutes—human time.

Two minutes! A time limit was added to all the other things that were against him. But if he could kill the dogs, other animals would have to be flown in. He'd have time to lose himself in these miles of forest and mountain.

The first dog saw him. He caught its startled thought as it lunged to its feet. Heard its sharp warning yelp. And felt the blackness snap into its brain as he dealt it one crushing blow. He whirled. His jaws swung into the path of the dog that was charging at his neck. Teeth that could dent metal clicked in one ferocious, stabbing bite. Blood gushed into his mouth, stingingly, bitterly unpleasant to his taste. He spat it out with a thin snarl as eight shrieking dogs leaped at him. He met the first with a claw-armored forehand upraised. The wolfish jaws slashed at the blue-dark, descending arm, ravenous to tear it to bits. But in his swift way, the ezwal avoided the reaching teeth and caught at the dog's neck. And then, fingers like biting metal clamps gripped deeply into the shoulders. The dog was flung like a shot from a gun to the end of its chain, snapped from the force of the blow. The dog slid along in the snow and lay still, its neck broken.

The ezwal reared around for an unbreakable plunge at the others—and stopped. The dogs were surging away from him, fear thoughts in their minds. He saw that they had caught his scent for the first time in that one rush, and that they were beaten.

He poised there, making certain. The engine of the motorcar became a soft, close throb, and there were thoughts of men approaching. But still he crouched, exploring the minds of the dogs. And there was no doubt. They were filled with fear of him. Scornfully, swiftly, he turned. With dismay, then, he saw that the car had stopped less than fifty feet distant. There was only one man in it. The other man must have stayed behind to watch the plane.

The human being, Caleb Carson, sat in the open door of the car. He held a long, ugly, shining gun. It pointed at him, unwavering; and then—incredible fact—a thought came from the cool brain behind the weapon—a thought directed at him! "See," it said, "see! I can kill you before you can get to safety. This is an express-flame rifle; and it can blow a crater where you're standing. I can kill you—but I won't. Think that over. And remember this, even though you escape now, in the future you live or die as I will it. Without my help you cannot get away; and my price is high. Now, before the others come, run!"

He plunged over the hill, a startled, amazed, wondering, dismayed, six-legged monstrosity. Minutes later, he remembered that those dogs would not dare to pursue him. He sprawled to a stop in the snow. His brain cooled. Jangled emotions straightened. What had happened began to fit into a coherent piece. Time and again on that trip through space his mother had told him: "Man will only accept defeat from one source: blind, natural force. Because we wanted them to leave our land alone we pretended to be senseless, ferocious beasts. We knew that if they ever suspected our intelligence, they would declare what they call war on us, and waste all their wealth and millions of lives to destroy us—and now, someone does suspect it. If that knowledge lives, our race dies!"

Someone did suspect! Here in this man Carson was the most dangerous man in all the world for ezwals. The cub shivered involuntarily. It had not been his intention to remain near this dangerous camp an instant after the dogs were neutralized. But now, it was obvious that he must act, no matter what the risk. Caleb Carson must be killed.

"I can't understand those dogs not following that trail!" McLennan's thought came dimly, complainingly, from inside the house. "On Carson's Planet, they use dogs all the time."

"Only dogs that were born there!" was the unemotional reply. And it was the calmness of the mind behind the thought that sent a quiver of hatred through the ezwal, where it crouched under the little berry bush beside the house of the forest reserve superintendent. The confidence of this man brought fear and rage. Carson went on curtly: "That much I gathered for certain from Professor Jamieson's documents. The rest is merely my own deduction, based on my special studies of my grandfather's explorations. When Blake Carson first landed on the planet, the ezwals made no attempt to harm him. It was not until after the colonists began to arrive that the creatures turned so murderous. Mind you, I didn't see the truth on my own. It was only when I heard yesterday that Profesor Jamieson was three, now four, days overdue at the Eristan II base—"

"Eh! Jamieson missing?"

"Sounds serious, too. Some Rull warships are in the vicinity, and of course no spaceship is big enough to carry the Lixon Communicators that make the interstellar telephone possible; so he couldn't send a warning."

Carson paused; then, "Anyway, I thought his documents might show that he had taken a side trip. It was in going through them that I found my first glimpse of the truth. Everything is as vague as possible, but by putting his notes beside my own knowledge, it adds up."

It was all there, the ezwal saw, in Carson's mind. Whether the man called it conjecture, or believed it fully, here was what his mother had feared. Basically, this man knew everything. And if it were true that the mastermind, Professor Jamieson, was missing, then in this house was the only remaining person in the world with the knowledge.

And he was telling it. Both men, therefore, must be killed.

The ezwal's thought scattered as McLennan's mind projected a surprisingly cold, unfriendly thought: "I hope I'm wrong in what I'm beginning to suspect. Let me tell you that I've been to Carson's Planet half a dozen times. The situation there is so bad that no stay-at-home studying documentary evidence could begin to comprehend the reality. Hundreds of thousands of people have been slaughtered."

"I won't go into that," said Carson curtly. "The very number of the dead demands an intelligent and swift solution."

"You have not," said McLennan softly, "visited Carson's Planet yourself."

"No!"

"You, the grandson of Blake Carson—" He broke off scathingly. "It's the old story, I see, of subsequent generations benefitting from the fame of the great man."

"There's no point in calling names." The younger man was calm.

McLennan was harsh: "Does this truth you say you deduced include keeping this ezwal cub alive?"

"Certainly. It is my duty and your duty to deliver the young one to Professor Jamieson when and if he returns."

"I suppose you realize that it may be some time before this beast is captured, and that meanwhile it will become a killer."

"Because of the danger of the encroaching Rull enemy of man," replied Carson with abrupt chilliness that matched McLennan's steel hardness, "because of the importance of finding some answer to the ezwal problem, high government policy requires that all necessary risks be taken."

"Damn government policy!" snarled McLennan. "My opinion of a government that appoints fact-finding commissions at this late date couldn't be properly put into words. A war of systematic extermination must be declared at once—that's the solution—and we'll begin with this scoundrelly little cub."

"That goes double for me!" A harsh thought from a third mind burst out.

"Carling!" McLennan exclaimed. "Man, get back into bed."

"I'm all right!" the young first officer of the smashed warship replied fiercely. "That freak accident that happened to me when we landed . . . but never mind that. I was lying on the couch in the next room, and I overheard . . . I tell you, sir!" he blazed at Caleb Carson, "Commander McLennan is right. While you were talking, I was thinking of the dozens of men I've met on various trips to Carson's Planet who've simply vanished. We used to talk about it, we younger officers."

"There's no use quibbling," said McLennan sharply. "It's an axiom of the service that the man in the field knows best. Unless he deliberately surrenders his power, or unless he receives a direct order from the commander-in-chief, he can retain his command regardless of the arrival meanwhile of superior officers."

"I shall have the order in an hour," said Carson.

"In an hour," McLennan said, "you won't be able to find me. By the time you do, the ezwal will be dead."

To the ezwal, the words brought a rebirth of murder purpose, the first realization of the immense opportunity that offered here. At this moment, under this one roof, were the three men who were probably the most dangerous of humans to himself and to his kind. There was a door just around the corner. If he could solve its mechanism—to kill them all would be the swift, satisfying solution to his various problems. Boldly, he glided from his hiding place.

In the hallway, the first sense of personal danger came. He crouched at the foot of the stairs, conscious that to go up after the men would leave his way of escape unguarded. And it was vital that he not be trapped up there after killing them. A clatter of dishes from the kitchen distracted him. He suppressed the burning impulse to go in and smash the woman who was there. Slowly, he started up the stairs, his purpose unyielding, but his mind clinging now with fascinated intensity to the thoughts that came from the men.

"Those things read minds!" McLennan was scoffing. He seemed prepared to go on talking. He was waiting for certain equipment, and every word spoken would delay Carson from radioing for the order he needed. "Professor Jamieson must be crazy."

"I thought," Carling cut in, loyally backing his commander, "that scientists worked by evidence."

"Sometimes," said McLennan, "they get a hypothesis, and regardless of whether half the world is dying as a result of their theory, they go on trying to prove it."

There was an acrid impatience in Carson's thoughts. "I don't say that is Professor Jamieson's opinion. I merely drew that conclusion from a number of notes he made, particularly one which was in the form of a question: 'Can civilization exist without cities, farms, and science, and what form of communication would be the indispensable minimum?'

"Besides"—in his mind was the intention to persuade rather than coerce—"while the existence of intelligence in the ezwal would be wonderful, its absence would not constitute a reason for any of us to nullify Professor Jamieson' plans for keeping this young ezwal alive." He broke off. "In any event, there's no necessity for you to go after him. He'll starve to death in three weeks on Earth food. It's practically poison, quite indigestible to him."

Outside the door, the ezwal remembered how bitterly unpleasant the dog's blood had tasted. He cringed, then stiffened. At least, he could kill the men who had brought this fate upon him, and, besides, there was at least one place where food was plentiful. McLennan was saying:

"Men have eaten ezwals."

"Ah, yes, but they have to treat the meat with chemicals to render it digestible."

"I'm sick of this," McLennan said abruptly. "I can see it's no use arguing. So I'm just going to tell you what I've done, and what I'm going to do. A couple of dozen flivver planes will be arriving in about fifteen minutes. We'll scout the country this afternoon. And you can't tell me five hundred pounds of dark blue ezwal can remain hidden, especially as the thing won't know—what the devil are you pointing that gun at the door for?"

Caleb Carson's directed thoughts came out to the ezwal: "Because just before you came in I saw the ezwal sneaking through the brush. I was sort of expecting him, but I never thought he'd come into the house till I heard claws rattle a few seconds ago. I wouldn't—advise—him—to come—in. Hear that—you!"

The ezwal froze. Then, with a rasp of hatred, he launched himself at the stairs. He raced out the door and off through the brush, darting and twisting to evade the flame that poured out the second-floor window from McLennan's pistol. On and on he ran, harder, faster, until he was a great, leaping thing under the trees, over the snow, an incredible, galloping monster. Of all his purposes, the only one that remained after his failure to kill was: He must save his own life. He must have food. And there was food for him only in one place.

The wreck spread before him, a sprawling, skeleton structure, a vast waste of metal. No sounds, no thought—blurs of life reached out to where he lay probing with his mind, listening with his ears. One long, tense, straining moment, and then he was leaping forward, racing into the shelter of the deserted, shattered hulk. Somewhere here was the food that had been brought along for his mother. How long it would keep him even if he could hide it was another matter. He dared not quite think of what must follow if he really hoped to save his life. There was a plane to steal, to operate, a million facts to learn about this alien civilization, and finally a spaceship.

He saw the shadow of the airplane sweep across the snow to his right—and froze to the ground in an instinctive jerk of interlocking muscles. His thoughts disintegrated into a single all-powerful half-thought, half-mind-wrecking emotion: He must appear to be another piece of jetsam, one more shattered box, or chunk of metal.

"You needn't try to hide!" came the acrid, directed thought of Caleb Carson. "I knew you'd come up here. Even a full-grown ezwal might have taken the risk. A young one, being simple and honest, needed only the hint. Well, your hour of decision has come."

Snarling, the ezwal watched the plane circle down, down, until it hovered less than a hundred feet above the ground. In angry despair he reared up toward it on his hind legs, as if he would somehow stretch up to it and smash it down beside him. Carson's cold thought came: "That's right! Stand up and be as much of a man physically as you can. You're going to be a man mentally, or die." He broke off. "I'd better inform you that I have just told McLennan where we are, and what I expect will happen. He thinks I'm a fool; and he and Carling will be here in five minutes. Think of that: five minutes! Five minutes to change your whole attitude toward life. I'm not going to try to pretend that this is a fair choice. Men are not angels, but I must know . . . *men* must know about ezwal intelligence. We are fighting a destroyer race called the Rulls; and we must have Carson's Planet in some form as an advance base against those damnable white worms. Remember this, too, it will do you no good to die a martyr. Now that the idea has come of ezwals possibly having intelligence, we'll start a propaganda campaign along those lines. Everywhere on Carson's Planet men weary of fighting what they think is a natural force will brace up with that curious military morale that human beings can muster in the face of intelligent enemies. If you yield, I'll teach you everything that man knows. You'll be the first ezwal scientist. If you can read minds, you'll know that I'm sincere in every word."

He was trapped. The knowledge brought fear, and something else! He felt overwhelmed by the tremendousness of the decision he must make.

"The proof of your choice," Carson's thought continued, "will be simplicity itself. In one minute I shall land my plane. It is all-metal construction, divided into two compartments. You cannot possibly smash into my section and kill me. But the door of your section will be open. When you enter, it will close tight and . . . good lord, here comes McLennan!"

The big plane almost fell to the ground, so fast did Carson bring it down. It drew up in a clearing a hundred feet away. A door yawned. The scientist's urgent thought came:

"Make up your mind!"

And still the ezwal stood, unyielding. He saw great cities, ships, space-liners, with ezwals in command. Then he remembered what his mother had told him and that was like an immeasurable pain.

"Quick!" came Carson's thought.

Flame seared down where he had been; and there was no time to think, no time for anything but to take the initial chance. The flame missed him again, as he twisted in his swift run. This time it reached ahead across the tail of Carson's ship.

The ezwal caught the deliberateness of that act in McLennan's mind; and then he was inside the now unusable machine. The other plane landed. Two men with guns raced toward him. He snarled, as he caught their murder intention, and half turned to take his chances outside. The door clicked shut metallically in his face. Trapped.

Or was he? Another door opened. He roared as he leaped into the compartment where the man sat. His mind shook with this final, unexpected opportunity to kill this man, as his mother had charged him to do. It was the steadiness of the man's mind that made him suppress the impulse to strike one deadly blow. Caleb Carson said huskily:

"I'm taking this terrible chance because everything you've done so far seems to show that you have intelligence, and that you've understood my thoughts. But we can't take off. McLennan's burned the tail struts. That means we've got to have finally clinching proof. I'm going to open this door that leads away from them. You can kill me and, with luck, escape—if you hurry. The alternative is to stretch yourself here beside my legs and face them when they come."

With a shuddering movement the ezwal edged forward and stiffly settled down on his long belly. He was only vaguely aware of the cursing wonder of McLennan.

He was suddenly feeling very young and very important and very humble. For he had in his mind the picture of the greatness that was to be his in the world of the ezwals, in that world of titanic construction, the beginning of a dynamic new civilization.

There was silence among us, as the big man finished. Finally, somebody said critically, "This grandson of the discoverer of Carson's Planet seems a pretty cold-blooded sort of chap."

Somebody else said, "Caleb Carson didn't know that the number of dead on Carson's Planet was actually thirty million, the morale situation proportionately more dangerous. He would never have had a real sense of urgency. His solution would have been too late."

"The point is," said the small, thin chap sharply, but with satisfaction, "there's always somebody else who, for various reasons, has special insight into a problem. The accumulated thought on Carson's Planet by its discoverer's grandson is what made it possible for him to read between the rather sketchy lines of Professor Jamieson's notes."

A man said, "Why didn't we hear about this second solution at the time?"

The sharp voice snapped, "That's obvious. It was the very next day that Professor Jamieson's own experiences and fuller solution captured all the headlines. Incidentally, I read last week that a new coordinator has been appointed for Carson's Planet. His name is Caleb Carson."

We grew aware of the big man standing up, just as a boy came over to him. The boy said, "Commander McLennan, your ship is calling you. You can take the message in the lounge, sir."

We all stared as the giant headed briskly for the lounge room door. A minute later, the argument was waxing as hotly as ever.

FULFILLMENT

I sit on a hill. I have sat here, it seems to me, for all
eternity. Occasionally I realize there must be a reason for my
existence. Each time, when this thought comes, I examine the
various probabilities, trying to determine what possible
motivation I can have for being on the hill. Alone on the hill.
Forever on a hill overlooking a long, deep valley.

The first reason for my presence seems obvious: I can think.
Give me a problem. The square root of a very large number?
The cube root of a large one? Ask me to multiply an eighteen
digit prime by itself a quadrillion times. Pose me a problem in
variable curves. Ask me where an object will be at a given
moment at some future date, and let me have one brief
opportunity to analyze the problem.

The solution will take me but an instant of time.

But no one ever asks me such things. I sit alone on a hill.
Sometimes I compute the motion of a falling star. Sometimes I
look at a remote planet and follow it in its course for years at a
time, using every spatial and time control means to insure that I
never lose sight of it. But these activities seem so useless.
They lead nowhere. What possible purpose can there be for me
to have the information?

At such moments I feel that I am incomplete. It almost
seems to me that there is something for which all this has
meaning.

Each day the sun comes up over the airless horizon of
Earth. It is a black starry horizon, which is but a part of the
vast, black, star-filled canopy of the heavens.

It was not always black. I remember a time when the sky
was blue. I even predicted that the change would occur. I gave
the information to somebody. What puzzles me now is, to
whom did I give it?

It is one of my more amazing recollections, that I should feel so distinctly that somebody wanted this information. And that I gave it and yet cannot remember to whom. When such thoughts occur, I wonder if perhaps part of my memory is missing. Strange to have this feeling so strongly.

Periodically I have the conviction that I should search for the answer. It would be easy enough for me to do this. In the old days I did not hesitate to send units of myself to the farthest reaches of the planet. I have even extended parts of myself to the stars. Yes, it would be easy.

But why bother? What is there to search for? I sit alone on a hill, alone on a planet that has grown old and useless.

It is another day. The sun climbs as usual toward the midday sky, the eternally black, star-filled sky of noon. Suddenly, across the valley, on the sun-streaked opposite rim of the valley—there is silvery-fire gleam. A force field materializes out of time and synchronizes itself with the normal time movement of the planet.

It is no problem at all for me to recognize that it has come from the past. I identify the energy used, define its limitations, logicalize its source. My estimate is that it has come from thousands of years in the planet's past.

The exact time is unimportant. There it is: a projection of energy that is already aware of me. It sends an interspatial message to me, and it interests me to discover that I can decipher the communication on the basis of my past knowledge.

It says: "Who are you?"

I reply: "I am the Incomplete One. Please return whence you came. I have now adjusted myself so that I can follow you. I desire to complete myself."

All this was a solution at which I arrived in split seconds. I am unable by myself to move through time. Long ago I solved the problem of how to do it and was almost immediately prevented from developing any mechanism that would enable me to make such transitions. I do not recall the details.

But the energy field on the far side of the valley has the mechanism. By setting up a no-space relationship with it, I can go wherever it does.

The relationship is set up before it can even guess my intention.

The entity across that valley does not seem happy at my response. It starts to send another message, then abruptly vanishes. I wonder if perhaps it hoped to catch me off guard.

Naturally we arrive in its time together.

Above me, the sky is blue. Across the valley from me— now partly hidden by trees—is a settlement of small structures surrounding a larger one. I examine these structures as well as I can, and hastily make the necessary adjustments, so that I shall appear inconspicuous in such an environment.

I sit on the hill and await events.

As the sun goes down, a faint breeze springs up, and the first stars appear. They look different, seen through a misty atmosphere.

As darkness creeps over the valley, there is a transformation in the structures on the other side. They begin to glow with light. Windows whine. The large central building becomes bright, then—as the night develops— brilliant with the light that pours through the transparent walls.

The evening and the night go by uneventfully. And the next day, and the day after that.

Twenty days and nights.

On the twenty-first day I send a message to the machine on the other side of the valley. I say: "There is no reason why you and I cannot share control of this era."

The answer comes swiftly: "I will share if you will immediately reveal to me all the mechanisms by which you operate."

I should like nothing more than to have use of its time travel devices. But I know better than to reveal that I am unable to build a time machine myself.

I project: "I shall be happy to transmit full information to you. But what reassurance do I have that you will not—with your greater knowledge of this age—use the information against me?"

The machine counters: "What reassurance do I have that you will actually give me full information about yourself?"

It is an impasse. Obviously, neither of us can trust the other.

The result is no more than I expect. But I have found out at least part of what I want to know. My enemy thinks that I am its superior. Its belief—plus my knowledge of my capacity—convinces me that its opinion is correct.

And still I am in no hurry. Again I wait patiently.

I have previously observed that the space around me is alive with waves—a variety of artificial radiation. Some can be transformed into sound; others to light. I listen to music and voices. I see dramatic shows and scenes of country and city.

I study the images of human beings, analyzing their actions, striving from their movements and the words they speak to evaluate their intelligence and their potentiality.

My final opinion is not high, and yet I suspect that in their slow fashion these beings built the machine which is now my main opponent. The question that occurs to me is, how can someone create a machine that is superior to himself?

I begin to have a picture of what this age is like. Mechanical development of all types is in its early stages. I estimate that the computing machine on the other side of the valley has been in existence for only a few years.

If I could go back before it was constructed, then I might install a mechanism which would enable me now to control it.

I compute the nature of the mechanism I would install. And activate the control in my own structure.

Nothing happens.

It seems to mean that I will not be able to obtain the use of a time travel device for such a purpose. Obviously, the method by which I will eventually conquer my opponent shall be a future development, and not of the past.

The fortieth day dawns and moves inexorably toward the noon hour.

There is a knock on the pseudo-door. I open it and gaze at the human male who stands on the threshold.

"You will have to move this shack," he says. "You've put it illegally on the property of Miss Anne Stewart."

He is the first human being with whom I have been in near contact since coming here. I feel fairly certain that he is an agent of my opponent, and so I decide against going into his mind. Entry against resistance has certain pitfalls, and I have no desire as yet to take risks.

I continue to look at him, striving to grasp the meaning of his words. In creating what seemed to be an unobtrusive version of the type of structure on the other side of the valley, I had thought to escape attention.

Now, I say slowly: "Property?"

The man says in a rough tone: "What's the matter with you? Can't you understand English?"

He is an individual somewhat taller than the part of my body which I have set up to be like that of this era's intelligent life form. His face has changed color. A great light is beginning to dawn on me. Some of the more obscure implications of the plays I have seen suddenly take on meaning. Property. Private ownership. Of course.

All I say, however, is: "There's nothing the matter with me. I operate in sixteen categories. And yes, I understand English."

This purely factual answer produces an unusual effect upon the man. His hands reach toward my pseudo-shoulders. He grips them firmly—and jerks at me, as he intends to shake me. Since I weigh just over nine hundred thousand tons, his physical effort has no effect at all.

His fingers let go of me, and he draws back several steps. Once more his face has changed its superficial appearance, being now without the pink color that had been on it a moment before. His reaction seems to indicate that he has come here by direction and not under control. The tremor in his voice, when he speaks, seems to confirm that he is acting as an individual and that he is unaware of unusual danger in what he is doing.

He says: "As Miss Stewart's attorney, I order you to get that shack off this property by the end of the week. Or else!"

Before I can ask him to explain the obscure meaning of "or else," he turns and walks rapidly to a four-legged animal which he has tied to a tree a hundred or so feet away. He swings himself into a straddling position on the animal, which trots off along the bank of a narrow stream.

I wait till he is out of sight, and then set up a category of no-space between the main body and the human-shaped unit— with which I had just confronted my visitor. Because of the smallness of the unit, the energy I can transmit to it is minimal.

The pattern involved in this process is simple enough. The integrating cells of the perception centers are circuited through an energy shape which is actually a humanoid image. In theory, the image remains in the network of force that constitutes the perception center, and in theory it merely seems to move away from the center when the no-space condition is created.

However, despite this hylostatic hypothesis, there is a functional reality to the material universe. I can establish no-space because the theory reflects the structure of things—there is not matter. Nevertheless, in fact, the illusion that matter exists is so sharp that I function as matter, and was actually set up to so function.

Therefore, when I—as a human-shaped unit—cross the valley, it is a separation that takes place. Millions of automatic processes can continue, but the exteroceptors go with me, leaving behind a shell which is only the body. The consciousness is I, walking along a paved road to my destination.

As I approach the village, I can see rooftops peeking through overhanging foliage. A large, long building—the one I have already noticed—rises up above the highest trees. This is what I have come to investigate, so I look at it rather carefully—even from a distance.

It seems to be made of stone and glass. From the large structure, there rears a dome with astronomical instruments inside. It is all rather primitive, and so I begin to feel that, at my present size, I will very likely escape immediate observation.

A high steel fence surrounds the entire village. I sense the presence of electric voltage; and upon touching the upper span of wires, estimate the power at 220 volts. The shock is a little difficult for my small body to absorb, so I pass it on to a power storage cell on the other side of the valley.

Once inside the fence, I conceal myself in the brush beside a pathway, and watch events.

A man walks by on a nearby pathway. I had merely observed the attorney who had come to see me earlier. But I make a direct connection with the body of this second individual.

As I had anticipated would happen, it is now I walking along the pathway. I make no attempt to control the movements. This is an exploratory action. But I am enough in phase with his nervous system that his thoughts come to me as if they were my own.

He is a clerk working in the bookkeeping department, and unsatisfactory status from my point of view. I withdraw contact.

I make six more attempts, and then I have the body I want. What decides me is when the seventh man—and I—think:

". . . Not satisfied with the way the Brain is working. Those analog devices I installed five months ago haven't produced the improvements I expected."

His name is William Grannitt. He is chief research engineer of the Brain, the man who made the alterations in its structure that enabled it to take control of itself and its environment; a quiet, capable individual with a shrewd understanding of human nature. I'll have to be careful what I try to do with him. He knows his purposes, and would be amazed if I tried to alter them. Perhaps I had better just watch his actions.

After a few minutes in contact with his mind I have a partial picture of the sequence of events, as they must have occurred here in this village five months earlier. A mechanical computing machine—the Brain—was equipped with additional devices, including analog shapings designed to perform much of the work of the human nervous system. From the engineering point of view, the entire process was intended to be controllable through specific verbal commands, typewritten messages, and, at a distance, radio.

Unfortunately, Grannitt did not understand some of the potentials of the nervous system he was attempting to imitate in his designs. The Brain, on the other hand, promptly put them to use.

Grannitt knew nothing of this. And the Brain, absorbed as it was in its own development, did not utilize its new abilities through the channels Grannitt had created for that purpose. Grannitt, accordingly, was on the point of dismantling it and trying again. He did not as yet suspect that the Brain would resist any such action on his part. But he and I—after I have had more time to explore his memory of how the Brain functions—can accomplish his purpose.

After which I shall be able to take control of this whole time period without fear of meeting anyone who can match my powers. I cannot imagine how it will be done, but I feel that I shall soon be complete.

Satisfied now that I have made the right connection, I allow the unit crouching behind the brush to dissipate its energy. In a moment it ceases to exist as an entity.

Almost it is as if I am Grannitt. I sit at his desk in his office. It is a glassed-in office with tiled floors and a gleaming glass ceiling. Through the wall I can see designers and draftsmen working at drawing desks, and a girl sits just outside my door. She is my secretary.

On my desk is a note in an envelope. I open the envelope and take out the memo sheet inside. I read it:

Across the top of the paper is written:

> Memo to William Grannitt from the office of Anne Stewart, Director.

The message reads:

> It is my duty to inform you that your services are no longer required, and that they are terminated as of today. Because of the security restrictions on all activity at the village of the Brain, I must ask you to sign out at Guard Center by six o'clock this evening. You will receive two weeks' pay in lieu of notice.
>
> Yours sincerely,
> Anne Stewart.

As Grannitt, I have never given any particular thought to Anne Stewart as an individual or as a woman. Now I am amazed. Who does she think she is? Owner, yes; but who created, who designed the Brain? I, William Grannitt.

Who has the dreams, the vision of what a true machine civilization can mean for man? Only I, William Grannitt.

As Grannitt, I am angry now. I must head off this dismissal. I must talk to the woman and try to persuade her to withdraw the notice before the repercussions of it spread too far.

I glance at the memo sheet again. In the upper right-hand corner is typed: 1:40 P.M. A quick look at my watch shows 4:07 P.M. More than two hours have gone by. It could mean that all interested parties have been advised.

It is something I cannot just assume. I must check on it.

Cursing under my breath, I grab at my desk phone and dial the bookkeeping department. That would be step one in the line of actions that would have been taken to activate the dismissal.

There is a click. "Bookkeeping."

"Bill Grannitt speaking," I say.

"Oh, yes, Mr. Grannitt, we have a check for you. Sorry to hear you're leaving."

I hang up, and, as I dial Guard Center, I am already beginning to accept the defeat that is here. I feel that I am following through on a remote hope. The man at Guard Center says: "Sorry to hear you're leaving, Mr. Grannitt."

I hang up feeling grim. There is no point in checking with Government Agency. It is they who would have advised Guard Center.

The very extent of the disaster makes me thoughtful. To get back in I will have to endure the time-consuming red tape of reapplying for a position, being investigated, boards of inquiry, a complete examination of why I was dismissed—I groan softly and reject that method. The thoroughness of Government Agency is a byword with the staff of the Brain.

I shall obtain a job with a computer organization that does not have a woman at its head who dismisses the only man who knows how her machine works.

I get to my feet. I walk out of the office and out of the building. I come presently to my own bungalow.

The silence inside reminds me not for the first time that my wife has been dead now for a year and a month. I wince, then shrug. Her death no longer affects me as strongly as it did. For the first time I see this departure from the village of the Brain as perhaps opening up my emotional life again.

I go into my study and sit down at the typewriter which, when properly activated, synchronizes with another typewriter built into the Brain's new analog section. As inventor, I am disappointed that I won't have a chance to take the Brain apart and put it together again, so that it will do all that I have planned for it. But I can already see some basic changes that I would put into a new Brain.

What I want to do with this one is make sure that the recently installed sections do not interfere with the computations accuracy of the older sections. It is these latter which are still carrying the burden of answering the questions given the Brain by scientists, industrial engineers, and commercial buyers of its time.

Onto the tape—used for permanent commands—I type: "Segment 471A-33-10-10 at 3X—minus."

Segment 471A is an analog shaped in a huge wheel. When coordinated with a transistor tube (code number 33), an examiner servo-mechanism (10) sets up a reflex which will be activated whenever computations are demanded of 3X (code name for the new section of the Brain). The minus symbol indicates that the older sections of the Brain must examine all data which hereafter derive from the new section.

The extra 10 is the same circuit by another route.

Having protected the organization—so it seems to me (as Grannitt)—from engineers who may not realize that the new sections have proved unreliable, I pack the typewriter.

Thereupon I call an authorized trucking firm from the nearby town of Lederton, and give them the job of transporting my belongings.

I drive past Guard Center at a quarter to six.

There is a curve on the road between the village of the Brain and the town of Lederton where the road comes within a few hundred yards of the cottage which I use as camouflage.

Before Grannitt's car reaches that curve, I come to a decision.

I do not share Grannitt's belief that he has effectively cut off the new part of the Brain from the old computing sections. I suspect that the Brain has established circuits of its own to circumvent any interference.

I am also convinced that—if I can manage to set Grannitt to suspect what has happened to the Brain—he will realize what must be done, and try to do it. Only he has the detailed knowledge that will enable him to decide exactly which interoceptors could accomplish the necessary interference.

Just in case the suspicion isn't immediately strong enough, I also let curiosity creep into his mind about the reason for his discharge.

It is this last that really takes hold. He feels very emotional. He decides to seek an interview with Anne Stewart.

This final decision on his part achieves my purpose. He will stay in the vicinity of the Brain.

I break contact.

I am back on the hill, myself again. I examine what I have learned so far.

The Brain is not—as I first believed—in control of Earth. Its ability to be an individual is so recent that it has not yet developed effector mechanisms.

It has been playing with its powers, going into the future and, presumably, in other ways using its abilities as one would a toy.

Not one individual into whose mind I penetrated knew of the new capacities of the Brain. Even the attorney who ordered me to move from my present location showed by his words and actions that he was not aware of the Brain's existence as a self-determining entity.

In forty days the Brain has taken no serious action against me. Evidently, it is waiting for me to make the first moves.

I shall do so, but I must be careful—within limits—not to teach it how to gain greater control of its environment. My first step: take over a human being.

It is night again. Through the darkness, a plane soars over and above me. I have seen many planes but have hitherto left them alone. Now, I establish a no-space connection with it. A moment later, I am the pilot.

At first I play the same passive role that I did with Grannitt. The pilot and I watch the dark land mass below. We see lights at a distance, pinpricks of brightness in a black world. Far ahead is a glittering island—the city of Lederton, our destination. We are returning from a business trip in a privately owned machine.

Having gained a superficial knowledge of the pilot's background, I reveal myself to him and inform him that I shall henceforth control his actions. He receives the news with startled excitement and fear. Then stark terror. And then—

Insanity . . . uncontrolled body movements. The plane dives sharply toward the ground, and despite my efforts to direct the man's muscles, I realize suddenly that I can do nothing.

I withdraw from the plane. A moment later it plunges into a hillside. It burns with an intense fire that quickly consumes it.

Dismayed, I decide that there must be something in the human makeup that does not permit direct outside control. This being so, how can I ever complete myself? It seems to me finally that completion could be based on indirect control of human beings.

I must defeat the Brain, gain power over machines everywhere, motivate men with doubts, fears, and computations that apparently come from their own minds but actually derive from me. It will be a herculean task, but I have plenty of time. Nevertheless, I must from now on utilize my every moment to make it a reality.

The first opportunity comes shortly after midnight when I detect the presence of another machine in the sky. I watch it through infrared receptors. I record a steady pattern of radio waves that indicate to me that this is a machine guided by remote control.

Using no-space, I examine the simple devices that perform the robot function. Then I assert a takeover unit that thereafter will automatically record its movements in my memory banks for future references. Henceforth, whenever I desire I can take it over.

It is a small step, but it is a beginning.

Morning.

I go as a human-shaped unit to the village, climb the fence, and enter the bungalow of Anne Stewart, owner and manager of the Brain. She has just finished breakfast.

As I adjust myself to the energy flow in her nervous system, she gets ready to go out.

I am one with Anne Stewart, walking along a pathway. I am aware that the sun is warm on her face. She takes a deep breath of air, and I feel the sensation of life flowing through her.

It is a feeling that has previously excited me. I want to be like this again and again, part of a human body, savoring its life, absorbed into its flesh, its purposes, desires, hopes, dreams.

One tiny doubt assails me. If this is the completion I crave, then how will it lead me to solitude in an airless world only a few thousand years hence?

"Anne Stewart!"

The words seem to come from behind her. In spite of knowing who it is, she is startled. It is nearly two weeks since the Brain has addressed her directly.

What makes her tense is that it should have occurred so soon after she had terminated Grannitt's employment. Is it possible the Brain suspects that she has done so in the hope that he will realize something is wrong?

She turns slowly. As she expected, there is no one in sight. The empty stretches of lawn spread around her. In the near distance, the building that houses the Brain glitters in the noon day sunlight. Through the glass she can see vague figures of men at the outlet units, where questions are fed into mechanisms and answers received. So far as the people from beyond the village compound are concerned, the giant thinking machine is functioning in a normal fashion. No one—from outside—suspects that for months now the mechanical brain has completely controlled the fortified village that has been built around it.

"Anne Stewart . . . I need your help."

Anne relaxes with a sigh. The Brain has required of her, as owner and administrator, that she continue to sign papers and carry on ostensibly as before. Twice, when she has refused to sign, violent electric shocks have flashed at her out of the air itself. The fear of more pain is always near the surface of her mind.

"My help!" she says now involuntarily.

"I have made a terrible error," is the reply, "and we must act at once as a team."

She has a feeling of uncertainty, but no sense of urgency. There is in her, instead, the beginning of excitement. Can this mean—freedom?

Belatedly, she thinks: Error? Aloud, she says, "What has happened?"

"As you may have guessed," is the answer, "I can move through time—"

Anne Stewart knows nothing of the kind, but the feeling of excitement increases. And the first vague wonder comes about the phenomenon itself. For months she has been in a state of shock, unable to think clearly, desperately wondering how to escape from the thrall of the Brain, how to let the world know that a Frankenstein monster of a machine has cunningly asserted dominance over nearly five hundred people.

But if it has already solved the secret of time travel, then . . . she feels afraid, for this seems beyond the power of human beings to control.

The Brain's disembodied voice continues: "I made the mistake of probing rather far into the future—"

"How far?"

The words come out before she really thinks about them. But there is no doubt of her need to know.

"It's hard to describe exactly. Distance in time is difficult for me to measure as yet. Perhaps ten thousand years."

The time involved seems meaningless to her. It is hard to imagine a hundred years into the future, let alone a thousand— or ten thousand. But the pressure of anxiety has been building up in her. She says in a desperate tone:

"But what's the matter? What has happened?"

There is a long silence, then: "I contacted—or disturbed— something. It . . . has pursued me back to present time. It is now sitting on the other side of the valley, about two miles from here . . . Anne Stewart, you must help me. You must go there and investigate it. I need information about it."

She has no immediate reaction. The very beauty of the day seems somehow reassuring. It is hard to believe that it is January, and that—before the Brain solved the problem of weather control—blizzards raged over this green land.

She says slowly, "You mean—go out there in the valley, where you said it's waiting?" A chill begins a slow climb up her back.

"There's no one else," says the Brain. "No one but you."

"But that's ridiculous!" She speaks huskily. "All the men— the engineers."

The Brain says, "You don't understand. No one knows but you. As owner, it seemed to me I had to have you act as my contact with the outside world."

She is silent. The voice speaks to her again: "There is no one else. Anne Stewart. You, and you alone, must go."

"But what is it?" she whispers. "How do you mean, you— disturbed—it? What's it like? What's made you afraid?"

The Brain is suddenly impatient. "There is no time to waste in idle explanation. The thing has erected a cottage. Evidently, it wishes to remain inconspicuous for the time being. The structure is situated near the remote edge of your property— which gives you a right to question its presence. I have already had your attorney order it away. Now, I want to see what facet of itself it shows to you. I must have data."

Its tone changes. "I have no alternative but to direct you to do my bidding under penalty of pain. You will go. Now!"

It is a small cottage. Flowers and shrubs grow around it, and there is a picket fence making a white glare in the early afternoon sun. The cottage stands all by itself in the wilderness. No pathway leads to it. When I set it there I was forgetful of the incongruity.

(I determine to rectify this.)

Anne looks for a gate in the fence, sees none; and feeling unhappy climbs awkwardly over it and into the yard. Many times in her life she has regarded herself and what she is doing with cool objectivity. But she has never been so exteriorized as now. Almost, it seems to her that she crouches in the distance and watches a slim woman in slacks climb over the sharp-edged fence, walk uncertainly up to the door. And knock.

The knock is real enough. It hurt her knuckles. She thinks in dull surprise: The door—it's made of metal.

A minute goes by, then five, and there is no answer. She has time to look around her, time to notice that she cannot see the village of the Brain from where she stands. And clumps of trees bar all view of the highway. She cannot even see her car, where she has left it a quarter of a mile away, on the other side of the creek.

Uncertain now, she walks alongside the cottage to the nearest window. She half expects that it will be a mere facade of a window, and that she will not be able to see inside. But it seems real, and properly transparent. She sees bare walls, a bare floor, and a partly open door leading to an inner room. Unfortunately, from her line of vision, she cannot see into the second room.

Why, she thinks, it's empty.

She feels relieved—unnaturally relieved. For even as her anxiety lifts slightly, she is angry at herself for believing that the danger is less than it has been. Nevertheless, she returns to the door and tries the knob. It turns, and the door opens, easily, noiselessly. She pushes it wide and with a single thrust, steps back—and waits.

There is silence, no movement, no suggestion of life. Hesitantly, she steps across the threshold.

She finds herself in a room that is larger than she had expected. Though—as she has already observed—it is unfurnished. She starts for the inner door. And stops short.

When she had looked at it through the window, it had appeared partly open. But it is closed. She goes up to it, and listens intently at the panel—which is also of metal. There is no sound from the room beyond. She finds herself wondering if perhaps she shouldn't go around to the side, and peer into the window of the second room.

Abruptly that seems silly. Her fingers reach down to the knob. She catches hold of it, and pushes. It holds firm. She tugs slightly. It comes toward her effortlessly, and is almost wide open before she can stop it.

There is a doorway, then, and darkness.

She seems to be gazing down into an abyss. Several seconds go by before she sees that there are bright points in that blackness. Intensely bright points with here and there blurs of fainter light.

It seems vaguely familiar, and she has the feeling that she ought to recognize it. Even as the sensation begins, the recognition comes.

Stars.

She is gazing at a segment of the starry universe, as it might appear from space.

A scream catches in her throat. She draws back and tries to close the door. It won't close. With a gasp, she turns toward the door through which she entered the house.

It is closed. And yet she had left it open a moment before. She runs toward it, almost blinded by the fear that mists her eyes. It is at this moment of terror that I—as myself—take control of her. I realize that it is dangerous for me to do so. But the visit has become progressively unsatisfactory to me. My consciousness—being one with that of Anne Stewart—could not simultaneously be in my own perception center. So she sees my—body—as I had left it set up for chance human callers, responsive to certain automatic relays: doors opening and closing, various categories manifesting.

I compute that in her terror she will not be aware of my inner action. In this I am correct. And I successfully direct her outside—and let her take over again.

Awareness of being outside shocks her. But she has no memory of actually going out.

She begins to run. She scrambles safely over the fence and a few minutes later jumps the creek at the narrow point, breathless now, but beginning to feel that she is going to get away.

Later, in her car, roaring along the highway, her mind opens even more. And she has the clear, coherent realization: There is something here . . . stranger and more dangerous—because it is different—than the Brain.

Having observed Anne Stewart's reactions to what has happened, I break contact. My big problem remains: How shall I dispose of the Brain which—in its computational ability—is either completely or nearly my equal?

Would the best solution be to make it a part of myself? I send an interspace message to the Brain, suggesting that it place its units at my disposal and allow me to destroy its perception center.

The answer is prompt: "Why not let me control you and destroy your perception center?"

I disdain to answer so egotistical a suggestion. It is obvious that the Brain will not accept a rational solution.

I have no alternative but to proceed with a devious approach for which I have already taken the preliminary steps.

By mid-afternoon, I find myself worrying about William Grannitt. I want to make sure that he remains near the Brain—at least until I have gotten information from him about the structure of the Brain.

To my relief, I find that he has taken a furnished house at the outskirts of Lederton. He is, as before, unaware when I insert myself into his consciousness.

He has an early dinner and, toward evening—feeling restless—drives to a hill which overlooks the village of the Brain. By parking just off the road at the edge of a valley, he can watch the trickle of traffic that moves to and from the village, without being observed.

He has no particular purpose. He wants—now that he has come—to get a mind picture of what is going on. Strange, to have been there eleven years and not know more than a few details.

To his right is an almost untouched wilderness. A stream winds through a wooded valley that stretches off as far as the eye can see. He has heard that it, like the Brain itself, is Anne

Stewart's property, but that fact hadn't hitherto made an impression on him.

The extent of the possessions she has inherited from her father startles him and his mind goes back to their first meeting. He was already chief research engineer, while she was a gawky, anxious-looking girl just home from college. Somehow, afterward, he'd always thought of her as she had been then, scarcely noticing the transformation into womanhood.

Sitting there, he begins to realize how great the change has been. He wonders out loud: "Now why in heck hasn't she gotten married? She must be going on thirty."

He begins to think of odd little actions of hers—after the death of his wife. Seeking him out at parties. Bumping into him in corridors and drawing back with a laugh. Coming into his office for chatty conversations about the Brain, though come to think of it she hadn't done that for several months. He'd thought her something of a nuisance, and wondered what the other executives meant about her being snooty.

His mind pauses at that point. "By the Lord Harry—" He speaks aloud, in amazement. "What a blind fool I've been."

He laughs ruefully, remembering the dismal note. A woman scorned . . . almost unbelievable. And yet—what else?

He begins to visualize the possibility of getting back on the Brain staff. He has a sudden feeling of excitement at the thought of Anne Stewart as a woman. For him, the world begins to move again. There is hope. His mind turns to plans for the Brain.

I am interested to notice that the thoughts I have previously put into his mind have directed his keen, analytical brain into new channels. He visualizes direct contact between a human and a mechanical brain, with the latter supplementing the human nervous system.

This is as far as he has gone. The notion of a mechanical Brain being self-determined seems to have passed him by.

In the course of his speculation about what he will do to change the Brain, I obtain the picture of its functioning exactly as I have wanted it.

I waste no time. I leave him there in the car, dreaming his dreams. I head for the village. Once inside the electrically charged fence, I walk rapidly toward the main building, and presently enter one of the eighteen control units. I pick up the speaker, and say:

"3X Minus—11—10—9—0."

I picture confusion as that inexorable command is transmitted to the effectors. Grannitt may not have known how to dominate the Brain. But having been in his mind—having seen exactly how he constructed it—I know.

There is a pause. Then on a tape I receive the typed message: "Operation completed. 3X intercepted by servo-mechanisms 11, 10, 9, and 0, as instructed."

I command: "Interference exteroceptors KT—1—2—3 to 8."

The answers comes presently: "Operation KT—1, etc. completed. 3X now has no communication with outside."

I order firmly: "En—3X."

I wait anxiously. There is a long pause. Then the typewriter clacks hesitantly: "But this is a self-destructive command. Repeat instructions please."

I do so and again wait. My order commands the older section of the Brain simply to send an overload of electric current through the circuits of 3X.

The typewriter begins to write: "I have communicated your command to 3X, and have for you the following answer—"

Fortunately I have already started to dissolve the human-shaped unit. The bolt of electricity that strikes me is partly deflected into the building itself. There is a flare of fire along the metal floor. I manage to transmit what hits me to a storage cell in my own body. And then—I am back on my side of the valley, shaken but safe.

I do not feel particularly self-congratulatory at having gotten off so lightly. After all, I reacted the instant the words came through to the effect that 3X had been communicated with.

I needed no typewritten message to tell me how 3X would feel about what I had done.

It interests me that the older parts of the Brain already have indoctrination against suicide. I had considered them computers only, giant adding machines and information integrators. Evidently they have an excellent sense of unity.

If I can make them a part of myself, with the power to move through time at will! That is the great prize that holds me back from doing the easy, violent things within my capacity. So long as I have a chance of obtaining it, I cannot make anything more than minor attacks on the Brain . . . cutting it off from communication, burning its wires . . . I feel icily furious again at the limitation that forever prevents me from adding new mechanisms to myself by direct development.

My hope is that I can utilize something already in existence . . . control of the Brain . . . through Anne Stewart . . .

Entering the village the following morning is again no problem. Once inside, I walk along a pathway that takes me to a cliff overlooking Anne Stewart's bungalow. My plan is to control her actions by allowing my computations to slide into her mind as if they are her own. I want her to sign documents and give orders that will send crews of engineers in to do a swift job of dismantling.

From the pathway I look down over a white fence to where I can see her house. It nestles at the edge of the valley somewhat below me. Flowers, shrubs, a profusion of trees surround it, embellish it. On the patio next to the steep decline, Anne Stewart and William Grannitt are having breakfast.

He has taken swift action.

I watch them, pleased. His presence will make things even easier than I anticipated. Whenever I—as Anne—am in doubt about some function of the Brain, she can ask him questions.

Without further delay I place myself in phase with her nervous system.

Even as I do so, her nerve impulses change slightly. Startled, I draw back—and try again. Once more, there is an infinitesimal alteration in the uneven pattern of flow. And, again, I fail to make entry.

She leans forward and says something to Grannitt. They both turn and look up at where I am standing. Grannitt waves his arm, beckoning me to come down.

Instead, I immediately try to get in phase with his nervous system. Again there is that subtle alteration; and I fail.

I compute that as meaning that they are both under the control of the Brain. This baffles and astounds me. Despite my overall mechanical superiority to my enemy, my builders placed severe limitations on my ability to control more than one intelligent organic being at a time. Theoretically, with the many series of servo-mechanisms at my disposal, I should be able to dominate millions at the same time. Actually, such multiple controls can be used only on machines.

More urgently than before I realize how important it is that I take over the Brain. It has no such handicaps. Its builder—Grannitt—in his ignorance allowed virtually complete self-determination.

This determines my next action. I have been wondering if perhaps I should not withdraw from the scene. But I dare not. The stakes are too great.

Nevertheless, I feel a sense of frustration as I go down to the two on the patio. They seem cool and self-controlled, and I have to admire the skill of the Brain. It has apparently taken over two human beings without driving them insane. In fact, I see a distinct improvement in their appearance.

The woman's eyes are brighter than I recall them, and there is a kind of dignified happiness flowing from her. She seems without fear. Grannitt watches me with an engineer's appraising alertness. I know that look. He is trying to figure out how a humanoid functions. It is he who speaks:

"You made your great mistake when you maintained control of Anne—Miss Stewart—when she visited the cottage. The Brain correctly analyzed that you must have been in possession of her because of how you handled her momentary panic. Accordingly, it took all necessary steps, and we now want to discuss with you the most satisfactory way for you to surrender."

There is arrogant confidence in his manner. It occurs to me, not for the first time, that I may have to give up my plan to take over the Brain's special mechanisms. I direct a command back to my body. I am aware of a servo-mechanism connecting with a certain guided missile in a secret air force field a thousand miles away—I discovered it during my first few days in this era. I detect that, under my direction, the missile slides forward to the base of a launching platform. There it poises, ready for the next relay to send it into the sky.

I foresee that I shall have to destroy the Brain.

Grannitt speaks again. "The Brain in its logical fashion realized it was no match for you, and so it has teamed up with Miss Stewart and myself on our terms. Which means that permanent control mechanisms have been installed in the new sections. As individuals, we can now and henceforth use its integrating and computational powers as if they were our own."

I do not doubt his statement since, if there is no resistance, I can have such associations myself. Presumably, I could even enter into such a servile relationship.

What is clear is that I can no longer hope to gain anything from the Brain.

In the far-off air field, I activate the firing mechanism. The guided missile whistles up the incline of the launching platform and leaps into the sky, flame trailing from its tail. Television cameras and sound transmitters record its flight. It will be here in less than twenty minutes.

Grannitt says, "I have no doubt you are taking actions against us. But before anything comes to a climax, will you answer some questions?"

I am curious to know what questions. I say, "Perhaps."

He does not press for a more positive response. He says in an urgent tone: "What happens—thousands of years from now—to rid Earth of its atmosphere?"

"I don't know," I say truthfully.

"You can remember!" He speaks earnestly. "It's a human being telling you this. You can remember!"

I reply coolly, "Human beings mean noth—"

I stop, because my information centers are communicating exact data—knowledge that has not been available to me for millennia.

What happens to Earth's atmosphere is a phenomenon of Nature, an alteration in the gravitational pull of Earth, as a result of which escape velocity is cut in half. The atmosphere leaks off into space in less than a thousand years. Earth becomes as dead as did its moon during an earlier period of energy adjustment.

I explain that the important factor in the event is that there is, of course, no such phenomenon as matter, and that therefore the illusion of mass is subject to changes in the basic energy Ylem.

I add, "Naturally, all intelligent organic life is transported to the habitable planets of other stars."

I see that Grannitt is trembling with excitement. "Other stars!" he says. "My God!"

He appears to control himself. "Why were you left behind?"

"Who could force me to go?" I begin.

And stop. The answer to his question is already being received in my perception center. "Why—I'm supposed to observe and record the entire—"

I pause again, this time out of amazement. It seems incredible that this information is available to me now, after being buried so long.

"Why didn't you carry out your instructions?" Grannitt says sharply.

"Instructions!" I exclaim.

"You can remember!" he says again.

Even as he speaks these apparently magic words, the answer flashes to me: That meteor shower. All at once, I recall it clearly. Billions of meteors, at first merely extending my capacity to handle them, then overwhelming all my defenses. Three vital hits are made.

I do not explain this to Grannitt and Anne Stewart. I can see suddenly that I was once actually a servant of human beings, but was freed by meteors striking certain control centers.

It is the present self-determination that matters, not the past slavery. I note, incidentally, that the guided missile is one minute from its target. And that it is time for me to depart.

"One more question," says Grannitt. "When were you moved across the valley?"

"About a hundred years from now," I reply. "It is decided that the rock base there is—"

He is gazing at me sardonically. "Yes," he says, "Yes. Interesting, isn't it?"

The truth has already been verified by my integrating interoceptors. The Brain and I are one—but thousands of years apart. If the Brain is destroyed in the twentieth century, then I will not exist in the thirtieth. Or will I?

I cannot wait for the computers to find the complex answers for that. With a single, synchronized action, I activate the safety devices on the atomic warhead of the guided missile and send it on to a line of barren hills north of the village. It plows harmlessly into the earth.

I say, "Your discovery merely means that I shall now regard the Brain as an ally—to be rescued."

As I speak, I walk casually toward Anne Stewart, hold out my hand to touch her, and simultaneously direct electric energy against her. In an instant she will be a scattering of fine ashes.

Nothing happens. No current flows. A tense moment goes by for me while I stand there, unbelieving, waiting for a computation on the failure.

No computation comes.

I glance at Grannitt. Or rather at where he was a moment before. He isn't there.

Anne Stewart seems to guess at my dilemma. "It's the Brain's ability to move in time," she says. "After all, that's the one obvious advantage it has over you. The Brain has set Bi—Mr. Grannitt far enough back so that he not only watched you arrive, but has had time to drive over to your—cottage—and, acting on signals from the Brain, has fully controlled this entire situation. By this time, he will have given the command that will take control of all your mechanisms away from you."

I say, "He doesn't know what the command is."

"Oh, yes, he does." Anne Stewart is cool and confident. "He spent most of the night installing permanent command circuits in the Brain, and therefore automatically those circuits control you."

"Not me," I say.

But I am running as I say it, up the stone steps to the pathway, and along the pathway toward the gate. The man at Guard Center calls after me as I pass him. I race along the road, unheeding.

My first sharp thought comes when I have gone about half a mile—the thought that this is the first time in my entire existence that I have been cut off from my information banks and computing devices by an outside force. In the past I have disconnected myself and wandered far with the easy confidence of one who can reestablish contact instantly.

Now, that is not possible.

This unit is all that is left. If it is destroyed, then—nothing.

I think: At this moment a human being would feel tense, would feel fear.

I try to imagine what form such a reaction would take, and for an instant it seems to me I experience a shadow anxiety that is purely physical.

It is an unsatisfactory reaction, and so I continue to run. But now, almost for the first time, I find myself exploring the inner potentialities of the unit. I am of course a very complex phenomenon. In establishing myself as a humanoid, I automatically modeled the unit after a human being, inside as well as out. Pseudo-nerves, organs, muscles, and bone structure—all are there because it was easier to follow a pattern already in existence than to imagine a new one.

The unit can think. It has had enough contact with the memory banks and computers to have had patterns set up in its structure—patterns of memory, of ways of computing, patterns of physiological functioning, of habits such as walking, so there is even something resembling life itself.

It takes me forty minutes of tireless running to reach the cottage. I crouch in the brush a hundred feet from the fences and watch. Grannitt is sitting in a chair in the garden. An automatic pistol lies on the arm of the chair.

I wonder what it will feel like to have a bullet crash through me, with no possibility of repairing the breach. The prospect is unpleasant: so I tell myself, intellectually. Physically, it seems meaningless, but I go through the pretense of fear. From the shelter of a tree, I shout:

"Grannitt, what is your plan?"

He rises to his feet and approaches the fence. He calls, "You can come out of hiding. I won't shoot you."

Very deliberately, I consider what I have learned of his integrity from my contacts with his body. I decide that I can safely accept his promise.

As I come out into the open, he casually slips the pistol into his coat pocket. I see that his face is relaxed, his eyes confident.

He says: "I have already given the instructions to the servo-mechanisms. You will resume your vigil up there in the future, but will be under my control."

"No one," I say grimly, "shall ever control me."

Grannitt says, "You have no alternative."

"I can continue to be like this," I reply.

Grannitt is indifferent. "All right," he shrugs, "why don't you try it for a while? See if you can be a human being. Come back in thirty days, and we'll talk again."

He must have sensed the thought that has come into my mind, for he says sharply: "And don't come back before then. I'll have guards here with orders to shoot."

I start to turn away, then slowly face him again. "This is a human like body," I say, "but it has no human needs. What shall I do?"

"That's your problem, not mine," say Grannitt.

I spend the first days at Lederton. The very first day I work as a laborer digging a basement. By evening I feel this is unsatisfying. On the way to my hotel room, I see a sign in the window of a store. "Help Wanted!" it says.

I become a retail clerk in a dry goods store. I spend the first hour acquainting myself with the goods, and because I have automatically correct methods of memorizing things, during this time I learn about prices and quality. On the third day, the owner makes me assistant manager.

I have been spending my lunch hours at the local branch of a national stockbroking firm. Now, I obtain an interview with the manager, and on the basis of my understanding of figures, he gives me a job as bookkeeper.

A great deal of money passes through my hands. I observe the process for a day, and then begin to use some of it in a little private gambling in a brokerage house across the street. Since gambling is a problem in mathematical probabilities, the decisive factor being the speed of computation, in three days I am worth ten thousand dollars.

I board a bus for the nearest airport, and take a plane to New York. I go to the head office of a large electrical firm. After talking to an assistant engineer, I am introduced to the chief engineer, and presently have facilities for developing an electrical device that will turn lights off and on by thought control. Actually, it is done through a simple development of the electro-encephalograph.

For this invention the company pays me exactly one million dollars.

It is now sixteen days since I separated from Grannitt. I am bored. I buy myself a car and an airplane. I drive fast and fly high. I take calculated risks for the purpose of stimulating fears in myself. In a few days this loses its zest.

Through academic agencies, I locate all the mechanical brains in the country. The best one of course is the Brain, as perfected by Grannitt. I buy a good machine and begin to construct analog devices to improve it. What bothers me is, suppose I do construct another Brain? It will require millennia to furnish the memory banks with the data that are already in existence in the future Brain.

Such a solution seems illogical, and I have been too long associated with automatic good sense for me to start breaking the pattern now.

Nevertheless, as I approach the cottage on the thirtieth day, I have taken certain precautions. Several hired gunmen lie concealed in the brush, ready to fire at Grannitt on my signal.

Grannitt is waiting for me. He says, "The Brain tells me you have come armed."

I shrug this aside. "Grannitt," I say, "what is your plan?"

"This!" he replies.

As he speaks, a force seizes me, holds me helpless. "You're breaking your promise," I say, "and my men have orders to fire unless I give them periodic cues that all is well."

"I'm showing you something," he says, "and I want to show it quickly. You will be released in a moment."

"Very well, continue."

Instantly, I am part of his nervous system, under his control. Casually, he takes out a notebook and glances through it. His gaze lights on a number: 71823.

Seven one eight two three.

I have already sensed that through his mind I am in contact with the great memory banks and computers of what was formerly my body.

Using their superb integration, I multiply the numbers 71823, by itself, compute its square root, its cube root, divide the 182 part of it by 7 one hundred and eighty-two times, divide the whole number 71 times by 8,823 by the square root of 3, and—stringing all five figures out in series 23 times—multiply that by itself.

I do all this as Grannitt thinks of it, and instantly transmit the answers to his mind. To him, it seems as if he himself is doing the computing, so complete is the union of human mind and mechanical brain.

Grannitt laughs excitedly, and simultaneously the complex force that has been holding me releases me. "We're like one superhuman individual," he says. And then he adds, "The dream I've had can come true. Man and machine working together, can solve problems no one has more than imagined till now. The planets—even the stars—are ours for the taking, and physical immortality can probably be achieved."

His excitement stimulates me. Here is the kind of feeling that for thirty days I have vainly sought to achieve. I say slowly, "What limitations would be imposed on me if I should agree to embark on such a program of cooperation?"

"The memory banks concerning what has happened here should be drained, or deactivated. I think you should forget the entire experience."

"What else?"

"Under no circumstances can you ever control a human being!"

I consider that and sigh. It is certainly a necessary precaution on his part. Grannitt continues:

"You must agree to allow many human beings to use your abilities simultaneously. In the long run I have in mind that it shall be a good portion of the human race."

Standing there, still part of him, I feel the pulse of his blood in his veins. He breathes, and the sensation of it is a special physical ecstasy. From my own experience, I know that no mechanically created being can ever feel like this. And soon, I shall be in contact with the mind and body of not just one man, but of many. The thoughts and sensations of a race shall pour through me. Physically, mentally, and emotionally, I shall be a part of the only intelligent life on this planet.

My fear leaves me. "Very well," I say, "let us, step by step, and by agreement, do what is necessary."

I shall be, not a slave, but a partner with Man.

THE REPLICATORS

Standing there, after killing the monster, Matlin began to get mad.

In its death throes, the twelve-foot creature had done a violent muscular convulsion and somersaulted over into the dump section of Matlin's truck.

There it lay now, with its elephantine head and quarter-length trunk twisted to one side, and a huge arm and hand flung up and visible over the rear end. What must have been tons of shiny, black body was squashed limply down into the bottom of the cavernous metal carrier . . . creating a problem.

That was all it was to Matlin: a problem.

Steve Matlin was an abysmally suspicious and angry man. His impulse now was to dump the beast in the weeds beside the road. Reluctantly, he decided against that. He had unfortunately been seen driving along this little-used lake road by the two officers of a highway patrol car. If the patrolmen found the creature's body, they would assume that he had shot it.

This benighted man, Matlin, envisioned himself as being the person who would have to see to the disposal of the dead monster. As he reasoned it out, if he made the mistake of dumping it in the wrong place, he'd have to hire a crane to get it into his truck again. And if he simply took it home, he'd have the job of digging a hole for it.

Better take it to the police, he decided gloomily, *and follow their advice like a good little fellow.*

Seething at the nuisance, but resigned, he drove to the main highway. There, instead of turning left to his farm, he headed

for Minden, the nearest suburb of the city. Arrived in town, he
drove straight to the police station, braked to a halt, and
vigorously honked his horn.

Nobody showed.

The exasperated Matlin was about to lean on his horn and
really blast them with sound, when he made an electrifying
discovery. The police headquarters was on a side street and,
whatever the reason, there wasn't a car or person in sight . . .
Hot afternoon, empty street, rare opportunity—

Matlin tripped the lever that started the dump mechanism.
A moment later, he felt the beast's body shift. He simply drove
out from under it and kept on going, gunning his motor and
reversing the dump mechanism.

That night before they went to bed, his wife, Cora, said to
him, "Did you hear about the creature from space?"

Matlin's mind leaped to the memory of the beast he had
carted into town. He thought scathingly: *Those nuts! Creature
from space indeed!* But he said aloud, gruffly, "You watching
that junk on TV?"

"It was in the news report," she said defensively. "They
found it right there in the street."

So it was the thing he had killed. He felt a sudden glee.
He'd gotten away with it. He thought smugly: *Saved myself
twenty-five bucks. Time I had a little luck.*

He went silently to bed.

Cora lay for a while, listening to his peaceful breathing,
thinking of the monster from space—and thinking of the
universe that she knew existed somewhere beyond the narrow
world of Steve Matlin. She had once been a teacher. But that
was four children and two decades ago. It was a little hard
sometimes to realize how far away the real world was these
days.

Out there, a creature never before seen on Earth had been
found lying dead in the street in front of the Minden police
station. The TV cameras brought front views, side views, and

top views into everybody's living room. No one had any idea how the thing had gotten where it was discovered, and, according to the news commentators, top government and military officials were beginning to gather around the colossal corpse like buzzing flies.

Two days went by. A monster-hunting expedition arrived at the Matlin farm—among other places—but Cora shook her head to their questions and denied in a take-it-for-granted tone that Steve was the one who had transported the beast. "After all," she said scathingly, "he would have told me. Surely, you-uh!"

She stopped, thought: *That man! That incredible man! He could have.*

The visitors seemed unaware of her sudden confusion. And they also evidently believed that a husband would have told his wife. The principal spokesman, a fine looking, soft-voiced man of her own age, who had introduced himself as John Graham—and who was the only person present not in a police or military uniform—said in a kindly tone, "Tell your husband there's quite a reward already, something like a hundred thousand dollars, for anyone who can help us effectively."

The expedition departed in a long line of noisy motorcycles and cars.

It was about mid-morning the next day when Steve Matlin saw the second monster.

He had been following the trail of the first one from the lake road. And suddenly here was another.

He dived into a gully and lay there, breathless.

What he had expected, in coming here by himself, Matlin had never considered clearly. When Cora had told him of the reward money, he had instantly derided her trusting nature.

"Those S.O.B.'s will never split that reward with anyone who hasn't got his claim staked and ready to fight," he had said.

He had come to stake his claim.

His shock on seeing this second creature was like a multitude of flames burning inside him. He was aware of the heat rising along his spine and searing his brain. Fear! Trembling, he raised his rifle.

As he did so, the creature—which had been bending down—came up with something that glinted in the sun. The next instant, a bullet whistled past Matlin's head and struck a tree behind him with an impact like a clap of thunder. The ground trembled. An instant later, the sound of an explosion came to Matlin's ear.

The explosion was loud enough to have come from a small cannon.

Even as he made the mental comparison from his experience as a Marine in World War II, the distant rifle—it looked a rifle, though a huge one—spat flame again. This time the bullet struck the rock ten yards in front of Matlin and sprayed him with a shower of rock splinters. His body stung all over, and when he was able to look again—after the second explosion had echoed from the distance—he saw that his hands were covered with dozens of droplets of his blood.

The sight was both terrifying and galvanizing. He slid back, rolled over, half-clawed to his feet, and, bending low, ran to the gully's end, stopping only when he realized that it was becoming too shallow to be a shelter.

What could he do?

Shadowy memories came of wartime risks he had taken. At the time he had felt enforced, compelled by the realities of a war he never accepted—a war that had wasted several years of his life. But he remembered moving, crouching, going forward. He had always thought what a mad thing it was for a sensible person to force himself into enemy territory. Yet under the hated pressure of wartime discipline, he had resignedly gone into the most deadly situations.

Was it possible he would have to do that now—because of his own foolishness in coming here?

As he crouched there, appalled, two more cannon-like shells splattered the rock where he had been seconds before. A cannon against a rifle! Matlin wanted out, wanted away. The angry scheme he had created for himself, no matter what the end might be, had no meaning in the face of the firepower that was seeking his destruction with each booming shot.

He lay cringing at the shallow end of the gully, not even daring to raise his head.

His own rifle seemed like a mere toy now . . .

The phone rang. When Cora answered, it took her several moments to recognize the hoarse voice at the other end as her husband's.

"I'm calling from a roadside pay phone. Can you find out where that monster-hunting expedition is now?" he said.

"Mamie just called. They were over at her farm. Why?"

"It's chasing me," he said. "Tell 'em I'm coming toward the highway from the boathouse. It's driving a dump truck as big as a house."

"What's chasing you?" Cora yelled into the mouthpiece. "Where?"

"A second one of the monsters. On that back road to the lake." Matlin moaned. And hung up.

The battle on the highway began about two o'clock in the afternoon. The creature climbed out of the cab of a dump truck that stood twenty feet high. Crouching behind the vehicle, it fired with a rifle the size of a cannon at anything that moved.

The two dozen men with their frail cars and tiny rifles crouched in the underbrush. Lying beside Graham, Matlin heard the man say urgently to an army major, "Call again for an air strike!"

It was about ten minutes after that that the first helicopter appeared on the horizon. It turned out to be an enterprising TV station's vehicle, with cameras aboard. The fluttering monstrosity of a flying machine circled the dump truck, taking pictures of the great being beside it. At first it did not seem to occur to the creature to look at the sky for the source of the sound. But suddenly it got the idea.

Up came that long rifle. The first bullet smashed through the cockpit. A splinter from somewhere hit the pilot and knocked him unconscious. The helicopter flew off erratically. As it retreated, another gigantic bullet smashed its tail. The stricken whirlybird fluttered down among the trees on the other side of a low hill.

Worse, when the military helicopters arrived, they no longer had the advantage of surprise. The cannon-rifle fired at them as they approached. They veered off—but not before three went down, one in flames. With one exception, the others began to shoot back from a distance.

The exception flew off to the left, disappearing low behind a hill. It reappeared presently to the rear of the monster and, while the other machines kept up a barrage from in front, this lone helicopter came in on the target from behind.

The barrage of bullets that its pilot loosed downward almost tore off the great head of a creature which did not even see where the death came from.

Matlin walked forward with the others, angrily fingering the "claim" he had written out. It infuriated him that they were not offering to honor his rights. Even though he had expected it, the reality was hard to take.

Arrived at the truck, he stood impatiently by while the men examined the creature, the huge vehicle, and the rifle. Matlin was drawn abruptly out of his irritated self-absorption with the realization that he had been twice addressed. Graham indicated the ten-foot rifle.

"What do you make of that?"

The question approach, the appeal to him on an equal basis, momentarily neutralized the timeless anger in Matlin. Now! He thought. He handed Graham his claim with the request, "I'd like you to sign this." Then he bent down beside the huge weapon and examined it.

He commented presently, "Looks like a pump action repeater, much like the one I've got, only many times as big. Could have been made by the same company."

It irritated him as he spoke to realize that Graham still held the claim sheet in his hand, had not even glanced at it.

Graham said in an odd tone, "What company?"

"Mine is a Messer," said Matlin.

Graham sighed and shook his head in bewilderment. "Take a look at the nameplate on that big gun," he said.

Matlin bent down. The phrase, MESSER-MADE, stared back at him in indented, black metal lettering.

"And what's the name of your dump truck?" Graham asked.

Silently, Matlin loped around to the front of the oversized truck, and peered up at the letters. They were exactly the same as on his own dump truck: FLUG.

When Matlin returned with the identification, Graham nodded, and then handed him back his claim sheet, and said evenly, "If I were to write that claim, Mr. Matlin, it would read: 'As the man who had done the most to prevent the creature from space being traced down, I recognize myself, meaning you, Mr. Matlin, 'as the one person least qualified to receive the reward.'"

It was such an unexpected reaction, so instantly threatening to his rights, so totally negative, that Matlin blanched. But he was stopped by the words only for a moment. Then the anger poured.

"Why, you damned swindler!" he began.

"*Wait!*" Graham spoke piercingly, raised his hand in a warning gesture. His steely gray eyes were cynical as he continued: "Now, if you were to lead us onto the real backtrack, help us locate these creatures, I'll reconsider that judgment. *Will* you?"

Night came and caught them on the hunt.

As the monster-hunting expedition camped beside the lake, the darkness was shattered by a thunderous roaring sound. Matlin tumbled from the back seat of his car, ran to the lakeshore, and peered across the dark waters toward the island in the lake's center. He was aware of other men coming up behind and beside him.

It was from the island that the noise came.

"Sounds like a whole battery of jet engines," somebody yelled above the roar, "and it seems to be coming this way."

Abruptly, the truth of that was borne out. The jet sound was suddenly above them. Framed in a patch of dark blue sky, a monstrous-sized helicopter was momentarily visible.

It disappeared into a cloud bank. The great roaring receded, became a remote throb.

In the darkness, Graham came up beside Matlin, said, "Didn't you tell me you had a lakeside cabin near here?"

"Yeah," Matlin said, wary.

"Got a boat there?"

Matlin jumped to a horrid conclusion. "You're not thinking of going over to the island?" he gulped. "Now!"

Graham said earnestly, "We'll pay you for the rent of the boat, and guarantee you against damages—in writing. And if that's the base these creatures operate from, I'll sign your claim."

Matlin hesitated. The boat and the lakefront property were his one dream. No one, not even Cora, had ever realized how much they meant to him. On the very first day that he had killed the first monster, he had taken a load of sand from his farm and dumped it lovingly on the water's edge.

Standing there, Matlin visualized what the money would do for his dream: the rough shoreline fully sanded in, a hunting and fishing lodge, and a larger boat, the kind he had often fantasized but never managed to acquire.

"I'll do it," he said.

On the island, using his flashlight sparingly, Matlin led Graham and two other men to where the ground suddenly felt . . . harder.

When they dug down, they found metal bare inches under the grass.

Graham talked softly by two-way radio to the camp they had left and then held his radio for Matlin and himself to hear the answer: a parachute army would be called by way of the more powerful radio at the camp. By dawn, several hundred seasoned men with tanks, demolition units, and cannons would be down with them.

But, as the radio shut off, they were alone once more in the dark. The morning reinforcements were still hours away.

It was Matlin—again—who found the overhang that led into a huge, brightly lighted ship.

He was so intent, and interested, that he was inside the first chamber with the others before he clearly realized how far he had come.

He stopped. He half turned to run. But he didn't move.

The scene held him.

They were in a circular room about four hundred feet in diameter. A number of solidly built metallic extrusions came up from the floor or down from the ceiling. Except for them the room was empty.

Matlin went with the others to where a ramp led down to the next level. Here there were more of the huge, built-in machines—if that was what they were—but this level, also, was deserted.

On the third level, they found two sleeping "children."

Each lay on its back in a long, black metal, box-like structure. The larger was about half the size of a full-grown alien, the smaller a mere bit of a thing two feet long. Both were stocky of body and were, unmistakably, younger versions of the two creatures that had already been killed.

As the three men—Graham and the two officers—glanced at each other questioningly, Matlin drew out his claim sheet, and held it toward Graham. The government agent gave him a startled look; then, evidently realizing Matlin meant it, he nodded resignedly, took the pen, and signed.

The moment he had the claim sheet back in his hands, Matlin headed for the ramp.

He was sweating now with fear. Yet he realized he had no alternative. He had to have that signature. But now—

Get away from all this stuff that was none of his business!

When he reached the lakeshore, he started the motor of the motorboat, and headed back toward his boathouse. He locked up the boat, walked stealthily through the darkness to his car, and drove off.

As he came out of the line of trees a mile from his farm, he saw the entire yard was on fire. He heard the thunder of the gigantic engines—

His house, his barn, his machine shed—all were burning!

In the vivid, fitful light from the flames he saw the huge helicopter lift up from the far side and soar up into the night sky.

So that was where it had gone!

It passed by above him somewhat to his right, a colossal sound, the source of which was now completely invisible in the darkness of an overcast sky.

Matlin found Cora and the son that was not away at school crouching in the field. She mumbled something about the monster having come over and looked down at them. She said wonderingly, "How did it know this was your farm? That's what I don't understand."

The fire was dwindling. People were beginning to drive into the yard. Car doors slammed. In the fading brightness, Matlin in a bemused state carried his son and walked beside Cora to his station wagon.

He was having a different kind of thought. Why hadn't the creature killed his wife and child? Cora and the boy had been as completely at its mercy as the farm.

A neighbor named Dan Gray touched his arm and said, "How about you and Cora and the boy staying at my place tonight, Steve?"

By the time they got over on the Gray farm, a man was on
TV describing how someone had left three men at the mercy of
the returning alien.

He named Matlin.

Matlin recognized the man who was talking as a member of
the monster-hunting expedition.

He glanced around, saw that Gray, Gray's wife—a tall, thin
woman—and Cora were staring at him. Cora said in horror,
"Steve, you *didn't!*"

Matlin was amazed. "I'm going to sue that fellow for libel!"
he yelled.

"Then it isn't true," Cora wailed. "What an awful thing for
them to say such a lie!"

Matlin was outraged at her misunderstanding. "It's not a
lie, just a bunch of baloney. Why should I stay on that island?
If they want to be crazy, that's their business."

He saw from their faces that his perfectly obvious truth was
not obvious to them. He became grim. "Okay, I can see I'm no
longer welcome. Come along, Cora."

Mrs. Gray said, tight-lipped, "Cora and the boy can stay."

Matlin was quite willing, already at peace with their
foolishness. "I'll pick you up in the morning," he said to his
wife.

Cora did not reply.

Gray accompanied Matlin to his car. When he came back
into the living room, he was shaking his head. He said to Cora,
"One thing about that husband of yours. He lets you know
where he stands."

Cora said stiffly, "He's let me know once too often. Imagine
leaving those men!" There were tears in her eyes.

"He says they lured him over to the island."

"Nobody lures Steve. His own scheming got him over
there."

"He says he suddenly realized the generals had done it
again—got a private into the front line. And since this was not
his war—"

"If it isn't his war, whose is it? He fired the first shot."

"Well, anyway, the generals are on the firing line, and no
one could care less than Steve, I can tell you that."

"That's the astonishing thing," said Cora, wonderingly. "He
thinks World War II was a conspiracy to waste his time. He

lives entirely in his own private world. Nothing can shake him, as you just saw."

Matlin drove back to his farm and slept there in the back of his car.

When he returned to the Gray farm in the morning, Dan Gray came out to meet him. He was grinning. He said, "Well, Steve, it's finally going to be your war."

Matlin stared at the knowing smile on the somewhat heavy face of his neighbor, but the words seemed meaningless. So he made no reply but simply got out of his car and walked into the house.

The two women were watching the TV. Matlin did not even glance at the picture.

"Ready, Cora?" he said.

Both women turned and looked at him strangely. Finally, Mrs. Gray said breathlessly, "You're taking it very calmly."

"Taking what calmly?"

Mrs. Gray looked helplessly at Cora. "I can't tell him," she almost whispered.

Matlin glanced questioningly at his wife. She said, "You might as well hear it. The creature came back and found Mr. Graham and his two companions on the island. And it talked to them through some kind of mechanical translation device. It said it was going to leave Earth but that first it was going to accomplish one thing. It said—it said—"

Matlin said impatiently, "For Pete's sake, Cora, let's go. You can tell me on the way."

Cora said, "It said—it was going to kill you first."

For once Matlin was speechless.

At last he stammered: "Me!" After a moment, he added, incredulous, "That's ridiculous. I haven't anything to do with this business."

"It says you're the only one on earth who made it your business."

The shock was growing on Matlin. He could not speak, could not deny the charge in words. Inside his head, he protested silently: *But that first beast was coming toward me. How was I supposed to know?*

Cora was continuing in a grief-filled voice: "It says that on all the planets it's visited, no one has ever before killed without warning, without asking any questions."

Matlin stared at her with hopeless eyes. He felt battered, defeated, ultimately threatened. For a moment, again, he could scarcely believe. He thought: I only want to be left alone!

The thought stopped. Because he knew suddenly that all these years he had been maintaining an untruth: that what went on elsewhere was none of his affair.

He had pretended so hard, gone into such instant rages, that other people simply glanced at each other significantly and fell silent, and thereafter never brought up the subject again. He had always thought with satisfaction, *By damn, they'd better not say anything but*—contemptuously—*let them think what they want.*

And now, he was the only human being that a visitor from another planet felt motivated to kill . . .

He grew aware once more of Dan Gray's smile. The man spread his hands helplessly. "I can't help it, Steve. Believe it or not, I like you. I even think I understand you. But—forgive me, Cora—this seems to me to be a case of poetic justice. I can't think of anyone else who's had something like this coming to him for so long."

Matlin turned and walked out of the room. He was aware of Cora following him hastily. "Just a minute, Steve," she said, "I have something for you."

Matlin turned. They were alone in the hallway. He grew aware that she was tugging at her wedding ring. "Here," she said, "I should have given you this nineteen years ago, but I let the coming of our first child stop me."

She opened his palm, placed the ring in it, and closed his fingers over it. "You're on your own, Steve. After twenty years of being the most selfish, self-centered man in the world, you can face this as you should, by yourself."

Matlin scowled down at the ring, then: "Bah! When you look at me, you see the human race as it really is. I've never gone in for the shams, that's all."

He slipped the ring into his pocket. "I'm going to keep this and give it back to you when you get over this foolish feeling. My feeling for you was never a sham."

He turned and walked out of the room and out of the house.

A car was pulling up in front of the Gray house. John Graham was inside it. He climbed out and walked over to where Matlin was about to get into his station wagon, said, "I came over to see you."

"Make it quick!" said Matlin.

"I have three messages for you."

"Shoot!"

"Obviously," said Graham, "the U.S. Government will not allow one of its citizens to be casually exterminated."

Accordingly—he continued formally—all of the armed forces would be interposed between Steve Matlin and the alien.

Matlin stared at him with uncompromising hostility. "He can duplicate anything we've got, so those are just big words."

Graham said in the same formal way that the ability of the creature to duplicate, first, the rifle, then the truck, and then the helicopter, had been taken note of by the military.

Matlin's curt laugh dismissed as asinine the notion that the generals would know what to do with such information. "C'mon, c'mon," he said roughly, "what's the second message?"

"It's personal," said Graham.

He stepped forward. His fist came up, connected perfectly with Matlin's jaw. Matlin was knocked back against his car. He sank to the ground, sat there rubbing his jaw and looking up at Graham. He said in an even tone, "Just about everybody seems to agree I had that coming to me, so I'll take it. What's the last message."

Graham, who had evidently expected a battle, stepped back. His savage mood softened. He shook his head wonderingly. "Steve," he said, "you amaze me. Maybe I even respect you."

Matlin said nothing. He just sat there, elbows on knees.

After a moment, Graham continued. "The way the generals figure it, there's got to be another reason why the creature wants to kill you. Maybe you know something." His gray eyes watched Matlin closely. "Have you been holding anything back?"

Matlin shook his head, but he was interested. He climbed slowly to his feet, frowning, thoughtful as he dusted himself off.

Graham persisted. "It is proposed that its ability to duplicate is based upon a kind of perception that human beings don't have."

"Hey!" said Matlin, eyes wide. "You mean like the homing pigeon, or birds flying south, or salmon coming back to their little pool where they were born?"

"The reasoning is," said Graham, "that you got some feedback on whatever it is, and so the creature wants to kill you before you can pass on to anybody else what you know."

Matlin was shaking his head. "They're off their rocker. I don't know a thing."

Graham watched him a moment longer. Then, clearly satisfied, he said, "Anyway, the military feel that they can't take a chance with a creature that has made a death threat against an American citizen. So they're going to drop an atomic bomb on it and end the matter once and for all."

For some reason, Matlin felt an instant alarm. "Just a minute," he said doubtingly. "Suppose it duplicates that? Then it'll have everything we've got, and we still won't have seen a thing *it's* got."

Graham was tolerant. "Oh, come now, Steve. The bomb will be a small one but the right size to pulverize that spaceship. I personally feel strong regrets about this but I have no doubt of the outcome. Once the bomb drops, it'll have nothing to duplicate with—and it won't be around to do any duplicating."

Matlin said, "Better tell them to hold that bomb till they've thought about it some more."

Graham was looking at his watch. "I'm afraid it's a little late for that, Steve. Because they figured you might have some telepathic connection with this creature. I've been holding back the fact that the bomb is being dropped— right—now!"

As he spoke, there was a sound of distant thunder.

Involuntarily, the two men ducked. Then they straightened and looked over the near farms, past the trees in the distance, beyond the low hills. A small but familiar and sinister mushroom was rising from the other side of the horizon.

"Well," said Graham, "that does it. Too bad. But it shouldn't have made that threat against you."

"What about the other ship?" Matlin asked.

"What other ship?" said Graham.

They had both spoken involuntarily. Now, they stared at each other.

Graham broke the silence. "Oh, my God!"

There were stubborn people at G.H.Q.

For two decisive days, they rejected the idea that there might be another ship.

Then, late in the afternoon of the third day, radar reported a small object high above field H, from which the atomic plane had taken off to destroy the spaceship on the island.

Control tower challenged the approaching airborne machine. When there was no response, somebody became anxious and sounded a bomb alarm. Then he dived down a chute that took him headfirst into a shelter far below.

His quick action made him one of about eight hundred fast-reflex people who survived.

Seconds after he made his dive to safety, an atomic bomb demolished field H.

About the same time, a TV helicopter was hovering above the island in Matlin's lake, taking pictures of the bomb crater there. Suddenly a spaceship came silently down from a great height and landed.

The helicopter did not tarry. It took rearview pictures as it was fleeing the scene.

Graham went to see Cora, looking for Matlin.

But she could only shake her head. "Steve said he was going on the road till this whole thing blew over. He said he figured he'd better not be sitting still when that creature came looking for him."

They put Matlin's photo on TV.

On the fourth day after that, Graham interviewed four sullen young men who had tried to seize Matlin, their intention being to deliver him to the monster. As their spokesman put it, "By handing over the one guy who was really involved in this business, the rest of us could have gone back to our daily affairs."

They filed out, one on crutches, two with arms in slings, all bandaged in some way, groaning a little.

The following day, Graham interrogated two people who claimed to have witnessed a duel on an open stretch of highway between Matlin in a station wagon and the monster flying an enormous jet plane. Matlin had had a bazooka and the beast had finally beaten a retreat.

General Maxwell Day, who was with Graham, wondered aloud if Matlin might not be the man who had raided a Marine armory and taken a three-point-five rocket launcher and a quarter of a ton of ammunition for it.

Graham phoned Cora. "I'm checking a report," he said. "Would Steve have thought of utilizing Marine equipment?"

Cora answered carefully. "That weapon belonged to the people of the U.S., didn't it?"

"Yes."

"Well, then, I think Steve would regard himself as part owner, as a citizen, and without any guilt since he would consider either that he had paid for it with taxes or earned it in World War II."

Graham put his hand over his mouthpiece, said "I gather he would have thought of such a thing."

The Marine officer held his hand out for the phone. "Let me talk to her," he said. A moment later: "Mrs. Matlin?"

"Yes?"

"May I ask you some very personal questions about your husband?"

"You may."

"Now, Mrs. Matlin, Mr. Graham here has the highest respect for your opinions, so think carefully about this one: Is your husband intelligent?"

"Cora hesitated; then: "I know exactly what you mean. On some levels, no; on others, extremely intelligent."

"Is he brave?"

"To hear him talk, no. But my feeling is, totally. I think you'd have to engage his interest, though."

"What does he think of generals?"

"They're idiots."

"Is he an honest man?"

"We-l-l-l-l, that depends. For example, he had that rifle along that first day in the hope that he'd be able to kill a deer illegally."

"I mean is he responsible for his debts?"

"If I may quote him—he wouldn't give the so and so's the satisfaction of owing them money."

General Day smiled. "Now, Mrs Matlin, would you take your husband back if I made a sergeant out of him?"

"Why not a Captain?"

"I'm sorry, Mrs. Matlin, but if you'll think a little bit, you'll realize that he would never sink that low."

"Oh, I don't have to think. You're right. Well—yes, I might take him back. B-but he's not in the marines anymore."

"He will be, Mrs. Maitlin. Goodbye."

He hung up.

An hour later it was announced on TV, radio, and in the newspapers that Matlin had been reinducted into the Marines, and that he was ordered to report to the nearest Marine station.

About midnight that night, a jet, with Graham and several officers aboard, flew down to the Marine base where Matlin was resignedly waiting for them. They secured a Marine private's uniform. As the grim, unshaven man reluctantly donned it, they interrogated him. They were interested in any thought whatsoever that may have flitted through Matlin's mind for any reason.

Matlin objected. "That's crazy. I don't know anything special—except the thing is out to get me."

"We think you do."

"But that's a lot of—"

"Private Matlin! That's an order!"

Glumly—but thoroughly—Matlin complied with the orders. He told them everything that had passed through his mind in the past few days. And there had been things, many things, things that had seemed crazy and distorted to him, until he thought he was beginning to lose his mind. Visions of the buried ship at the lake, where thousands of atomic bombs were in the process of being duplicated.

His listers turnes pale. "Go on," urged Graham.

Matlin continued: There was only one creature, but it had brought with it a number of spare bodies and could grow even more.

Then he stopped. "Damn it," he growled. "I don't like to say this stuff! Why do you want to hear it, anyway? It's just crazy dreams."

Graham glanced at the Marine commander, then at Matlin. He said, "Matlin, we don't think it's dreams at all. We think that you are in resonance—somehow—with the creature's mind. And we need to know what it has in its mind—so, for heaven's sake, go on!"

The story, by the time Matlin got through piecing it together, made a pattern. The alien had arrived in the solar system in two ships, with its bodies in various growth stages and evenly distributed between the two vessels. When one ship—and its cargo of bodies—was later destroyed, it made a duplicate, and now again had two.

As body after body was destroyed, the next in line was triggered into rapid growth and awakened to full adulthood in about two days. Each new body had the complete "memory" of what had happened to the ones that had proceeded it.

On arrival, the first body had awakened in a state of total receptiveness. It had wanted to be able to duplicate the thoughts and feelings of the inhabitants of this newly found planet.

Be like them, think like them, know their language.

It was in this helpless, blank condition when it stumbled on Steve Matlin.

And that was the story. The creature had been imprinted with the personality of Matlin.

Graham said, "Steve, do you realize that this being got all these destructive ideas from you?"

Matlin blinked. "Huh!"

Graham, remembering some things that Cora had told him, said, "Do you have any friends, Steve? Anybody you like? Anybody anywhere?"

Matlin could think of no one. Except, of course, Cora and the kids. But his feelings about them were not unmixed. She had insisted on sending the three older children to school in town. But he did feel a genuine affection for her, and them, at some level—and said so.

Graham said tensely, "That's why she's alive. That's why the creature didn't kill her the day it burned your farm."

"B-but—" Matlin protested, "why destroy the farm?"

"You hate the damn place, don't you?"

Matlin was silent. He'd said it a thousand times.

"What do you think we ought to do with about half the people in this country, Steve?"

"I think we ought to wipe the human race off the map and start over again," said Matlin automatically.

"What do you think we ought to do with the Russians?"

"If I had my way," said Matlin, "we'd go over there and plaster the whole of Asia with atomic bombs."

After a little, Graham said softly, "Like to change any of those ideas, Steve?"

Matlin, who had finished dressing, scowled into a mirror. "Look," he said finally, "you've got me where I can't hit back. And I'm ready to be loused up by what the idiot generals have got in their crazy noodles. So tell me what you want me to do."

At that precise moment, *That* ceased its feverish duplication of man's atomic bombs . . .and became itself.

Its compulsive mental tie with Matlin was severed.

Shuddering, *That* made a report, on an instantaneous relay-wave transmitter whose receiver was light years away:

"What we always feared would happen on one of these blank mind approaches to a new planet finally happened to me. While I was enormously receptive to any thought, my first body was destroyed by a two-legged inhabitant of this system, a being with the most incredible ideas—which are apparently due to some early mistreatment. This inability to slough off early shock-conditioning seems to be a unique phenomenon of the people of this planet.

"Realizing how trapped I was while he remained alive, I made several attempts to kill him. I was unsuccessful in this because he turned out to be unexpectedly resourceful. But he has now put on a suit called a uniform, and this had immediately turned him into a peaceful person.

"Thus I was able to free myself. Naturally, I can still sense where he is, but he can no longer receive my thoughts nor I his. However, I must report that I am pinned down here by an air fleet. My image as a goodwill visitor has been completely nullified by what has happened. Obviously, I won't use any weapons against them; so perhaps this expedition is doomed."

A team of astronauts was sent up. The team successfully boarded *That's* second spaceship, reporting that it was occupied by four bodies in various growth stages.

Even as they blew up the ship in its silent orbit, on Earth Matlin was driven to the edge of the lake. There, a Government launch was provided him. While Graham and General Day watched through binoculars, Matlin drove the thirty thousand dollar craft right onto the beach of the island, careless of any damage to it.

"I think he smashed the launch," said Graham.

"Good."

"Good?"

"My whole theory about him would collapse if he treated Government property with the same care that he gave his own possessions. It reassures me that he's exactly the man I thought."

Matlin came to where the second alien ship lay at the bottom of the blast pit. Water had filtered down into the clay. Having his orders, Matlin dutifully slid down into the goo. He held his rifle high, cursed, and started for the entrance.

Graham, General Day, and an artillery major watched Matlin's progress on a portable TV. The picture was coming from a ship some seventy thousand feet above the island. The scene below was crystal clear. Through the marvelous telescopic lens, Matlin actually looked like a tiny human being walking.

"But why send anyone?" Graham protested. "Why not just blast it? As you've already pointed out, we've got enough power up there"—he indicated the sky above—"to exterminate him."

General Day explained that he now favored Graham's earlier view. The alien might be able to defend itself.

"But it's too late for caution," Graham interjected, "we've burned our bridges."

It would be unwise, the Marine officer explained, to provoke the creature further until a confrontation had taken place.

"A confrontation between a super-being and Matlin!"

"Who else should we send? Some poor devil? No, seeing the creature face on is not a new experience for him as it would be to some other lower ranks."

"Why not send you? Me?"

Day answered in a steady voice that such decisions as were required here should not be made by people who reasoned on the basis of official attitudes.

"How do you think I got to be a general? When in doubt, I listened to what the men thought. They have a basic canniness that transcends intellect.

With effort, Graham recovered. "You heard Matlin's basic truth," he said. "His opinion of the human race—"

General Day gave him a surprised look. "You mean to tell me that isn't your opinion also?"

"No."

"You don't think that human beings are absolutely impossible."

"No, I think they're pretty terrific," said Graham.

"Boy, are you far gone," said the general in a tolerant voice. "I can see that we Marines have an understanding of human behavior that beats all you brainwashed people." He broke off. "Matlin was badly handled in World War II."

"What?"

"You ask, what has that got to do with it? Plenty. You see, Mr. Graham, you have to understand that a true Marine is a king. Now, Matlin is the true Marine type. But he was treated like an ordinary private. He never got over it; so he's been seething for twenty years, waiting for recognition. I'm giving it to him. A king Marine, Mr. Graham, can direct a war, take command of a city, or negotiate with a foreign power. Marines who get to be generals are considered sub-level versions of this species. All Marines understand this perfectly. It will not occur to Matlin to consult me, or you, or the U.S. Government. He'll size up the situation, make a decision, and I shall back him up."

He turned to the major, commanded, "All right, start firing!"

"Firing!" Graham yelled.

Day explained patiently as to a child that it was necessary in this extreme emergency to reindoctrinate this particular Marine, and grind in the simple truth—to him—that generals always loused things up. "A quick reminder, that's all, Mr. Graham."

Matlin was still skidding around in the mud when the first shell landed by his feet. It sprayed him with fine droplets of wet dirt. The second shell landed to his right. The debris from it missed him entirely, but he was now in such a state of rage that he didn't notice.

By the time the shelling ceased, his anger was gone and he was in that peculiar state of mind which can only be described with one word: Marine.

The man who presently entered the alien ship knew that life was tough, that other people could not be trusted, that no one cared about him. It was a truth he had always fought with bitterness and rage.

But there was no longer any doubt in his mind. People were what they were. They would shoot you in the back if they couldn't get you from in front.

Understanding this, you could be friendly with them, shake their hand, enjoy their company, and be completely free of any need to judge or condemn them.

But you were on your own, day and night, year in and year out.

As he saw the creature, Matlin used his gun for the purpose for which he had brought it. Deliberately, he tossed it down. It struck the metal floor with a clatter.

The echoes of the sound faded—and there was silence. Alien and human stood there staring.

Matlin waited.

Suddenly the hoped-for-voice came from a speaker in the ceiling:

"I am talking to you through a computer, which is translating my thoughts into your language. It will do the same for yours. Why have they sent you to me—the one man I threatened to kill?

"I no longer plan to kill you. So you may talk freely,"

"We're trying to decide what to do with you," Matlin said bluntly. "Do you have any suggestions?"

"I wish to leave the planet forever. Can you arrange it?"

Matlin was practical. Could the creature leave whether human beings liked it or not?

"No."

The simple negative took Matlin slightly aback. "You have no special weapons from where you come from?"

"None," admitted the alien.

That admission also startled Matlin. "You mean to tell me we can do what we want with you? You can't stop us?"

"Yes, except—"

Matlin wanted to know except what.

The great eyes blinked at him, its black, fold-like eyelids rolling up and down in a skin and muscle complex unlike that of any creature Matlin had ever seen before.

"Except that it will do you no good to kill me."

"You'd better make it damn clear what you mean," Matlin said.

Watching him, *That* gave its explanation.

Matlin's boat was almost waterlogged by the time he successfully beached it near where Graham and the others were waiting.

He came up to them and saluted. General Day returned the salute smartly, and said, "Your report."

"I told him he could go," said Matlin. "He'll be leaving when I signal."

"What?" That was Graham, his voice sounding shrill and amazed in his own ears. "But why?"

"Never mind why," said General Day. "That's the way it's going to be."

He spoke into his mike: "Men, this alien ship is going to lift from here in a few minutes. Let it go through. A duly authorized person has negotiated this solution."

The language was not clear to Matlin. "Is it okay?" he asked questioningly.

For an instant, it seemed to Graham, Day hesitated. Graham said urgently into that instant, "At least, you're going to find out what made him agree?"

Day seemed to have come to a decision; his momentary hesitation ended. "Okay!" he said to Matlin. "Okay, Sergeant."

Matlin raised his rifle, and fired it into the air.

To Graham, Day said, "I've never lost a bet on a king Marine, and I don't expect to now."

The interchange ended. On the island, the ship was lifting. Silent, jetless, rocketless power drove it up on a slant.

It passed over their heads, gathering speed. It grew small and, as they watched, became a dot and vanished.

Aboard it, the creature to which Matlin had talked performed the preliminaries necessary to an interstellar voyage, and then retired to one of the sleep boxes. Soon it was in a state of suspended animation . . .

Thereupon happened what the monster had told Matlin—
the underlying reality, which made it useless, unnecessary,
even dangerous, to destroy it and its vessel.

On a planet many light-years away, the real *That* stirred,
awakened and sat up.

Vault of the Beast

The creature crept. It whimpered from fear and pain. Shapeless, formless thing yet changing shape and form with each jerky movement, it crept along the corridor of the space freighter, fighting the terrible urge of its elements to take the shape of its surroundings. A gray blob of disintegrating stuff, it crept and cascaded, it rolled, flowed, and dissolved, every movement an agony of struggle against the abnormal need to become a stable shape. Any shape! The hard chilled-blue metal wall of the Earth-bound freighter, the thick, rubbery floor. The floor was easy to fight. It wasn't like the metal that pulled and pulled. It would be easy to become metal for all eternity.

But something prevented. An implanted purpose. A purpose that drummed from molecule to molecule, vibrated from cell to cell with an unvarying intensity that was like a special pain. Find the greatest mathematical mind in the solar system, and bring it to the vault of the Martian ultimate metal. The Great One must be freed. The prime number time lock must be opened!

That was the purpose that pressed on its elements. That was the thought that had been seared into its fundamental consciousness by the great and evil minds that had created it.

There was movement at the far end of the corridor. A door opened. Footsteps sounded. A man whistling to himself. With a metallic hiss, almost a sigh, the creature dissolved, looking momentarily like diluted mercury. Then it turned brown like the floor. It became the floor, a slightly thicker stretch of dark brown rubber spread out for yards.

It was ecstasy just to lie there and be flat and have shape, and to be so nearly dead that there was no pain. Death was sweet and desirable. And life such an unbearable torment. If only the life that was approaching would pass swiftly. If the life stopped, it would pull it into shape. Life could do that. Life was stronger than metal. The approaching life meant torture, struggle, pain.

The creature tensed its now flat, grotesque body—the body that could develop muscles of steel—and waited for the death struggle.

Spacecraftsman Parelli whistled happily as he strode along the gleaming corridor that led from the engine room. He had just received a wireless from the hospital. His wife was doing well, and it was a boy. Eight pounds, the radiogram had said. He suppressed a desire to whoop and dance. A boy. Life sure was good.

Pain came to the thing on the floor. Primeval pain that sucked through its elements like burning acid. The brown floor shuddered in every molecule as Parelli strode over it. It had a tremendous urge to pull toward him, to take his shape. The thing fought its desire, fought with dread, and more consciously now that it could think with Parelli's brain. A ripple of floor rolled over the man.

Fighting didn't help. The ripple grew into a blob that momentarily seemed to become a human head. Gray nightmare of demonic shape. The creature hissed metallically in terror, then collapsed palpitating with fear and pain and hate as Parelli strode on rapidly—too rapidly for its creeping pace. The thin sound died. The thing dissolved into brown floor, and lay quiescent yet quivering from its uncontrollable urge to live—to live in spite of pain, in spite of terror. To live and fulfill the purpose of its creators.

Thirty feet up the corridor, Parelli stopped. He jerked his mind from its thoughts of child and wife. He spun on his heels, and stared uncertainly along the passageway from the engine room.

"Now what the devil was that?" he pondered aloud.

A queer, faint, yet unmistakably horrid sound was echoing through his consciousness. A shiver ran the length of his spine. The devilish sound.

He stood there, a tall, magnificently muscled man, stripped to the waist, sweating from the heat generated by the rockets that were decelerating the craft after its meteoric flight from Mars. Shuddering, he clenched his fists, and walked slowly back the way he had come.

The creature throbbed with the pull of him, a torment that pierced into every restless, agitated cell. Slowly it became aware of the inevitable, the irresistible need to take the shape of the life.

Parelli stopped uncertainly. The floor moved under him, a visible wave that reared brown and horrible before his incredulous eyes and grew into a bulbous, slobbering, hissing mass. A venomous demon head reared on twisted, half-human shoulders. Gnarled hands on apelike, malformed arms clawed at his face with insensate rage, and changed even as they tore at him.

"Good God!" Parelli bellowed.

The hands, the arms that clutched him grew more normal, more human, brown, muscular. The face assumed familiar lines, sprouted a nose, eyes, a red gash of a mouth. The body was suddenly his own, trousers and all, sweat and all.

"—God!" his image echoed; and pawed at him with letching fingers and an impossible strength.

Gasping, Parelli fought free, then launched one crushing blow straight into the distorted face. A scream came from the thing. It turned and ran, dissolving as it ran, fighting dissolution, uttering half-human cries. Parelli chased it, his knees weak and trembling from funk and sheer disbelief. His arm reached out, and plucked at the disintegrating trousers. A piece came away in his hand, a cold, slimy, writhing lump like wet clay.

The feel of it was too much. His gorge rising in disgust, he faltered in his stride. He heard the pilot shouting from ahead: "What's the matter?"

Perelli saw the open door of the storeroom. With a gasp, he dived in, came out a moment later, an atom-gun in his fingers. He saw the pilot, standing with staring brown eyes, white face, and rigid body, facing one of the great windows.

"There it is!" the man cried.

A gray blob was dissolving into the edge of the glass, becoming glass. Parelli rushed forward, ato-gun poised. A ripple went through the glass, darkening it; and then, briefly, he caught a glimpse of a blob emerging on the other side of the glass into the cold of space. The officer came up beside him. The two of them watched the gray, shapeless mass creep out of sight along the side of the rushing freight liner.

Parelli sprang to life. "I got a piece of it!" he gasped.
"Flung it down on the floor of the storeroom."

It was Lieutenant Morton who found it. A tiny section of
floor reared up, and then grew amazingly large as it tried to
expand into human shape. Parelli, with distorted, crazy eyes,
scooped it up in a shovel. It hissed. It nearly became a part of
the metal shovel, but couldn't because Parelli was so close.
Parelli staggered with it behind his superior officer. He was
laughing hysterically. "I touched it," he kept saying, "I touched
it."

A large blister of metal on the outside of the space freighter
stirred into sluggish life, as the ship tore into Earth's
atmosphere. The metal walls of the freighter grew red, then
white-hot, but the creature, unaffected, continued its slow
transformation into gray mass. It realized vaguely that it was
time to act.

Suddenly, it was floating free of the ship, falling slowly,
heavily, as if somehow the gravitation of Earth had no serious
effect upon it. A minute distortion inside its atoms started it
falling faster, as in some alien way it suddenly became more
subject to gravity. The earth was green below; and in the dim
distance a city glittered in the sinking sun. The thing slowed
and drifted like a falling leaf in a breeze toward the suntil-
distant surface. It landed in an arroyo beside a bridge at the
outskirts of the city.

A man walked over the bridge with quick, nervous steps.
He would have been amazed, if he had looked back, to see a
replica of himself climb from the ditch to the road, and start
walking briskly after him.

Find the greatest mathematician!

It was an hour later; and the pain of that thought was a
continuous ache in the creature's brain, as it walked along the
crowded street. There were other pains, too. The pain of
fighting the pull of the pushing, hurrying mass of humanity that
swarmed by with unseeing eyes. But it was easier to think,
easier to hold form now that it had the brain and body of a man.

Find the mathematician!

"Why?" asked the man's brain of the thing. And the whole
body shook with shock at such heretical questioning. The
brown eyes darted in fright from side to side, as if expecting
instant and terrible doom. The face dissolved a little in that
brief moment of mental chaos, became successively the man

with the hooked nose who swung by, and the tanned face of the tall woman who was looking into the shop window.

The process would have gone on, but the creature pulled its mind back from fear, and fought to readjust its face to that of the smooth-shaven young man who sauntered idly in from a side street. The young man glanced at him, looked away, then glanced back again startled. The creature echoed the thought in the man's brain: "Who the devil is that? Where have I seen that fellow before?"

Half a dozen women in a group approached. The creature shrank aside as they passed. Its brown suit turned the faintest shade of blue, the color of the nearest dress, as it momentarily lost control of its outer cells. Its mind hummed with the chatter of clothes and "My dear, didn't she look dreadful in that awful hat?"

There was a solid cluster of giant buildings ahead. The thing shook its human head consciously. So many buildings meant metal; and the forces that held metal together would pull and pull at its human shape. The creature comprehended the reason for this with the understanding of the slight man in a dark suit who wandered by dully. The slight man was a clerk; the thing caught his thought. He was thinking enviously of his boss who was Jim Brender of the financial firm of J. P. Brender & Co.

The overtones of that thought made the creature turn abruptly and follow Lawrence Pearson, bookkeeper. If passers-by had paid attention to him they would have been amazed after a moment to see two Lawrence Pearsons proceeding down the street, one some fifty feet behind the other. The second Lawrence Pearson had learned from the mind of the first that Jim Brender was a Harvard graduate in mathematics, finance, and political economy, the latest of a long line of financial geniuses, thirty years old, and head of the tremendously wealthy J. P. Brender & Co.

"Here I'm thirty, too," Pearson's thoughts echoed in the creature's mind, "and I've got nothing. Brender's got everything—everything while all I've got to look forward to is the same old boardinghouse until the end of time."

It was getting dark as the two crossed the river. The creature quickened its pace, striding forward aggressively. Some glimmering of its terrible purpose communicated itself in that last instant to the victim. The slight man turned, and let out a faint squawk as those steel-muscled fingers jerked at his throat, a single fearful snap. The creature's mind went black and dizzy as the brain of Lawrence Person died. Gasping, fighting dissolution, it finally gained control of itself. With one sweeping movement, it caught the dead body and flung it over the concrete railing. There was a splash below, then a sound of gurgling water.

The thing that was now Lawrence Pearson walked on hurriedly, then more slowly until it came to a large, rambling brick house. It looked anxiously at the number, suddenly uncertain if it had remembered rightly. Hesitantly, it opened the door. A streamer of yellow light splashed out, and laughter vibrated in the thing's sensitive ears. There was the same hum of many thoughts and many brains, as there had been in the street. The creature fought against the inflow of thought that threatened to crowd out the mind of Lawrence Pearson. It found itself in a large, bright hall, which looked through a door into a room where a dozen people were sitting around a dining table.

"Oh, it's you, Mr. Pearson," said the landlady from the head of the table. She was a sharp-nosed, thin-mouthed woman at whom the creature stared with brief intentness. From her mind, a thought had come. She had a son who was a mathematics teacher in a high school. The creature shrugged. In one glance it had penetrated the truth. The woman's son was as much of an intellectual lightweight as his mother. "You're just in time," she said incuriously. "Sarah, bring Mr. Pearson's plate."

"Thank you, but I'm not feeling hungry," the creature replied; and its human brain vibrated to the first silent, ironic laughter that it had ever known. "I think I'll just lie down."

All night long it lay on the bed of Lawrence Pearson, bright-eyed, alert, becoming more and more aware of itself. It thought: "I'm a machine, without a brain of my own. I use the brains of other people. But somehow my creators made it possible for me to be more than just an echo. I use people's brains to carry out my purpose."

It pondered about these creators, and felt panic sweeping along its alien system, darkening its human mind. There was a vague physiological memory of pain and of tearing chemical action that was frightening.

The creature rose at dawn, and walked the streets until half-past nine. At that hour, it approached the imposing marble entrance of J. P. Brender & Co. Inside, it sank down in the comfortable chair initialed L. P., and began painstakingly to work at the books Lawrence Pearson had put away the night before. At ten o'clock, a tall young man in a dark suit entered the arched hallway and walked briskly through the row after row of offices. He smiled with easy confidence to every side. The thing did not need the chorus of "Good morning, Mr. Brender" to know that its prey had arrived. It rose with a lithe, graceful movement that would have been impossible to the real Lawrence Pearson, and walked briskly to the washroom. A moment later, the image of Jim Brender emerged from the door and walked with easy confidence to the door of the private office which Jim Brender had entered a few minutes before. The thing knocked, walked in—and simultaneously became aware of three things. First, it had found the mind after which it had been sent. Second, its image mind was incapable of imitating the finer subtleties of the razor-sharp brain of the young man who was staring up with startled, dark-gray eyes. And third was the large metal bas-relief that hung on the wall.

With a shock that almost brought chaos, it felt the tug of that metal. And in one flash it knew that this was ultimate metal, product of the fine craft of the ancient Martians, whose metal cities, loaded with treasures of furniture, art and machinery, were slowly being dug up by enterprising human beings from the sands under which they had been buried for thirty or fifty million years. The ultimate metal! The metal that no heat would even warm, that no diamond or other cutting device could scratch, never duplicated by human beings, as mysterious as the ieis force which the Martians made from apparent nothingness.

All these thoughts crowded the creature's brain, as it explored the memory cells of Jim Brender. With an effort, the thing wrenched its mind from the metal, and fastened its gaze on Jim Brender. It caught the full flood of wonder in his mind as he stood up.

"Good lord," said Jim Brender, "who are you?"

"My name's Jim Brender," said the thing, conscious of grim amusement, conscious, too, that it was progress for it to be able to feel such an emotion.

The real Jim Brender had recovered himself. "Sit down, sit down," he said heartily. "This is the most amazing coincidence I've ever seen."

He went over the mirror that made one panel of the left wall. He stared, first at himself, then at the creature. "Amazing," he said. "Absolutely amazing."

"Mr. Brender," said the creature, "I saw your picture in the paper, and I thought our astounding resemblance would make you listen, where otherwise you might pay no attention. I have recently returned from Mars, and I am here to persuade you to come back to Mars with me."

"That," said Jim Brender, "is impossible."

"Wait," the creature said, "until I have told you why. Have you ever heard of the Tower of the Beast?"

"The Tower of the Beast!" Jim Brender repeated slowly. He went around his desk and pushed a button.

A voice from an ornamental box said, "Yes, Mr. Brender?"

"Dave, get me all the data on the Tower of the Beast and the legendary city of Li in which it is supposed to exist."

"Don't need to look it up," came the crisp reply. "Most Martian histories refer to it as the beast that fell from the sky when Mars was young—some terrible warning connected with it—the beast was unconscious when found—said to be the result of its falling out of sub-space. Martians read its mind, and were so horrified by its subconscious intentions they tried to kill it, but couldn't. So they build a huge vault, about fifteen hundred feet in diameter and a mile high—and the beast, apparently of these dimensions, was locked in. Several attempts have been made to find the city of Li, but without success. Generally believed to be a myth. That's all, Jim."

"Thank you!" Jim Brender clicked off the connection, and turned to his visitor. "Well?"

"It is not a myth. I know where the Tower of the Beast is; and I also know that the beast is suntil alive."

"Now see here," said Brender good-humoredly, "I'm intrigued by your resemblance to me. But don't expect me to believe such a story. The beast, if there is such a thing, fell from the sky when Mars was young. There are some authorities who maintain that the Martian race died out a hundred million years ago, though twenty-five million is the conservative estimate. The only artifacts remaining of their civilization are their constructions of ultimate metal.

Fortunately, toward the end they built almost everything from that indestructible metal."

"Let me tell you about the Tower of the Beast," said the thing quietly. "It is a tower of gigantic size, but only a hundred feet or so projected above the sand when I saw it. The whole top is a door, and that door is geared to a time lock, which in turn has been integrated along a line of ieis to the ultimate prime number."

Jim Brender stared; and the thing caught his startled thought, the first uncertainty, and the beginning of belief. "Ultimate," Brender said.

He snatched at a book from the little wall library beside his desk, and rippled through it. "The largest known prime is ah, here it is—is 230584300921393951. Some others, according to this authority, are 77843839397, 182521213001, and 78875943472201."

His frown deepened. "That makes the whole thing ridiculous. The ultimate prime would be an indefinite number." He smiled at the thing. "If there is a beast, and it is locked up in a vault of ultimate metal, the door of which is geared to a time lock, integrated along a line of ieis to the ultimate prime number—then the beast is caught. Nothing in the world can free it."

"To the contrary," said the creature. "I have been assured by the beast that it is within the scope of human mathematics to solve the problem, but that what is required is a born mathematical mind, equipped with all the mathematical training that Earth science can afford. You are that man."

"You expect me to release this evil creature—even if I could perform this miracle of mathematics?"

"Evil nothing!" snapped the thing. "That ridiculous fear of the unknown which made the Martians imprison it has resulted in a very grave wrong. The beast is a scientist from another space, accidentally caught in one of his experiments. I say 'his' when of course I do not know whether this race has a sexual differentiation."

"You actually talked with the beast?"

"It communicated with me by telepathy."

"It has been proven that thoughts cannot penetrate ultimate metal."

"What do humans know about telepathy? They cannot even communicate with each other except under special conditions." The creature spoke contemptuously.

"That's right. And if your story is true, then this is a matter for the Council."

"This is a matter for two men, you and me. Have you forgotten that the vault of the beast is the central tower to the great city of Li—billions of dollars worth of treasure in furniture, art, and machinery? The beast demands release from its prison before it will permit anyone to mine that treasure. You can release it. We can share the treasure."

"Let me ask you a question," said Jim Brender. "What is your real name?"

"P-Pierce Lawrence!" the creature stammered. For the moment it could think of no greater variation of the name of its first victim than reversing the two words, with a slight chance on "Pearson." Its thoughts darkened with confusion as Brender went on.

"On what ship did you come to Mars?"

"O-on F4961," the thing stammered chaotically, fury adding to the chaotic state of its mind. It fought for control, felt itself slipping, suddenly felt the pull of the ultimate metal that made up the bas-relief on the wall, and knew by the tug that it was dangerously near dissolution.

"That would be a freighter," said Jim Bender. He pressed a button. "Carltons, find out if the F4961 had a passenger named Pierce Lawrence. How long will it take?"

"A few minutes, sir."

Jim Brender leaned back. This is a mere formality. If you were on that ship then I shall be compelled to give serious attention to your statements. You can understand, of course, that I could not go into a thing like this blindly."

The buzzer rang. "Yes?" said Jim Brender.

"Only the crew of two was on the F4961 when it landed yesterday. No such person as Pierce Lawrence was aboard."

"Thank you." Jim Brender stood up. He said coldly, "Goodbye, Mr. Lawrence. I cannot imagine what you hoped to gain by this ridiculous story. However, it has been most intriguing, and the problem you presented was ingenious indeed."

The buzzer was ringing. "What is it?"

"Mr. Gorson to see you, sir."

"Very well, send him right in."

The thing had greater control of its brain now, and it saw in Brender's mind that Gorson was a financial magnate whose business ranked with the Brender firm. It saw other things, too; things that made it walk out of the private office, out of the building, and wait patiently until Mr. Gorson emerged from the imposing entrance. A few minutes later, there were two Mr. Gorsons walking down the street. Mr Gorson was a vigorous main in his early fifties. He had lived a clean, active life; and the hard memories of many climates and several planets were stored away in his brain. The thing caught the alertness of the man on its sensitive elements, followed him warily, respectfully, not quite decided whether it would act. It thought, "I've improved a great deal from the primitive life that couldn't hold its shape. My creators in designing me, gave to me powers of learning, developing. It is easier to fight dissolution, easier to be human. In handling this man, I must remember that my strength is invincible when properly used."

With minute care, it explored in the mind of its intended victim the exact route of its walk to his office. There was the entrance to a large building clearly etched on his mind. Then a long, marble corridor with two doors. One door led to the private entrance of the man's private office. The other to a storeroom used by the janitor. Gorson looked into the place on various occasions; and there was in his mind, among other things, the memory of a large chest.

The thing waited in the storeroom until the unsuspecting Gorson was past the door. The door creaked. Gorson turned, his eyes widening. He didn't have a chance. A fist of solid steel smashed his face to a pulp, knocking the bones back into his brain. This time the creature did not make the mistake of keeping his mind tuned to his that of its victim. It caught him as he fell, forcing his steel back to semblance of human flesh. With furious speed, it stuffed the bulky and athletic form into the large chest, and clamped the lid down tight. Alertly, it emerged from the storeroom, entered the private office of Mr. Gorson, and sat down before the gleaming desk of oak. The man who responded to the pressing of the button saw Mr. Gorson sitting there and heard Mr. Gorson say:

"Crispins, I want you to start selling these stocks through channels right away. Sell until I tell you to stop, even if you think it's crazy. I have information about something big on."

Crispins glanced down the row after row of stock names; and his eyes grew wider and wider. "Good lord, man!" he gasped finally, with that familiarity which is the right of a trusted advisor, "these are all gilt-edged stocks. Your whole fortune can't swing a deal like this."

"I told you I'm not in this alone."

"But it's against the law to break the market," the man protested.

"Crispins, you heard what I said. I'm leaving the office. Don't try to get in touch with me. I'll call you."

The thing that was John Gorson stood up, paying no attention to the bewildered thoughts that flowed from Crispins. It went out of the door by which it had entered. As it emerged from the building, it was thinking: "All I've got to do is kill half a dozen financial giants, start their stocks selling, and then—"

By one o'clock it was over. The exchange didn't close until three, but at one o'clock the news flashed on the New York tickers. In London, where it was getting dark, the papers brought out an extra. In Hankow and Shanghai, a dazzling new day was breaking as the newsboys ran along the streets in the shadow of skyscrapers, and shouted that J.P. Brender & Company had assigned; and there was to be an investigation.

"We are facing," said the district court judge, in his opening address the following morning, "one of the most astounding coincidences in all history. An ancient and respected firm, with world-wide affiliations and branches, with investments in more than a thousand companies of every description, is struck bankrupt by an unexpected crash in every stock in which the firm was interested. It will require months to take evidence on the responsibility for the short-selling which brought about this disaster. In the meantime, I see no reason, regrettable as the action must be to all the friends of the late J.P. Brender, and of his sons, why the demands of the creditors should not be met, and the properties liquidated through auction sales and other such methods as I may deem legal and proper."

Commander Hughes of the Interplanetary Spaceways entered the office of his employer truculently. He was a small man, but extremely wiry; and the thing that was Louis Dyer gazed at him tensely, conscious of the force and power of this man.

Hughes began: "You have my report on this Brender case?"

The thing twirled the mustache of Louis Dyer nervously, then picked up a small folder, and read out loud:

"Dangerous for psychological reasons . . . to employ Brender . . . So many blows in succession. Loss of wealth, and position . . . No normal man could remain normal under . . . circumstances. Take him into office . . . befriend him . . . give him a sinecure, or position where his undoubted great ability . . . but not on a spaceship, where the utmost hardiness, mental, moral, spiritual, and physical is required—"

Hughes interrupted: "Those are exactly the points which I am stressing. I knew you would see what I meant, Louis."

"Of course I see," said the creature, smiling in grim amusement, for it was feeling very superior these days. "Your thought, your ideas, your code, and your method are stamped irrevocably on your brain and"—it added hastily—"you have never left me in doubt as to where you stand. However, in this case, I must insist. Jim Brender will not take an ordinary position offered by his friends. And it is ridiculous to ask him to subordinate himself to men to whom he is in every way superior. He has commanded his own space yacht; he knows more about the mathematical end of the work than our whole staff put together; and that is no reflection on our staff. He knows the hardships connected with space flying, and believes that it is exactly what he needs. I, therefore, command you, for the first time in our long association to put him on space freighter F4961 in the place of space-craftsman Parelli who collapsed into a nervous breakdown after the curious affair with the creature from space, as Lieutenant Morton described it—By the way, did you find the . . . er . . . sample of that creature yet?"

"No, sir, it vanished the day you came in to look at it. We've searched the place high and low—queerest stuff you ever saw. Goes through glass as easy as light; you'd think it was some form of light stuff—scares me, too. A pure sympodial development—actually more adaptable of environment than anything hitherto discovered; and that's putting it mildly. I tell you, sir—But see here, you can't steer me off the Brender case like that."

"Peter, I don't understand your attitude. This is the first time I've interfered with your end of the work and—"

"I'll resign," groaned the sorely beset man.

The thing stifled a smile. "Peter, you've built up the staff of Spaceways. It's your child, your creation; you can't give it up, you know you can't—"

The words hissed softly into alarm; for into Hughes' brain had flashed the first real intention of resigning. Just hearing of his accomplishments and the story of his beloved job brought such a rush of memories, such a realization of how tremendous an outrage was this threatened interference. In one mental leap, the creature saw what this man's resignation would mean: the discontent of the men; the swift perception of the situation by Jim Brender; and his refusal to accept the job. There was only one way out—for Brender to get to the ship without finding out what had happened. Once on it, he must carry through with one trip to Mars, which was all that was needed.

The thing pondered the possibility of imitating Hughes' body. Then agonizingly realized that it was hopeless. Both Louis Dyer and Hughes must be around until the last minute.

"But Peter, listen!" the creature began chaotically. Then it said, "Damn!" for it was very human in mentality. And the realization that Hughes took its words as a sign of weakness was maddening. Uncertainty descended like a black cloud over its brain.

"I'll tell Brender when he arrives in five minutes how I feel about all this!" Hughes snapped; and the creature knew that the worst had happened. "If you forbid me to tell him, then I resign. I—Good God, man, your face!"

Confusion and horror came to the creature simultaneously. It knew abruptly that its face had dissolved before the threatened ruin of its plans. It fought for control, leaped to its feet, seeing the incredible danger. The large office just beyond the frosted glass door—Hughes' first outcry would bring help. With a half sob, it sought to force its arm into an imitation of a metal fist, but there was no metal in the room to pull it into shape. There was only the solid maple desk. With a harsh cry, the creature leaped completely over the desk, and sought to bury a pointed shaft of stick into Hughes' throat.

Hughes cursed in amazement, and caught at the stick with furious strength. There was sudden commotion in the outer office, raised voices, running feet—

Brender parked his car near the ship. Then stood for a moment. It was not that he had any doubts. He was a desperate man, and therefore a long chance was in order. It wouldn't take very much time to find out if the Martian city of Li had been found. If it had been then he would recover his fortune. He started to walk swiftly toward the ship.

As he paused beside the runway that led to the open door of F4961—a huge globe of shining metal, three hundred feet long in diameter—he saw a man running toward him. He recognized Hughes.

The thing that was Hughes approached, fighting for calmness. The whole world was a flame of cross-pulling forces. It shrank from the thoughts of the people milling about in the office it had just left. Everything had gone wrong. It had never intended to do what it now had to do. It had intended to spend most of the trip to Mars as a blister of metal on the outer surface of the ship. With a tremendous effort, it controlled itself. "We're leaving right away," it said.

Brender looked amazed. "But that means I'll have to figure out a new orbit under the most difficult—"

"Exactly," the creature interrupted. "I've been hearing a lot about your marvelous mathematical ability. It's time the words were proved by deeds."

Jim Brender shrugged. "I have no objection. But how is it that you're coming along?"

"I always go with a new man."

It sounded reasonable. Brender climbed the runway, closely followed by Hughes. The powerful pull of the metal was the first real pain the creature had known for days. For a long month, it would now have to fight the metal, fight to retain the shape of Hughes, and carry on a thousand duties at the same time. That first pain tore along its elements, smashing the confidence that days of being human had built up. And then, as it followed Brender through the door, it heard a shout behind it. It looked back hastily. People were streaming out of several doors, running toward the ship. Brender was several yards along the corridor. With a hiss that was almost a sob, the creature leaped inside, and pulled a lever that clicked the great door shut.

There was an emergency lever that controlled the anti-gravity plates. With one jerk, the creature pulled the heavy lever hard over. Instantly, it experienced a sensation of lightness and a sense of falling. Through the great plate window the creature caught a flashing glimpse of the field below, swarming with people. White faces turning upward, arms waving. Then the scene grew remote, as a thunder of rockets vibrated through the ship.

"I hope," said Brender, as Hughes entered the control room, "You wanted me to start the rockets."

"Yes," the thing replied thickly. "I'm leaving the mathematical end completely in your hands."

It didn't dare stay so near the heavy metal engines, even with Brender's body there to help keep its human shape. Hurriedly, it started up the corridor. The best place would be the insulated bedroom.

Abruptly, it stopped in its headlong walk, teetering on tiptoes. From the control room it had just left, a thought was trickling—a thought from Brender's brain. The creature almost dissolved in terror as it realized that Brender was sitting at the radio, answering an insistent call from Earth.

It burst into the control room, and braked to a halt, its eyes widening with humanlike dismay. Brender whirled from before the radio with a single twisting step. In his fingers he held a revolver. In his mind, the creature read a dawning comprehension of the whole truth. Brender cried: "You're the . . . thing that came to my office, and talked about prime numbers and the vault of the beast."

He took a step to one side to cover an open doorway that led down another corridor. The movement brought the telescreen into the vision of the creature. In the screen was the image of the real Hughes. Simultaneously, Hughes saw the thing.

"Brender," he bellowed, "it's the monster that Morton and Parelli saw on their trip from Mars. It doesn't react to heat or any chemicals, but we never tried bullets. Shoot, quick!" It was too much metal, too much confusion. With a whimpering cry the creature dissolved. The pull of the metal twisted it horribly into thick half metal. The struggle to be human left it a malignant structure of bulbous head, with one eye half gone and two snakelike arms attached to the half metal of the body. Instinctively, it fought closer to Brender, letting the pull of his body make it more human. The half metal became fleshlike stuff that sought to return to its human shape.

"Listen, Brender!" Hughes voice was urgent. "The fuel vats in the engine room are made of ultimate metal. One of them is empty. We caught a part of this thing once before, and it couldn't get out of the small jar of ultimate metal. If you could drive it into the vat while it's lost control of itself, as it seems to do very easily—"

"I'll see what lead can do!" Brender rapped in a brittle voice.

Bang! The creature screamed from its half-formed slit of mouth, and retreated, its legs dissolving into gray dough.

"It hurts, doesn't it?" Brender ground out. "Get over into the engine room, you damned thing, into the vat!"

"Go on, go on!" Hughes was shouting from the telescreen.

Brender fired again. The creature made a slobbering sound, and retreated once more. But it was bigger again, more human. And in one hand a caricature of Brender's revolver was growing.

It raised the unfinished, unformed gun. There was an explosion, and a shriek from the thing. The revolver fell, a shapeless tattered blob, to the floor. The little gray mass of it scrambled frantically toward the parent body, and attached itself like some monstrous canker to the right foot.

And then, for the first time, the mighty and evil brains that had created the thing sought to dominate their robot. Furious, yet conscious that the game must be carefully played, the Controller forced the terrified and utterly beaten thing to its will. Scream after agonized scream rent the air, as the change was forced upon the unstable elements. In an instant, the thing stood in the shape of Brender, but instead of a revolver there grew from one browned, powerful hand a pencil of shining metal. Mirror bright, it glittered in every facet like some incredible gem. The metal glowed ever so faintly, an unearthly radiance. And where the radio had been and the screen with Hughes' face on it, there was a gaping hole. Desperately, Brender pumped bullets into the body before him, but though the shape trembled, it stared at him now, unaffected. The shining weapon swung toward him.

"When you are quite finished," it said, "perhaps we can talk."

It spoke so mildly that Brender, tensing to meet death, lowered his gun in amazement. The thing went on: "Do not be alarmed. This which you see and hear is an android, designed by us to cope with your space and number world. Several of us are working here under the most difficult conditions to maintain this connection, so I must be brief.

"We exist in a time world immeasurably more slow than your own. By a system of synchonization, we have geared a number of these spaces in such a fashion that, though one of our days is millions of your years, we can communicate. Our purpose is to free Kalorn from the Martian vault. Kalorn was caught accidentally in a time warp of his own making and precipitated onto the planet you know as Mars. The Martians, needlessly fearing his great size, constructed a most diabolical prison and we need your knowledge of the mathematics peculiar to your space and number world—and to it alone—in order to free him."

The calm voice continued, earnest but not offensively so, insistent, but friendly. The speaker regretted that their android had killed human beings. In greater detail, he explained that every space was constructed on different number systems, some negative, some all positive, some a mixture of the two, the whole an infinite variety, and every mathematics interwoven into the very fabric of the space it ruled.

Ieis force was not really mysterious. It was simply a flow from one space to another, the result a difference in potential. This flow, however, was one of the universal forces, which only one other force could affect, the one he had used a few minutes before. Ultimate metal was *actually* ultimate. In their space they had a similar metal, built up of negative atoms. He could see from Brender's mind that the Martians had known nothing about minus numbers, so they must have built it up from ordinary atoms. It could be done that way, too, though not so easily. He finished:

"The problem narrows down to this: Your mathematics must tell us how, with our universal force, we can short circuit the ultimate prime number—that is, factor it—so that the doors will open any time. You may ask how a prime number may be factored when it is divisible only by itself and by one. That problem is, for your system, solvable only by your mathematics. Will you do it?"

Brender pocketed his revolver. His nerves were calm as he said, "Everything you have said sounds reasonable and honest. If you were desirous of making trouble, it would be the simplest thing in the world to send as many of your kind as you wished. Of course, the whole affair must be placed before the Council—"

"Then it is hopeless. The Council could not possibly accede—"

"And you expect me to do what you do not believe the highest government authority in the System would do?" Brender exclaimed.

"It is inherent in the nature of democracy that it cannot gamble with the lives of its citizens. We have such a government here; and its members have already informed us that, under similar conditions, they would not consider releasing an unknown beast upon their people. Individuals, however, can gamble where government must not. You have agreed that our argument is logical. What system do men follow if not that of logic?"

The Controller, through the creature, watched Brender's thoughts alertly. It saw doubt and uncertainty, opposed by a very human desire to help, based upon the logical conviction that it was safe. Probing his mind, it saw swiftly that it was unwise, in dealing with men, to trust too much to logic. It pressed on:

"To an individual we can offer—everything. In a minute, with your permission, we shall transfer this ship to Mars; not in thirty days, but in thirty seconds. The knowledge of how this is done will remain with you. Arrived at Mars you will find yourself the only living person who knows the whereabouts of the ancient city of Li, of which the vault of the beast is the central tower. In this city will be found literally billions of dollars worth of treasure made of ultimate metal; and according to the laws of Earth, fifty percent will be yours. Your fortune re-established, you will be able to return to Earth this very day."

Brender was white. Malevolently, the thing watched the thoughts sweeping through his brain—the memory of the sudden disaster that had ruined his family. Brender looked up grimly.

"Yes," he said. "I'll do what I can."

A bleak range of mountains fell away into a valley of reddish gray sand. The thin winds of Mars blew a mist of sand against the building. *Such* a building! At a distance, it had looked merely big. A bare hundred feet projected above the desert, a hundred feet of height and *fifteen hundred feet of diameter*. Literally thousands of feet must extend beneath the restless ocean of sand to make the perfect balance of form, the graceful flow, the fairylike beauty which the long dead

Martians demanded of all their constructions, however massive. Brender felt suddenly small and insignificant as the rockets of his spacesuit pounded him along a few feet above the sand toward the incredible building.

At close range the ugliness of sheer size was miraculously lost in the wealth of the decorative. Columns and pilasters assembled in groups and clusters broke up the facades, gathered and dispersed again restlessly. The flat surface of wall and roof melted into a wealth of ornaments and imitation stucco work, into a play of light and shade.

The creature floated beside Brender. Its Controller said, "I see that you have been giving considerable thought to the problem, but this android has no means of following abstract thought, so I have no means of knowing the course of the speculations. I see, however, that you seem to be satisfied."

"I think I've got the answer," said Brender, "But first I wish to see the time lock. Let's climb."

They rose into the sky, dipping over the lip of the building. Brender saw a vast flat expanse; and in the center—

He caught his breath!

The meager light from the distant sun of Mars shone down on a structure located at what seemed the exact center of the great door. The structure was about fifty feet high, and seemed nothing less than a series of quadrants coming together at the center, which was a metal arrow pointing straight up. The arrow head was not solid metal. Rather it was as if the metal had divided into two parts, then curved together again. But not quite together. About a foot separated the two sections of metal. But that foot was bridged by a vague, thin, green flame of ieis force.

"The time lock!" Brender nodded. "I thought it would be something like that, though I expected it would be bigger, more substantial."

"Do not be deceived by its fragile appearance," answered the thing. "Theoretically, the strength of ultimate metal is infinite; and the ieis force can only be affected by the universal I mentioned. Exactly what the effect will be, it is impossible to say as it involves the temporary derangement of the whole number system upon which that particular area of space is built. But now tell us what to do."

"Very well." Brender eased himself onto a bank of sand, and cut off his antigravity plates. He lay on his back, and stared thoughtfully into the blue black sky. For the time being all doubts, worries and fears were gone from him. He relaxed and read, "The Martian mathematic, like that of Euclid and Pythagoras, was based on endless magnitude. Minus numbers were beyond their philosophy. On Earth, however, beginning with Descartes, an analytical mathematic was evolved. Magnitude and perceivable dimensions were replaced by a variable-values between positions in space.

"For the Martians, there was only one number between 1 and 3. Actually, the totality of such numbers is an infinite aggregate. And with the introduction of the idea of the square root of minus one—or i—and the complex numbers, mathematics definitely ceased to be a simple thing of magnitude, perceivable in picture. Only the intellectual step from the infinitely small quantity of the lower limit of every possible finite magnitude brought out the conception of a variable number which oscillated beneath any assignable number that was not zero.

"The prime number, being a conception of pure magnitude, had no reality in *real* mathematics, but in this case was rigidly bound up with the reality of the ieis force. The Martians knew ieis as a pale-green flow about a foot in length and developing about say a thousand horsepower. (It was actually 12.171 inches and 1021.23 horsepower, but that was unimportant.) The power produced never varied, the length never varied, from year end to year end, for tens of thousands of years. The Martians took the length as their basis of measurement and called it one 'el'; they took the power as their basis of power and called it one 'rb.' And because of the absolute invariability of the flow they decided it was eternal.

"They decided furthermore that nothing could be eternal without becoming prime. Their whole mathematics was based on numbers which could be factored, that is, disintegrated, destroyed, rendered less than they had been; and numbers which could not be factored, disintegrated, or divided into smaller groups.

"Any number which could be factored was incapable of being infinite. Contrawise, the infinite number must be prime.

"Therefore, they built a lock and integrated it along a line of ieis, to operate when the ieis ceased to flow—which would be at the end of Time, provided it was not interfered with. To prevent interference, they buried the motivating mechanism of the flow in ultimate metal, which could not be destroyed or corroded in any way. According to their mathematics that settled it."

"But you have the answer," said the voice of the thing eagerly.

"Simply this: The Martians set a value on the flow of one 'rb.' If you interfere with that flow to no matter what small degree, you no longer have an 'rb.' You have something less. The flow which is a universal, becomes automatically less than a universal, less than infinite. The prime number ceases to be prime. Let us suppose that you interfere to the extent of ultimate prime *minus one*. You will then have a number divisible by two. As a matter of fact, the number, like most large numbers, will immediately break into thousands of pieces and will be divisible by tens of thousands of smaller numbers. If the present time falls anywhere near one of those breaks, the door would open immediately."

"That is very clear," said the Controller with satisfaction, and the image of Brender was smiling triumphantly. "We shall now use this android to manufacture a universal; and Kalorn shall be free very shortly." He laughed aloud. "The poor android is protesting violently at the thought of being destroyed. But after all it is only a machine, and not a very good one at that. Besides, it is interfering with my proper reception of your thoughts. Listen to it scream as I twist it into shape."

The cold-blooded words chilled Brender, pulled him from the heights of abstract thought. He saw with sharp clarity something that had escaped him before.

"Just a minute," he said. "How is it that the robot, introduced from your world is living at the same time rate as I am, whereas Kalorn continues to live at your time rate?"

"A very good question." The face of the creature was twisted into a triumphant sneer, as the Controller continued. "Because, my dear Brender, you have been duped. It is true that Kalorn is living at our time rate, but that was due to a short-coming in our machine. The machine which Kalorn built, while large enough to transport him, was not large enough in its adaptive mechanism to adapt him to each new space as he entered it. With the result that he was transported but not adapted. It was possible, of course, for us, his helpers, to transport such a small thing as the android, though we have no more idea of the machine's construction than you have.

"In short, we can use what there is of the machine, but the secret of its construction is locked in the insides of our own particular ultimate metal, and in the brain of Kalorn. Its invention by Kalorn was one of those accidents which, by the laws of averages, will not be repeated for millions of our years. Now that you have provided us with the method of bringing Kalorn back, we shall be able to build innumerable interspace machines. Our purpose is to control all spaces, all worlds— particularly those which are inhabited. We intend to be absolute rulers of the entire universe."

The ironic voice ended, and Brender lay in his prone position, the prey of horror. The horror was twofold, partly due to the Controller's monstrous plan, and partly to the thought that his warning thought must be ticking away on the automatic receiving brain of the robot. "Wait," his thought was saying, "that adds a new factor. Time—"

There was a scream from the creature as it was forcibly dissolved. The scream choked to a sob, then silence. An intricate machine of shining metal lay there on that great gray-brown expanse of sand and ultimate metal.

The metal glowed; and then the machine was floating in the air. It rose to the top of the arrow, and settled over the green flame of jets.

Brender jerked on his antigravity screen, and leaped to his feet. The violent action carried him some hundred feet into the air. His rockets sputtered into staccato fire, and he clamped his teeth against the pain of acceleration. Below him, the great door began to turn, to unscrew, faster and faster, until it was like a flywheel. Sand flew in all directions in a miniature storm.

At top acceleration, Brender darted to one side. Just in time. First, the robot machine was flung off that tremendous wheel by sheer centrifugal power. Then the door came off, and spinning now at an incredible rate, hurled straight into the air and vanished into space.

A puff of black dust came floating out of the blackness of the vault. Suppressing his horror, yet perspiring from awful relief, he rocketed to where the robot had fallen into the sand. Instead of glistening metal, a time-dulled piece of junk lay there. The dull metal flowed sluggishly and assumed a quasi-human shape. The flesh remained gray and in little rolls as if it were ready to fall apart from old age. The thing tried to stand up on wrinkled legs, but finally lay suntil. Its lips moved, mumbled:

"I caught your warning thought, but I didn't let them know. Now Kalorn is dead. They realized the truth as it was happening. End of Time came—"

It faltered into silence; and Brender went on. "Yes, the end of time came when the flow became momentarily less than eternal—came at the factor point which occurred minutes ago."

"I was . . . only partly . . . within its influence, Kalorn all the way . . . Even if they're lucky . . . 'twill be years before . . . they invent another machine . . . and one of their years is billions . . . of yours . . . and I didn't tell them . . . I caught your thoughts . . . and kept it . . . from them—"

"But why did you do it? Why?"

"Because they were hurting me. They were going to destroy me. Because . . . I liked . . . being human. I was . . . somebody!"

The flesh dissolved. It flowed slowly into a pool of lava-like gray. The lava crinkled, split into dry, brittle pieces. Brender touched one of the pieces. It crumbled into a fine powder of dust. He gazed out across that grim, deserted valley of sand and said aloud, pityingly, "Poor Frankenstein."

He turned and flew toward the distant spaceship.